INCLINED TO SCANDAL

ZOË MULLINS

Inclined to Scandal
ISBN # 978-1-83943-886-8
©Copyright Zoë Mullins 2018
Cover Art by Posh Gosh ©Copyright July 2018
Interior text design by Claire Siemaszkiewicz
Totally Bound Publishing

Published in 2020 by Totally Bound Publishing, United Kingdom.

Totally Bound Publishing is an imprint of Totally Entwined Group Limited.

INCLINED TO SCANDAL

Dedication

It has been nearly three decades since I read my first
historical romance, and decided that one day, I
would put pen to paper and create my own
Regency drama. From the ballroom to the bedroom,
from the tall ships to the country gardens, I was
entranced. I want to thank Totally Bound for giving
me the opportunity to fulfill that dream.

Chapter One

Rath was surprised that Lisette recognized him when he presented himself at the private entrance to her personal rooms at *Chez de Sauveterre*. The last leg of the trip had been difficult, the storms seeming endless. He hadn't shaved in weeks, his hair needed a good wash and his clothes, though still well-cut, were caked with dirt, saltwater and blood. He did not look the part of a peer of the realm, or a partner in Sinclair Knolls, one of the most prosperous shipping and import interests in England.

Lisette had taken one look at him, seen behind the filth and grime and flung herself into his arms. His former mistress was ten years his senior but nothing in her countenance betrayed her age. Though in her mid-forties now, she still looked fresh and carefree, with her white-blonde hair pulled back in a loose knot. Her blue eyes swam with tears at the sight of him.

It was always at Lisette's home that he regained his land legs. His coachman followed behind him with a small trunk filled with the clothes and toiletries that would turn the feared Captain Wrath into the Rowan Grayson Sinclair, the Earl of Rathbridge or that devilish Lord Sin, as some still called him.

He assured her of his health and general well-being before being seen up to a private guest room. He was relieved to see Gisele and Richards awaiting him in his room. They must have received word that his ship had at last made port.

He wrapped an arm around Richards' shoulders and kissed Gissy on the forehead. They had been his faithful servants for years and appreciating their company, he regretted that he saw so little of them.

He'd met Richards when he had been a footman in his parents employ, but the young man had shown potential. Upon setting up his own lodgings in Albany, Rath had asked him to become his personal valet. By then, Gisele went where Richards went, and had taken on the role of housekeeper, cook and maid.

Tonight, the two worked together, putting to rest the fearsome Lord Wrath and revealing the gentleman beneath. Richards stripped him out of the offensive rags, and Gisele ran to dispose of them. Richards was nothing if not serious about his work, and Rath knew by the look he gave the sodden clothing that Richards was planning to take them out back and burn them. Rath hid a grin. He would never see the 'offensive garments' again. Richards set them by the door and turned back to the trunk, pulling out Rath's more fashionable London attire.

"Not the jacket, not tonight."

Richards lifted his brow as if to admonish him. The world, however, would not end if he showed up downstairs in his waistcoat and shirtsleeves. He glared back at Richards, who frowned, but silently relented.

Gisele laughed at them both. "You two have the same argument each time you come home."

"That was hardly an argument," Richards grumbled. "It's hard to argue with a man who looks like a naked caveman. We must do something about that hair and beard, my lord."

"Of course, Richie."

"Come on, caveman." Gisele held out her hand. "I happen to like you naked and hairy. Though not so filthy as you are now."

"I thought you liked me dirty?" he teased, and saw a look pass between her and Richards. "Good lord, has she finally taken pity on you and agreed to marry you, Richie?"

"Aye, my lord. I've made her my wife."

"You should have said, man." He reached out to grab a towel and wrapped it around his waist.

Gisele tugged the towel off him playfully. "Pssh, my lord. He's seen you tup me. He's helped you tup me. There is no need to be missish about showing me your stick now."

Richards laughed. "No, my lord. Modesty would be quite out of place. Get in your tub and let Gissy and I clean you up."

Rath shook his head but couldn't stop from grinning. He had always expected the two would wed, had encouraged it after Gisele had birthed Richards' second child. That she'd finally consented was a cause for celebration.

He leaned back in the hot tub and let them take care of him. Gissy washed his hair first, then moved on to washing his body with a scented cloth. Richards had pulled a stool close to the tub side and had prepared a basin of hot water. He began the process of shaving him, which meant cutting the length of whiskers first.

Rath never considered himself a prissy man. He wasn't a fop. He did for himself for months at a time while at sea, but he did enjoy the feeling of another running a razor or a soft cloth over his skin.

Gisele rang for more water and a parade of young boys brought hot pots into the room. When he stood, she and Richards took turns rinsing him clean with the hot water, before Gissy wrapped him in soft towels. She led him over to the dressing table where Richards completed his transformation by trimming his unruly hair to a respectable, but still unfashionable length.

"You will always look the pirate, my lord," Gisele said, crawling onto his lap as Richards continued to towel his hair dry.

"Sssh, that's our secret, Gis." He laughed as she kissed his newly shaven chin and jaw.

"You will always be Captain Wrath, my lord, scourge of the high seas." Richards laughed and leaned over his shoulder to kiss Gissy himself. Then he turned a kiss to Rath's jaw. Rath caught his eye and could not fail to miss the hint of challenge there. He took Richie's lips in a hungry kiss, their tongues dueling for control as Gissy purred and began releasing him from his prison of towels. She trailed her lips down his chest.

It was his turn to growl as he threaded his fingers through her fair hair. He pulled his lips from Richards. "I know you like your caveman, but you may find manliness a little too wild, even for you, my love," he warned.

She grinned up at him, skimming his abdomen with her hand then settling it between his thighs. "Should we clean this up so I can suck you proper, my lord?"

"You have the best ideas, Gissy." He looked from her to Richards then spread his legs wide. His aching cock twitched earnestly.

"You hold it still, Gis, and I'll expose it." Richards knelt between his thighs, the snick, snick of his scissors a disturbingly arousing type of foreplay, followed by the scrape of the razor over his aching sac. He held his breath as Gissy's small hands stroked his cock, her thumb circling its tip as his valet palmed the sensitive skin of his denuded balls.

"Water to rinse, Gissy?" Richards asked. "We need to make sure the captain is every bit the gentleman down here."

"That cock ain't never been a gentleman, my love." She placed a bowl beneath him and poured warm water from the pitcher over his crotch. The preparation was decadent in its deliberateness. "That's why I can't get enough of sucking it. He's so long and thick I can barely breathe around him when he shoves it down my throat."

Richards used the cotton towels to dry him as Gissy disposed of the basin and pitcher. Richie stroked the towel with arousing intent over Rath's cock. It twitched in response.

"Really, Gis, it's just a matter of practice. Isn't that right, my lord?" Richards ran his tongue over Rath's balls, then up the length of his cock.

Gissy knelt on the outside of Rath's thigh, her chin resting on it as she and Rath both watched Richie soak its length with his saliva and his tongue tease the tip before opening his mouth to devour it whole.

Rath's hands instinctively flew to both Richards' and Gisele's heads, his fingers tightening in their hair. "Fuck, Richards, yes, take it like that." He bucked his hips, as Richards swallowed against its head.

Gisele whimpered and he opened his eyes to see she had pulled up her skirts and had one hand down between her thighs, rubbing her clit hard with her palm.

"She needs you to fuck her." He pushed Richie away so he could see his wife's gleaming cunt. She was wet with desire for them both.

"Oh, yes, my pirate," she agreed, her voice husky. "I need you to fuck my mouth as my man takes my cunny."

"I need that too, Gis," he agreed, standing. "Come to the bed. Let me see him eat you before he fucks you."

Gisele ran to the bed, threw herself onto her back, with her thighs wide. Richards stalked toward her, a feral grin on his lips. He bunched up her skirts and spread her legs wide. Richie's shoulders fit between her stockinged feet as he pushed her legs open. Rath's gaze fell to her splayed thighs, watching as Richards bent his head to her softly furred quim. Her arousal glistened, and he moaned with the sweet taste of her.

The sounds of passion beat a happy cacophony in his head and his nostrils flared with the scent of arousal in the room. Gisele's sweet moans increased with her husband's lascivious attentions.

Rath smiled and began dressing as he watched them. Gis had led Richie on a merry chase these last seven years. He was going to have to talk to Richards about his plans, and whether they wanted to continue in his service. It was a little unusual for his staff to be married, but his was an unusual household. While he was at sea, he'd given them leave to raise their boys there. He would miss the family should they decide to retire from his employ, and not just because of the carnal pleasures he had shared with them.

Rath was tucking in his shirt when Gissy squealed her release.

"Jesus, Gissy, you made me fight for that one." Richards laughed and rolled her over, tossing her skirts up over her arse. "Were you trying to hold out for his lordship's cock in your mouth, or mine in your cunny?"

He had a wicked gleam in his eye when he looked Rath's way. He released his placard and pulled out his long, hard erection. He pumped it in his hand, his thumb brushing over its glistening tip.

"My lord, will you help me fuck Gissy?"

Rath flicked the button on the front of his pants and his cock sprang free. He knelt on the bed in front of Gisele. With one finger beneath her chin, he tilted her face up to him. "Do you want that, Gissy? You want my cock down your throat?"

She sighed and opened her mouth as Richards plunged his cock into her hard and deep. The momentum propelled her forward and she swallowed against Rath's cock as it slid across her palate.

Rath let Richards set the rhythm, Gissy taking more of him each time her husband slammed into her. Rath alternated between looking at Gissy, her eyes glassy with desire, her mouth stretched around his girth, her blonde hair tumbling over her shoulders, to Richards. Where Gissy looked wanton, Richards was a testament of restraint. His shirt and waistcoat were still tucked. He looked intent and relieved as he fucked into her.

Rath's balls drew up tight. He had missed this. The scent of woman's arousal, her heady cries. His orgasm raced down his spine and through his cock a second before he erupted with a shout.

His shout was followed by Richard's, as they poured into poor Gissy, drowning her with their seed.

He stumbled off the bed as Richards and Gisele collapsed atop it. Richie gathered Gis in his arms, and he could just make out his whispers of reassurance and love. Rath rubbed at some distant pain on the skin over his heart.

Rath finished dressing.

"You don't have to go, sir," Richards said, straightening up.

"I need to try my hand at the tables. I'm out of practice." He smiled. "You two take your time. I'll heading back to the ship soon, but my trunks are already on their way to the townhouse. When you are done here, head there and begin sorting things out, if you don't mind."

"No trouble at all, sir. Everything will be well and in its place by the time you arrive," Gisele promised, as she pushed her skirts back over her bare legs.

"I can always count on you, Gissy." He grabbed his jacket and his cane before leaving in search of a different game.

* * * *

Chez de Sauveterre was located in an unassuming town home in a reputable part of London. She'd purchased it with the help of Lords Rathbridge, Hunton and Palmer, who understood her desire to provide a safe haven, a *sauve terre*.

Lisette had created a sanctuary where her like-minded, well-born and deep-pocketed friends could relax and indulge their vices without interference, censure or fear. If you weren't Lisette's friend, you were never going to get through its gilded doors. She didn't allow just any young rakehell intent on random gaming and whoring into her home. Membership was sponsored, and hard to come by, considering the standard of discretion to which she held its members.

No one lost their fortune at her tables. Lisette was close to every banker in this city, and if you couldn't afford to lose, you weren't allowed to play. And lo to the card shark or cheat who tried to ply their skill at her tables. She had some of the best pugilists in England at her disposal to take care of their ilk.

She also prided herself on the quality of companions she provided for her clients. She didn't employ whores. Lisette had been one and wouldn't facilitate that life for anyone else. What she provided were educated men and women, many down on their luck and in search of better circumstances. They offered conversation, flirtation, and if they chose, they could invite a guest back to their rooms for more intimate diversions.

Lisette prided herself on the number of her staff who had found better opportunities outside of *Chez de Sauveterre*. While some took long-term engagements as mistresses, others had gone on to become secretaries, housekeepers and even shop owners, having found investors among Lisette's 'friends'. One of the most skilled and sought-after milliners on Conduit Street had begun as a companion at *Chez de Sauveterre*.

There was nothing tawdry about *Chez de Sauveterre*. And yet, it wasn't quite respectable, either. Certainly, it wasn't the usual haunt of an unmarried society miss, even if she was considered safely on the shelf.

Georgiana had practically grown up in Lisette's home. Mrs. Cooke, Lisette's housekeeper, was the first nanny she remembered. Her brother Kit and his friends had been Lisette's first investors nearly two decades ago. Georgiana had learned to play, and to win, at cards while still sitting on her brother's knee. She knew she would always be welcome here, even if it was no longer wise to come.

Since returning to England from their plantation in Tortola more than two years ago, she had only visited a handful of times and she'd only dared to sit at a card table once before. But she didn't care if she was recognized. Having passed twenty-one, she was beyond the age when most ladies of the ton found a husband. She was happy with her books and her horses and was waiting, albeit impatiently, for her brother to take her home.

Somehow, he'd gotten it into his head that because she had some silly title, Viscountess Belstratten, she needed a proper coming out. That was prefaced by a year at Lady Hilbert's Academy for Young Ladies, upon the conclusion of which, Lady Sarah Hilbert had declared her a hoyden and unfit for society.

She didn't care. She wanted to be back on the island. Riding her horse astride, the wind in her hair, not tucked tightly beneath a bonnet. She wanted to be able to go out without a chaperone and work the fields. Or she wanted to join Kit on his ship and sail. What good was it to be heiress to a shipping fortune when she hadn't been able to step aboard one in over two years?

She wanted to growl in frustration. It was no wonder after the disastrous afternoon she'd spent with her aunt and uncle that she had ordered her carriage to take her here. She'd had to have her butler, Satterswaite, eject them from her home before the tea had been served. And ejecting her aunt was no easy task. Constance was as wide as she was tall, and Georgiana was always surprised she actually fit through doorways. The thought made her smile, though she knew it was petty.

"He threatened to marry me to some ancient minor baron whose land abuts his," she told Lisette as she paced Lisette's private drawing room.

"Lord Carver?" Lisette grimaced.

"So you know the sweaty, round little man with the piggy eyes and turned-up nose."

"I know of him, yes. Kit pointed him out to me once at a ball, and mentioned that he'd cheated him out of some prime horseflesh. And you forgot his stale, fetid breath."

Georgiana shuddered. She could never forget his breath. Ugh! "I don't understand. I did everything that was asked. I even had my come out even though I was the oldest one that season. I can't help if it didn't take. How can Lord Carver be my reward?"

"Kit would never allow that to happen," Lisette consoled her.

"Kit's not here," she reminded her. "And Aunt Constance threatened to put me in a hospital if I didn't do as I was told. As if my reluctance to marry was a disease of the mind."

Georgiana flopped in front of Lisette, kneeling upon the floor. "I won't let them send me back there." She knew they couldn't send her back 'there'. Kit and his connections had made sure that 'there' had been closed down after he'd rescued her when she was only five years old. The thought of any facility of the sort filled with dread, a cold so deep that she thought ice water instead of blood ran in her veins.

"Of course not." Lisette shook her head. "That is ridiculous. I would never allow it. Cleo would never allow it. No one would allow it."

Cleo was her brother's former lover, and supposed to be her guardian while she was in London. "But only Kit could stop it."

"Pfft," she huffed. "No. *C'est impossible.* I would hide you first." She grinned. "You would be my chatelaine, Marie, and you would order around my staff, just like you played at when you were a little girl. If the officers came and asked for Georgiana, I would say no, no, no. There is no one here by that name."

"Thank you, Lise." She hugged her.

"*Oui.* We will deal with your English relations if the need arises." She squeezed her back, and Georgiana let herself relax in her arms a moment. "And so, you want to play cards tonight?"

"Maybe a little." She shrugged. It was the atmosphere and the freedom more than the cards that drew her here.

"You know Cleo will try to gut me if she discovers you here, Ana."

Lisette was the only one to shorten Georgiana down to Ana, having declared years ago that Georgie was a name for a boy. "I cannot call you such. You are Ana," she'd said.

"But Cleo isn't here tonight, is she?" She had spent many evenings with Cleo and Kit here during their misspent youth. She knew Cleo still regularly attended if not for the tables then for the gentlemen company.

"No. Not tonight. She had dinner plans, I believe with Dr. Wright."

"And the theater after. I begged off because of a headache." A headache caused by her extended family.

Lisette shook her head. "All right. Cover your hair and wear a mask and you may go play. I will prepare the excuses for your chaperone."

"*Merci*, Lisette." She bussed a kiss across the older woman's cheek and allowed herself to be escorted to the gaming room.

Chapter Two

Rath poured himself a glass of gin and looked around small gaming parlor. There were a number of games underway, but his eyes rested on one table. "She is decidedly out of place," he told Lisette who had joined him.

Lisette followed his gaze, and he heard her sharp intake of breath.

"Since she is masked, I take it she is not one of yours."

"No, but she and her family have always been special friends." She put her gloved hand on his sleeve. "I hold a special *tendre pour la petite fille.*"

"You hold a special fondness for me, too, Lise." He grinned down at her. "She is not your daughter, is she?"

She glared at him and he laughed. "I will take care," he offered. "I won't even try to seduce her, but I do plan to join her table. Does she need money or is she here for fun?"

"She does not need money." Lisette frowned, and Rath knew it was killing her to hold to her principles of privacy. She wouldn't just tell him who she was, but he would find out.

He motioned the footman for another drink, and winked at Lisette before stalking toward the table and taking an empty chair. The play was deep, and he joined just in time to see *la jeune fille* lose a ton. She may be flushed, but a hundred pounds in just one hand was steep. He would not have been as sanguine as she appeared if his hand had turned so quickly.

She raised her gaze to look at him, her violet eyes made more striking by the half mask obscuring her features. The mask did nothing to hide her rich, chestnut curls. She obviously eschewed fashion since she'd chosen not only to wear her hair down, but she wore no bonnet, only a jeweled bandeau woven into her hair. The ends brushed the swell of her ample breasts. The empire waist of her gown seemed to present the creamy globes for best display, and he wondered if she truly wasn't for sale as Lisette had claimed.

He sighed and looked over his cards, playing cautiously as he watched his opponent. She had considerable skill, but also a heavy dose of luck, and for the next hour the winning was divided evenly between himself and her. One by one their companions withdrew from the game, and formed a small ensemble watching the competition between them, as the stakes grew higher.

He leaned back in the generous leather chair and rolled his shoulders. He addressed her directly for the first time. "You've played well," he complimented her, as he nimbly flipped his cards onto the table one by one. "Until now."

A slow murmur ran through the group of onlookers. She'd lost a monkey on that last hand, more than five hundred pounds, and he saw her swallow hard. He wondered how she was planning to explain the loss to her banker or perhaps to her protector.

"I hope you put my money to good use," she demurred, trying to be graceful, but her jaw clenched, and a quiver about her lips.

He laughed. "I have every intention to," he said as he called for the footmen to open their best champagne and make sure everyone had a glass. With the small cheer that greeted his pronouncement, the crowd swarmed Lisette, effectively cutting her off from *la petite mysterieuse*.

Rath quickly stood, his weight only slightly supported on his pewter and ebony cane. He took the dark-haired beauty by the elbow and discreetly removed her from the main salon into a small private chamber beyond. He locked the door behind him.

The room was well appointed in shades of burgundy that coordinately nicely with the burgundy and copper striped gown she wore. She stood in the middle of the room, awkwardly, as he went to the sideboard and poured them both a snifter of brandy.

She was trying to look brave, but her hand shook slightly as she took the glass.

"You don't do this often, do you?"

"Excuse me?"

"Frequent this type of establishment," he clarified.

"Oh." She smiled, a bit of her bravado returning. "I thought you meant lose at piquet. That was quite tiresome of you to beat me. And the answer is no, to both."

The corner of his mouth lifted and he gave a short, derisive laugh. "It shows."

This had been, Georgiana decided, a no-good, horrible day. She had just lost five hundred pounds. Her stern Methodist uncle was bound to find out and Kit would likely tear a strip off her as well. Not that Kit would care that she'd played, just that she'd lost. He'd taught her better than that.

She looked at her opponent with consternation. She felt as if she should know him, but she couldn't place him. He wasn't fashionable, though his clothes were obviously from the best tailor. *No one with that much money should look like that,* she thought.

From his wide-shouldered, well-sculpted chest, narrow waist and muscled thighs, he was built like a laborer but he dressed better than the prince regent. His shirt was of a fine cambric. His waistcoat, a green and black brocade, was double breasted and emphasized the impressive width of his chest. He wore fitted pantaloons tucked into hessians that were, she'd bet another monkey on it, made by Hoby.

You'd almost think he were a gentleman, she thought, *except for his raven hair, which though gleaming, is too long to be fashionable, falling past his shoulders.*

"Do I know you?" she finally asked as she watched him lean back imperiously, glass in hand, in one of the velvet wingback chairs in front of the hearth.

"I am sure beyond a doubt that I would have remembered meeting you," he told her as he crossed an ankle over his knee. "I am only just returning to London."

"I heard someone call you 'Captain'." She took a seat across from him in a matching chair. She tossed back the last of her brandy with an unladylike swig. "Who are you, then?"

"I've been known by many names," he hedged, "but I am a captain of a small merchant ship."

She looked again at the boots. He may say small, but obviously profitable. If he sailed, that could explain his swarthy complexion.

"And you are called?" she asked again.

"You can call me Gray."

"Captain Gray?" she wondered.

He smiled, and he looked very disarming. "Just Gray for now."

She shrugged, but gave up. *Let him keep his secrets.* "I should be going, Gray."

"I was hoping you'd be up for another game." He leaned forward in his chair and raised an eyebrow arrogantly. She wondered if they taught that look to men in school. Her brother could give her the same look. Usually when he knew she was lying about something.

"As much as I would love not to have to explain to my uncle why I need to withdraw the funds, I really shouldn't play with you. I have nothing left to offer," she drawled, then chastised herself. She should not be flirting with this man. She had no excuse. *Your aunt and uncle are trying to marry you off to an old goat,* a little voice in her head reminded her. *That is no excuse,* she told it.

"Darling," he purred, "I think you have a lot to offer."

Goosebumps rose where his dark eyes roamed over her, caressing her. Her chest flushed when his gaze lingered on her breasts.

"But I am unwilling to wager my body to your pleasure."

He laughed, a throaty chuckle, and jumped up from his chair as he quickly grabbed the brandy from the sideboard and brought it back to the table between them.

"I like your frankness," he said as he filled her glass and his. "I am sure I'm not the first to say you are a most unusual woman."

At nearly three and twenty, that was probably the nicest description she'd heard in a while. Wild, hoydenish, eccentric, blue-stocking, original, on-the-shelf and spinster were more casually thrown about.

"I attest to the description."

He sat back down. His forearms resting on his thighs as he leaned forward. "I promise you, when you give yourself to me it will be for pleasure not because you lost a wager. When I take you to bed, it will be because you want to be there, beneath me. You want to feel me inside of you."

She was spellbound by his bold words, and the heat uncurling in her belly. She didn't notice when he reached out and pulled on the ties of her mask. It dropped to her lap.

"No hiding, love." He grinned at her. "The choice is yours."

He didn't have piggy eyes or fetid breath, she'd give him that. He was strong and virile, and she realized she was being offered an unparalleled opportunity. With the safety of anonymity inside this room, she could afford whatever the evening held. She thought of her uncle threatening to marry her off. She thought of how soon she could make it to *Belle Fleur*, their island plantation. She was a spinster after all, and had only been kissed three times. *How can I afford to say no?* she wondered.

"Deal the cards, Captain."

He smiled and opened a little drawer in the table next to them, producing a pack of cards. "Let's make it easy. A few hands of *vingt-et-un*, twenty-one. The winner can choose his prize." His brow rose again in question and she struggled not to roll her eyes as she nodded.

He dealt the cards. In the first hand, he had two tens, but she had a jack and an ace. He was forced to return her allowance.

"Feel better now, love?"

"You could always win it back on the next hand," she reminded him

"I'm not playing for your money." He dealt again and won the hand.

"What forfeit do you require?" she asked coyly.

"A secret. One you've never shared with anyone."

"You know you don't play fair?" she scolded. "A secret?"

She sighed finally. "I've never done anything quite like this before. I mean, I've gambled here on occasion, when I can convince Lisette to let me in. But I've never done anything like this" — she looked around the private room, then at him — "before."

"Darling, that's no secret." He smiled. "But you can tell me how a society miss, one who is yet unmarried, ever came to be a patron of Lisette's."

"How do you know I am not married?" she snapped.

"Are you?"

"No. I'm considered quite on the shelf."

"Then the question stands." His tone was firm.

She sighed. "I've never been a proper member of society. I wasn't raised in England. I wasn't raised to be a lady, per se. I had an unusual upbringing." She worded it carefully. "I was already past the time of what should have been my coming out when my family realized that I should return to England and learn to be a lady. It hasn't taken."

"Did you want it to?"

She grinned. "Lord, no."

"Good, because I like you wild," he told her, as he dealt the cards again. Losing this hand, she requested the same forfeiture from him.

He pretended to think about. "I've spent my whole life running from responsibility, spending time I didn't need to on my business, and at sea. All to avoid something that, although I can do it quite competently, I have no interest in."

"What is it that's expected of you?"

"That would be telling, and for that, you have to make another wager." But it would be a few hands before she would win again.

When her next forfeit came, he asked for her to leave her chair and to sit on his lap. Her heart began to thunder again, but she moved toward him. His thighs were thick and solid, she discovered, and he pulled her into a thoughtful embrace. Sitting sideways, she was just able to curl her shoulder under his. And had she wanted to, she could lean her head onto his shoulder. She didn't, but she could have.

She was very close to him. She could see the rough stubble already growing on his freshly shaven jawline, and she smelled the clean scent of sandalwood from his hair. She fought the urge to rub her cheek against him. She caught her breath and tried to regain her composure, knowing she was out of her depth tonight.

When he won again, he begged a kiss. She was going to remind him that they weren't wagering for sexual favors but she wanted that kiss.

He stroked her cheek. "Have you kissed many men, love?"

She thought of the kisses she had experienced, some sloppy, some boyish. "A few," she admitted, "but none that were still strangers to me."

He touched his lips to hers. His lips were warm and insistent. *Persuasive,* she thought, as she tangled her hand into his hair. He didn't try to overpower her with the kiss. He didn't suck on her mouth as others had tried. It was tender, gentle but sure, and she hated when he pulled away. She heard herself whisper his name. "Gray."

"Next time, you will kiss me," he promised.

She looked at him, confused. Hadn't she just been doing that? But no, she had been letting him do the leading. "If I win, you will teach me how to kiss you."

They both won. "Keep your hand on my shoulder like that," he said, taking her hand and resting it on the nape of his neck. He pushed his hair out of the way.

"Can you feel my pulse here?" He placed her hand over the vein in his neck. "I didn't know my heart could beat so fast," he confessed, surprised. "Now, kiss my lips as I kissed yours."

As she did, he pulled her tighter to him, wrapping his arms around her back, pressing her into him.

"Now, open your mouth just a little."

As she followed his instruction, the warmth of his tongue slid between her lips. She melted against him.

"Now, my love, give me your tongue."

She slipped her tongue into his mouth. She had never kissed like this before. She wasn't sure she should. A warmth unfurled deep in her belly, and her skin grew sensitive all over. She wanted to mold herself to him, when he gently pushed her away.

He loved the sound of her gentle sigh that said she was as reluctant to break apart as he was. But this was a game. A dangerous one and he knew better than to play it. She may be convinced that she was on the shelf, a hoyden whose family wouldn't care if he debauched her, but he knew wealthy families rarely just didn't care about their unmarried daughters. There was likely a father, or brother, out there ready to chop his balls off if he compromised her. But he couldn't help himself. There was something familiar about her, and yet unique. And he'd been away too long.

He dealt the cards again, but she won.

Lucky, too, he thought, as he was about to ask for her breasts, uncovered for his touch and his taste. She requested a more innocent forfeit, a token to remember him by.

He didn't have a lot to offer her. He reached up and pulled off his neatly tied cravat. He could hear the scolding Richards was going to give him, but he didn't care. He tossed it aside and took out a thin leather rope that was hidden inside his shirt. On it was a silver raven. He pulled it over her head. It fell between her breasts.

"It's beautiful," she said, taking it in her hands, admiring it. "What is its significance to you?"

He thought about telling her that it was the name of his first ship, but that would have garnered more questions because *The Raven* was the flagship in their fleet. That and his partner's ship, *The Eagle.* "On one of my first trips to sea, I came upon a skilled silversmith. I liked the intricacies and how he captured the bird in flight. It represented freedom."

"I like it," she said, letting the lucky bird fall into the crescent between her breasts.

He wanted to be that bird, and when he won next hand, he did ask for her breasts to be bared for him.

He watched her struggle with propriety, but only for a moment. She shifted on his lap to present the pristine little pearl buttons in the back and he took great care as he slid the first six tiny buttons through their holes, loosening the gown enough for the bodice and chemise to be slipped down beneath her breasts.

"Beautiful," he whispered and touched his tongue to one nipple. She stiffened but she did not pull away, and he lapped with greater fervor at her nipple, then pulled it into his mouth to suckle upon.

A soft moan escaped her lips as her hands curled into his long dark hair, and she pulled him closer to her.

He plumped her breasts together in his hands and trailed his lips from one to the other and back again. upon His fingers played where his mouth had been, pinching and tugging as she squirmed on his lap. She was pressing her thighs together in a futile attempt to release the ache his attentions has created. He prayed she wasn't successful. He wanted to be the one to relieve her ache.

He pulled away with a growl, leaving his hand covering one soft, round mound. His erection was growing more uncomfortable in his trousers, as she squirmed. "You had better deal the next hand."

With shaking hands, she dealt out the cards. "Do you know what you want for forfeit?" she asked breathlessly before deciding whether she'd take another card.

"I want you out of that dress." His voice was husky with wanting.

"We can't wager for sex," she replied.

"Take your clothes off and we'll see what happens."

She held on seventeen, but Sin took another card to improve his fourteen. An eight lost him the hand. "What do you want?" he asked.

She swallowed hard. "I want to know why."

He looked perplexed. "Why?"

"There are women here who are guaranteed to bring you pleasure tonight. Why do you want to play this little game?"

"You want to know why I'm picking on you." He played with one of her errant curls, resting just above her nipple. "I'm not sure I even know," he confided.

"That's not an answer."

He squeezed his eyes shut. "You have fire, and tonight I needed fire." He slipped his hand around her waist, turning her to him just slightly, so that he caressed her buttocks and down her thighs. "And I knew you wouldn't break, but you would — you will — bend."

"We have one hand left in our game." Each card carried great weight. Their game could soon be over. He watched her deal herself a natural twenty-one.

"What will it be, love?" he whispered in her ear as she looked at the cards. "Will you request your freedom?"

He knew she was warring with the impulse to run. "Or will you stay with me a little longer?" His breath was hot on her temple. "No more games."

"I should leave," she whispered, and as a gentleman, he lifted his wandering hands from her body.

"Then go."

She hesitated a long moment but just when he thought she'd change her mind, she stood, straightening her dress.

He strode to the sideboard and poured himself another brandy. She stalled, touching the raven medallion she had won. "What are you waiting for?" he asked roughly, letting the brandy soothe the ache in his belly. He wished it were gin.

"Don't let me go."

It was the invitation he had been waiting for, and he damned himself for not bringing her to a room with a proper bed. The brandy was forgotten as he pulled her toward him.

"Touch me," he whispered, and guided her hand to the erection beneath his trousers. "Tell me it's what you want."

"I don't know what I'm supposed to want, but I don't want you to stop touching me," she whispered.

He groaned and kissed her hard, his tongue exploring her mouth.

With a swiftness that belied experience, he slid her dress from her body, leaving her in her chemise, stockings and kid slippers, standing before the fire. Its light shadowed the curve of her body beneath the thin silk.

He guided her hands to his waistcoat, helping her shaking hands undo buttons before shrugging it off. Next, he pulled his shirt over his head as she watched him, eyes wide.

"Trust me," he told her, kissing her hands, stroking her fingertips with his tongue. He pulled her to the floor with him, cushioned by the soft fur rug before the fire.

He guided her hand back to his arousal. "Feel how hard you make me. How ready I am to be inside you." Fire leapt to her eyes. "Do you want me inside you, love?"

She nodded. "Please."

Her chemise was no barrier, and he pulled it out of his way, slipping his hand through the nest of curls at the juncture of her thighs. He slid one finger then two inside her sleek passage, as he kissed her breasts. She

31

writhed and moaned, chewing on his shoulder. Biting him.

"You are so sweet and tight, my little hell cat," he told her, looking down at her. "Let it go," he urged her, knowing she was nearing release. He stroked her more insistently, and slid a third finger inside her.

Her body released. She moaned and purred against him, her juices spilling over his fingers. He fumbled with his trousers, ready to follow her to heaven, despite the insistent knocking at the door.

"The room is occupied," he shouted.

"Captain," a voice called to him, behind the door. "Captain. It's an emergency."

"Shit," he swore as he hung his head, catching his breath.

"Hold a minute," he yelled in response then looked down at the woman before him. "I'm sorry, love. But I will be right back." He knelt up away from her and pulled her chemise over her thighs. He rushed to the door, opening it a fraction. It was a hurried conversation. He let out a litany of curses under his breath once the door was closed again. "I have to go."

"I don't understand," she said, her brows knitting together as she sat up, clasping the chemise to her breasts.

"Those damn responsibilities, I'm afraid." He paused, shaking his head and wondering why he was about to offer an explanation. "My cabin boy took a hard fall, broke his leg three days out. It's set well, but there's infection spreading. He almost lost his leg, but we thought we had it licked. Seems the fever is back, which could mean the infection is back. The doc may have to amputate, and if that happens, I need to be there." He returned to her, kneeling over her to take her lips in a gentle kiss. "Were it anything less, I would not leave you."

"I understand," she said, taking his hand and letting him help her off the floor. He pulled on his shirt and helped her back into her dress, playing an accomplished role as her lady's maid, as he made sure each button was fastened and she was presentable again. No one needed to know what had been about to happen here, but he would never forget. He touched his pendant, which now hung around her neck.

"Remember me, love?" he asked. "I will find you again."

He gave her one more kiss, pulling her hard against him, forcing her hips against his, so she could feel the proof of his attraction. Then he slipped out the door.

Chapter Three

It's not going to be a good day, Rath decided as his carriage arrived at the dock where *The Raven* had put in the day before. He was pleased to at least still have the bottle of brandy in his hand.

He saw Gabe already on deck and sighed with some relief. If the boy's leg could be saved, then Gabe would do it. He had promised Lonny that he wouldn't let them take his leg without a fight, and as only a nine-year old could, he believed in him without question.

Lonny was a precocious boy, always in trouble. Hanging off the rigging. Getting under foot. Truth told, he wasn't much of a cabin boy, but he would be a good sailor one day. He loved *The Raven*, almost as much as Rath himself did. Lonny still considered it a treat to wax down the wheel. Rath had even let him guide the ship once or twice on calm nights, with him standing by.

It had been a week since he had broken his shin bone, falling from the rigging. Rath had seen the wound set himself by Roy Johnson, the ship's sawbones. He ensured the calf was bound in place, to prevent, if he could, lameness from setting in.

Rath had long ago decided to leave the earldom to his brother and any of his heirs. It wasn't that he didn't like children, he adored them, but it was the responsibility he hated. He had taken on Lonny after his mother, a lightskirt whom many of his men enjoyed, had died.

"You have to save the leg, Gabe." He greeted his old friend with a hug.

"I should be able to do that," he assured him. "He may limp a little at first, but he should get past the worst of it. He's young, and still growing. He'll compensate effectively for whatever impact this has now."

Better to walk with a limp than not to walk at all, Rath thought. It was what he had to tell himself after his injury. He caressed the well-worn cane that he used infrequently now. His own leg grew near useless if the weather was chill and damp. The muscles would cramp and tighten, and a dull ache would set in. *It's the main reason,* he told himself, he had taken to sailing south so often and for so long.

"I'm going to go see him," Rath said, clapping Gabe on the shoulder.

"I should warn you," Gabe called after him. "Cleo is with him now."

"She's what?" he asked, incredulous that Viscountess Welles should be anywhere but in bed at sunrise.

"When she heard you were back, and Lonny was hurt, I couldn't keep her away."

"You could have fucking tried."

"Restraining Cleo is like trying to stop a typhoon, you know that."

Gabe wasn't kidding. For a little woman, Cleo was a regular dervish, unable to let go of an idea once she got it. "She wanted to see Lonny, but she also said she needed to speak to you."

"No doubt to box my ears for letting Lonny get hurt."

"Likely. I'll give you a minute and then I will be down to change Lonny's dressing."

It was not lost on him that the only way Cleo could know he was in port was because she had been with Gabe. Not the jealous type, he was happy for them both. It had been many years since Cleo had warmed his bed. And Gabe, who had saved his life on at least two occasions, was due for some pleasure. A woman like Cleo would be good for him.

Cleo sat on the cot next to Lonny. He saw a smudge of blood on her skirt and Lonny's dirty bandages on the floor by the bed. She never shied away from getting dirty. He lay a hand on her shoulder, and smiled at her before greeting Lonny.

"How you doing, son?" He tussled Lonny's hair.

"It's like you promised, Capt'n. I can keep my leg, doc says."

"So I hear." He knelt by Lonny's cot. "But it's not over yet, you know. Dr. Gabe still has to poke and prod and that won't be fun. Then you got to do exactly like he says, even if it means no fishing for a while, and no climbing in the rigging."

"Yes, Capt'n." He smiled. "Miss Cleo says she gonna send me a cake, sir. With strawberries on top. But only if I'm real brave."

"That's right, Lonny," she cooed. "You're going to be my brave little man, and I will make sure you have all the cake you want." She smiled down at the little boy she had helped Rath save from the streets a few years before.

With a knock at the door, Gabe interrupted asking, "What does the good doctor get? I hope I get some strawberries, too." He grinned at Lonny.

"Yes, sir, doc." Lonny laughed. "You can have some of my cake."

"Well, I will like that immensely." He looked at both Cleo and Rath. "Ship out, you two," he ordered. "Lonny and I have some work to do."

Rath took Cleo's arm and escorted her to his cabin. "Can I get you a drink, or order you up some breakfast?" he asked.

"Cook is already preparing a light repast for us," she told him. "Buns, fresh fruit and the like, now that you are back in port."

Cleo Allstead, the Viscountess Welles, was a petite and graceful woman, with long curling white-blonde hair. She always wore jewel-tone colors to highlight her best feature, her soft, cream complexion. At thirty-eight, she was a commanding presence. She evoked an iron will that had spirited her from her country beginnings to the London ton more than twenty years ago.

Cleo, he marveled, never seemed to age and appeared very much as she had when she'd first arrived in London at seventeen, when her father, a country squire, had found a wealthy bidder for his daughter's hand. After two years of forced confinement to a cold and often brutal marriage bed, she was freed when her nearly seventy-year-old husband had a brain seizure and died. Indeed, no one missed the ancient viscount, his children having all shuffled off their mortal coil before him.

He nodded. "How long have you two been..." He let the question hang in the air.

"Gabe is a good friend," she confided. "And it's been a while, though what we have is between us, no one needs to know."

"Is that your choice, or his?" Gabe was from a good family with money, and while his family had hoped a military career would be in his future, they were not unduly put out when he'd become a physician. "He's a fine man."

"I know he is." She smiled. "I only wish I knew it then. We've wasted so much time."

"You're in love with him," he accused, recognizing the gentleness in her voice. He had spent too many nights with her not to know her well. They had formed the core of a set of hellions nearly fifteen years ago. She the young widow with him and four other good friends, including his brother Ash, Gabe, his business partner, Kit, and Olivia. Olivia had gone on to marry Gabe's eldest brother.

"Does this mean you are finally going to get your happily ever after?" he teased.

"I wouldn't go that far. But he does make me exceedingly happy." She frowned. "At least he does when I let him."

"You should let him." He shook his head. "I know your first marriage was hell, but it wouldn't be the same with Gabe."

"I know it wouldn't, but I also know he could and should find someone with more to offer."

"No one has more to offer than you."

She laughed at him. "You know I wasn't talking about my cunt."

"I wasn't, either. You are beautiful, and wealthy. He is your match in every way."

"He's also eternally optimistic and should have a young wife on his arm."

"Bah," Rath scoffed, shaking his head. She was not as jaded as she pretended and Gabe was too experienced to desire some miss straight from her come-out.

Cook arrived with breakfast and set it on the table between them. "If it's not to gush over you and Gabe, and I really don't think you'd put me through that, then what is it you wanted to discuss with me? Gabe said you had something important on your mind."

As much as Cleo did want to gush about her relationship with Gabe, since Rath was one of the few who would understand not just her joy but her hesitation, she had come to request Rath's help on another matter.

"It's Kit."

By the look on Rath's face, she knew she wasn't playing fair. There was nothing Rath wouldn't do for Kit, his best friend. They had been raised together, their fathers having been business partners. They had later nearly died protecting each other during the Napoleonic War. "More accurately, it's Kit's sister, Georgiana. Do you remember her?"

She waited until Rath could conjure up any memory of her. It had been a long time. "Braids and breeches, and she used to try to out race me on her pony," he said finally.

"She must have been eight or nine, just Lonny's age the last time you saw her. I think it was that weekend at Kit's country house. Before you went east for the first time."

"I do remember her vaguely, she must be what, nearly eighteen now?"

Cleo laughed. "Try twenty-three."

Rath was horrified. "When the hell did that happen?"

"When none of us were looking, I fear. And she is still in breeches half the time. Kit asked me to be her confidante and chaperone of sorts when she is in England. In truth, she's done amazingly well. She's turned into quite a stunner, but every bit as outrageous as Kit."

"Now that is a scary thought." He laughed. "Usurped of our roguish title by a little sister. Sounds like she needs a good husband to keep her in line."

"She absolutely refuses to marry or even consider it." She didn't have to remind Rath of her own experience with marriage for him to understand that Kit, who had raised his sister since she was six years old, would never force her into marriage. She would have a love match or nothing at all.

"She sounds spoiled, charming and dangerous." He sighed as he leaned back in his chair, popping a tart into his mouth. "So, tell me, what mess has she gotten into, and how can I help?"

* * * *

"Not now," Georgiana murmured as someone continued to push back and forth at her shoulder, trying to wake her. She hadn't gone straight home after Gray had left her last night. She'd had to sit through a very long lecture from Lisette, and she'd done her best to lie through her teeth so no one was the wiser as to what almost happened with Captain Gray. "Nothing happened," she continued to remind herself, even in her state of half-sleep.

The shaking did not stop and she opened one eye to spy her maid, looking harried, standing next to her bed.

"Miss Georgie, please wake up." She shook her again. "Your uncle, Mr. Norris, is downstairs bellowing," she persisted. "And Lady Welles is here, too."

Through the clouds in her head, Georgiana realized her life, and it seemed her household, was suddenly out of control. She sat up in bed, looking around for her dressing gown. "They're all here?" she asked, seeing her gown on the end of the bed where she'd discarded it last night.

When Leda nodded, Georgiana turned and buried her face in the pillow once more. It was not going to be a good day. She screamed into her pillow.

"Has Gladys been informed?" she asked once she finished screaming. Gladys Rucker, the ancient widow of some country squire, was her official companion.

"She is down there, too, but likely asleep in her chair," Leda confided.

Georgiana rolled her eyes. She had no doubt Gladys could sleep through her uncle's shouts and recriminations. She slept more than she was awake, and she was only her companion for two reasons — to give the poor woman a comfortable home to die in, and to give Georgiana some semblance of propriety since living on her own just wasn't done.

She sighed, and looked beseechingly at her maid. "Fine. Grab my blue morning dress. The silk one with yellow flowers and my yellow cap," she told Leda as she hurried to the basin to wash her face. She could make herself decent in very little time. Especially since she didn't need to worry about even combing her hair.

"What fool thing have you gotten yourself into now?" Leda asked as she helped Georgiana into a fresh chemise and the gown.

"What haven't I done?" She shrugged, wondering just what they had discerned this time.

"Lady Welles was telling your uncle to shut his mouth and wait for explanations. She called for tea in the salon, but I don't think tea is going to do it."

"What time is it?" Surely it wasn't already tea time?

"Nearly midday. But you were out late, weren't you?" Leda swooped up the very wrinkled, hastily discarded dress that Georgiana had worn the night before, off the bedroom floor.

"You already know the answer to that." Georgie frowned. "Tell them I will be down directly."

It was a half an hour before Georgiana finally descended the staircase, but it was not to shouting, cursing or even a sermon.

Cleo sat waiting for her on the bottom stair. "Five minutes sooner, and you'd be hearing the wrath of Charles. Now, come, thank me, drink your tea and tell me what the hell you thought you were doing at *Chez de Sauveterre*."

Georgie plodded along behind the woman she considered her surrogate mother. She had taken over raising Georgiana after her parents had died more than fifteen years ago, while involved with the infamous Kit Knolls. It was to Cleo that Georgiana was sent two years ago, in need of a formal lady's education. And it was to Cleo whom Georgie had always confided in, no matter the escapade, until now.

"How did they find out?"

"That, I don't know. I found out from my maid, who is seeing the valet of a certain viscount whom you

42

fleeced out of a quarterly allowance last night. Now, explain yourself."

"He was an extremely poor card player."

"You know that is not the explanation I am looking for." Cleo glared. "Had you received another note?"

Ah, the notes. There had been six so far. Suggesting she meet the anonymous sender if she wanted to prevent him, or her she supposed, from releasing some salacious *on-dit* to the ton and ruining her brother's reputation and business, and possibly seeing him jailed. She hadn't ignored them, but neither had she met the writer. She'd taken them to Cleo to manage as she saw fit.

"I hardly need some feckless blackmailer leading me astray. I do that well enough on my own," she offered. "I ran scared after my aunt and uncle threatened to marry me off to a piggy-eyed man with bad breath?"

Cleo frowned. "You must have been upset, because you are usually smart enough not to get caught." She laughed then said, "What in particular made you food for gossip this morning?"

"I was doing very well at piquet." She shrugged, sipping her tea. "I must have offended someone's sensibilities when I took their money, I mean besides Lord Harte."

"With whom were you playing?"

"The usual suspects. Viscount Varleigh and Viscount St. James. And you know that dear Chadwick. And that architect of Countess Farnsworth. What's his name? He played quite well, actually." She deliberately left out any mention of Captain Gray.

"I took the usual precautions. Lisette took great care to make sure I had a mask. I wasn't even wearing my usual jewelry. If Uncle Charles found out I was at

Lisette's, it must be all over London, because he never hears the gossip."

"I don't think it all over town. But it is very curious that he discovered you were there. He doesn't have contacts with our crowd. That is just one more mystery we'll have to figure out."

"How did you get dear Uncle Charles to leave?"

"I promised him I had you in hand, and could make all this go away for good."

She hugged the woman tightly in gratitude. She was always able wrap Charles around her finger. "Oh, Cleo, how do you do it?"

"I knew him when he wasn't a stodgy old grouch, and I may know a few secrets of his that he'd rather I kept." She winked. "But don't thank me yet. We still need a plan."

Georgiana looked at her. "What do you mean?"

"You weren't the first to mention the most inappropriate match that has been found for you."

Georgiana's heart pounded in her throat. Not this again. "They can't."

"They probably can, but won't. We won't let them, but you need to trust me." Cleo looked at the teapot with undisguised disgust. "Do you have anything stronger than tea?"

Georgiana laughed and moved to the small bookcase in the corner behind the chair where Gladys sat dozing. She reached behind a set of books and pulled out a bottle of sherry. She poured it into both their teacups.

Cleo took a healthy sip, then another. "So much better than tea." She sighed. "So let's try to figure out who recognized you and decided to spread gossip. I will visit Lisette this afternoon and get her working on it from her end. Her clients know better than to gossip. And if they've forgotten, she will remind them."

Georgiana started making a list of all the ways her foray to *Chez de Sauveterre* could be known. Between the three of them, they could ferret out the source. She also trusted Cleo to obstruct her aunt and uncle's plan.

* * * *

He laughed into his porter as he looked over his latest letter. He was tired of the chit having access and protection from the highest echelons of the ton. *This should limit her protectors.* He grinned. Especially once it was printed in the gossip column of *La Belle Assemblée.* He would be sure to send it to the *Times*, the *Morning Post* and even the *Gentleman's Magazine.*

Yes, he thought gleefully, *this will drag her into the open.* Expose her for the weak-willed whore she was.

He hadn't expected her to be so careful. Women, in his experience, were not thinking creatures, but she had thought of everything—disguises, hired carriages, alibis. But last night she'd been careless. She'd played with the wrong man, one who could be bought, and one who knew exactly who was behind the mask. It was marvelous, and it hadn't even been his idea. She'd walked into that trap by herself.

When his spy had informed him that she was at *Chez de Sauveterre,* he knew he had her. He had witnesses, bought and paid for, who would bring her down. It wasn't enough yet, but it was a pattern. A little more money and he could convince his witnesses to place her at the Cyprian's Ball and Vauxhall. That should look good in the pages of the paper. He could ensure that her guardianship and well-being was left to her aunt and uncle, and that her fortune found its way to him.

That would teach them a lesson. There was no escaping their history.

Chapter Four

There were a number of things Rath had expected to see when he arrived at the family mansion in Grosvenor Square, but his brother's bare buttocks were not one. He stopped short at the door to the library.

He reviewed the scene quickly. His baby brother, Ashleigh, pants around his ankles, was fucking—was that a maid? He really couldn't see her well from the door—a young woman with admirably long, creamy thighs, across what had been their father's, and now his oak desk.

"Tupping a wench upon my desk," the Earl of Rathbridge scolded. "I expected better from my heir. At least bring a second for me to enjoy."

"Bugger it, Rath," Ash snarled. "Shut your eyes as I help my wife to dress."

Rath did not move. *I must be hearing things,* he thought, *Ash did not just call the chit his wife, did he? My brother is married. The half-naked woman is my sister-in-law?* Too many thoughts were racing through his brain at once, and he didn't close his eyes. Ash pulled her skirts back down, and his pants up, as the uncommonly pretty, ginger-haired young woman hastily adjusted her gaping bodice, giggling and looking adoringly at Ash.

"What the damn hell do you mean your wife?" Rath demanded as soon as he could express words again.

"Exactly as it sounds." He raked his fingers through his mussed blond hair, then helped his wife gather hers back into its braid. "Maggie, or should I say Margaret Frances McCurdy, Lady Sinclair, may I present you to Rowan Grayson Sinclair, the Earl of Rathbridge, also known as Lord Wrath, or Lord Sin, depending on who you ask. My brother, the much loved but totally jaded merchant shipper, and all-round pain in my arse."

With her legs and breasts once again concealed, Maggie visually stiffened her spine and bolstered her courage. Extending her hand, she dropped to a polite curtsy. "'Tis pleased I am to finally meet you," she said, not bothering to hide her lilting Scottish brogue. "I shall leave you both to catch up. I will send a footman to you. And I am sure, my lord, you must be hungry. I will have a small luncheon prepared."

Ash squeezed her hand encouragingly and watched her dash from the room.

"Explain," Rath demanded, slapping his leather gloves on his defiled desk.

"I take it our letter never found you, or you would know that Maggie and I were married nearly six weeks ago."

"Six weeks?"

Ash tucked his shirt, still grinning. "And the best six weeks it has been."

Rath could but stare at his little brother. This was not the young man he had left two years ago. Catching his brother in flagrante delicto was commonplace enough, though he usually saved that behavior for their bachelor quarters, but the brother he had left was serious and stern, and had sworn never to marry.

This new Ash was positively giddy with, he hesitated to think it, love. Rathbridge men did not marry for love, not when the earldom was at stake. *But then again,* he reminded himself, *Ash isn't the earl and can marry where he pleases.* He had never seen his brother happier.

"Do I know her family? Does Mother approve? I'm sorry, Ash, but I can think of a thousand questions, and for the first time I'm thinking that I've been away too long." He sighed, leaning against the desk. It hadn't been much more than two years this time.

"You *have* been away too long," Ash agreed, pulling out a bottle of gin from the desk drawer and moving their conversation to a pair of chairs by the fireplace. "I'll give you the short version." He poured a glass for himself and passed one to Rath, who sat down across from him, squeezing his wide frame into the delicate chair.

"Just after you left for the east, I bought the most magnificent stallion from the Scottish Highlands, and even managed to convince Baron Drake's horse trainer, a fabulous man who talks to horses, to come to work for our stables. Angus did not come alone, nor did the stallion, as Maggie, his niece, came with him. She was only seventeen at the time, and wild. But she had a way with horses and Mother took to her like chocolate.

"Well, Mother couldn't leave well enough alone, and convinced Angus to let her send Maggie to finishing school. And when she came back, she was nothing like the wild creature that had gone. She was ravishing. And with a little coaxing from Mother, Maggie and Maggie's meddling best friend, well, I fell head over heels for her. And in about seven months, maybe a little less" — he smiled rakishly — "you should be an uncle."

"Bloody Christ," he swore.

"You don't sound pleased, brother."

"Hell, of course I'm pleased. It's just—" He didn't know how to end that statement. It's just that he had lost his last partner in depravity, his best friend. He saw the anxious look in Ash's eyes. "It's just that I should have been here for the wedding."

Ash frowned. "If we knew when you were returning, we may have been able to wait, but—"

Rath held up his hand to stop his brother. "I know. I'm not faulting you both, I just would have liked to see you wed. I have a lovely piece of jade aboard ship that should make you both a beautiful wedding present."

Ash laughed. "That would be lovely, I'm sure, but having you here is a much better gift. I worried that we'd never see you home again."

Rath tried his best not to growl at that dig. He did not like to be taken to task by his brother. They had made the decision together that his efforts were best spent in the Far East.

"I hope I did not embarrass her too much earlier," Rath apologized.

"Hell, that's nothing compared to being caught by Angus the week before the wedding. It took two weeks for the bruise from that horse whip to disappear from my ass." He chuckled suddenly, obviously remembering. "But you would probably like to catch up on less malicious gossip, and my wife will blister my ears if she catches me telling that particular tale."

Rath shook his head. "It's going to take me a few days to get used to you as a married man."

"You will have a little time. Next Friday, we're throwing our first ball here. It's just a small one now that we're back in London, to celebrate her birthday, and of course, our wedding. Mother has promised no more than two hundred people."

"A small event, then." He rolled his eyes, but was laughing. Their mother had a tendency to go overboard. "Now that I'm home I should maybe learn more about the estate business, since you'll soon have your hands full with my nephew."

"Niece," Ash corrected. "Maggie swears it's a girl to torment and bewitch me, and of course, Mother agrees with her."

"My niece then. If you're throwing a ball, then Mother and Felicia must be in London."

"They are still at Rosehaven, but they are arriving this week, and will be joining us here at Sinclair House so they can help Maggie prepare for the party. Are you staying here?"

"Thank you, no. Gisele and Richards are aware of my return. And I think I will be more comfortable at my townhouse."

"Well, let's get a quick luncheon, and then I will fill you in on estate business and any other gossip you've missed. I think you'll be pleased with the progress of the shipyards. We added another ship, *The Eclipse*, to the American route."

After lunch, Rath sat behind his father's desk. He was happy to be back at the family's London home. He was not yet over his shock, of that he was sure. The last day and a half had taken on a surreal quality, with Rath sensing himself as only a bit player in the drama.

He had, of course, told Cleo that he would help Kit's sister any way he could, and discovered that Kit was still in the Caribbean, having become the unlikely heir to his neighbors' estate.

"It must be contagious," Rath grumbled under his breath, thinking of the number of his friends who had married since he'd last seen them. At least Cleo was still giving Gabe a merry chase.

And now his sister and mother were on their way from Rosehaven. It would soon be a full house. He considered a moment what it was like to be back 'home'. It had been nearly three years since he had visited, and longer than that since he spent any real time in England. He felt as if he'd been thrown into another world. Everyone's lives had changed so much. Everyone's but his.

"Damn me, but I need a woman," he swore, tossing back another glass of gin.

He needed time to adjust to all the changes in the lives of his family and friends. *It will be a better time if I can find that copper-haired vixen,* he thought. What a thoroughly enjoyable diversion she could have turned out to be. But he didn't even know her name. Not that he had given her his real name, either.

Still, he could press up on Lisette, and if not Lisette, then perhaps one of her footmen for her direction. He decided to get on that straight away. A few hours between her legs would definitely improve his mood. He recalled his brother usually kept a runner or two in his employ. He smiled. By this time tomorrow, he could be balls deep in pleasure.

* * * *

It had been two days, and still Georgiana had heard nothing about this grand plan of Cleo's to save her reputation. Nor had she had any more anonymous letters. *Perhaps they've grown bored with my ignoring them,* she thought, *and moved on to another.*

She had hesitated to tell Cleo of the ever-increasing number of nasty letters she'd been receiving. At Lady Hilbert's she had gotten used to receiving nasty letters from the other girls, telling her to go home, calling her an island whore or worse. No, she'd decided long ago that nasty letters were to be expected when one was unconventional and monied.

Unfortunately, Georgie realized she had not come away from her momentary folly at *Chez de Sauveterre* unscathed. She could tell from the cool stares she received when out shopping, that rumor was making its way the titled masses.

She did not put a lot of stock in rumor herself and had hoped for some enlightened minds among the ton, but it did not seem like many would be forthcoming. Yesterday she had run into one of the few girls from school she could call a friend, Lady Eliza Rumsford, the youngest daughter to the Earl of Rumsford. But as they began to chat, her mother had bellowed out, "Eliza, it is time to leave."

Eliza had given her mother an inquiring look, but beneath the weight of her mama's forbidding stare, she had turned to Georgie with a promise to call soon then followed her mother from the store.

It was a pleasant surprise when she arrived home to discover her best friend waiting to have tea with her. Maggie understood her and would forgive her anything.

"Maggie, thank goodness, at least you are still my friend."

"Why wouldn't I be?" Then a light of understanding grew in her eyes. "They've found out about your late-night escapades, haven't they?"

Georgiana nodded. "And at least one of them is causing a stir." She explained that her uncle had gotten word of her visits to *Chez de Sauveterre* and if he did, that must mean it was grist for the rumor mill, since her uncle never had any idea of what went on in the city.

"And still no word from the mysterious correspondent?" Maggie questioned.

"I won't meet with him, and Cleo assures me there is nothing damning he may have on Christopher. My parents have been dead now nearly twenty years, and I'm assured they did not lead sordid lives, beyond a bit of sanctioned piracy."

"I believe they called it privateering during the war. And my own husband and his family, having been partners with yours, would be accused of that, as well," Maggie suggested.

"But still that's not enough for blackmail. It's just that I know very little about his rakehell days. Once it was pointed out to him that teaching his little sister to gamble, sail and curse were considered improper, he became quite respectable around me."

"Too bad it was too late by then." She snorted.

"Don't get snippy with me. And don't you start complaining. My 'knowledge' proved useful when helping you land Ash."

"Speaking of that, did you hear that the earl has arrived home again?"

"Yes, Cleo plans to enlist him to help my cause and give me some respectability." She snorted. "From what

I remember of him, he was quite disreputable. What have you heard of him?"

"I'm not sure anyone knows him very well anymore. He's been away for so long. It's probably a good thing he's to give you respectability because I don't think he believes Ash and I to be all that respectable right now. When he arrived home we were, well, you know, in the library."

"You shameless hussy." Georgiana pretended to be indignant but smiled at her friend. She had been so glad when the Countess of Rathbridge decided to sponsor Maggie's education at Lady Hilbert's Academy. It meant she had at least one friend who was as new to London and new its rules as she was. And Maggie could always be persuaded to participate in a good escapade.

"I know but Ash has become so delightfully wicked, where he used to be so serious. Rathbridge thought I was Ash's mistress. You should have heard the yelling. He was really quite insulting. But once Ash explained that we were married, he became almost friendly."

"I hear he can be a tyrant, and he used to have the most abominable reputation. Even worse than Kit's. I'm surprised that he complained that there was a mistress in his house. Rumor has he has had more than his share."

"That was one of the insults. He said that if Ash was going to bring his 'ladies' home, then he had to be prepared to share." She tried to look offended, but just smiled. "But you know Ash, he was very calm about it. He just pulled down my skirt and pulled up his pants and sent me to get tea so he could take care of his brother. He is so efficient."

Efficient, Georgie harrumphed, remembering when that wasn't a positive quality and had been instead a cruel sticking point to Maggie who was trying to garner his attention. Georgie had thought him cold and obtuse. He had put Maggie off time and again with ease. *Thank you very much for your help with the horses. Thank you very much for being a friend to my mother, to my sister, whatever.* They had put an end to that. They had made Maggie into a raving beauty who couldn't be ignored. What with her lush curves, and her striking red-blonde hair, she was a hit even without an ample dowry.

"Oh, Georgie, you should find such efficiency. It is so time consuming, you wouldn't be left any chance to get into trouble."

She thought of Gray, and how he had caressed her. "Oh, Maggie, you must promise not to tell anyone, but I have a secret that I must share." She clasped her friend's hands. "I did meet someone."

"How exciting! Who is he? Do I know him? Is he that dashing Lord Hurley who's just come back from the Americas?"

"No, it is not Lord Hurley, who kisses like a fish, by the by." She mimicked fish lips and sent them both into a fit of giggles. "I met him on my ill-fated escapade to *Chez de Sauveterre,* and I don't know his name."

"How romantic, but are you sure he's not the blackmailer?"

"No, but if the blackmailer knew what happened, then maybe he'd have something to blackmail me with."

"You didn't!"

"Of course not," she exclaimed. She'd never tell how Maggie how close she'd come to being lost in his arms.

She stood and strode to the sideboard to pour herself a glass of sherry. "But oh, he was so handsome," she told her. "Not like Ash is handsome. He was dark and menacing, but also gentle with an irrepressible spark of wit."

"You had better be pouring two glasses, because I want to hear all about this dashing stranger." Maggie giggled.

She brought back a glass for them both and settled in to share with her best friend what she could tell no one else.

* * * *

Rath arrived at Cleo's townhouse unannounced. He had just met the runner to discover that while he'd not yet found her, he was chasing down a rumor of a young woman who had been seen frequenting a gaming hell earlier this week. He had told the runner to keep looking and inform him as soon as she was found.

Cleo's housekeeper showed him into the salon, and he helped himself to a glass of gin from the decanter on the sideboard.

The door to the library swung open and Cleo swanned into the room. "You must have been busy not to come before now. Have the mamas already discovered that an eligible Earl has returned to the market?"

He caught Cleo in a light embrace. "The invitations have been overflowing. I had forgotten how quickly word travels."

Cleo slipped from his arms and poured herself a glass of sherry. "Speaking of travels, I had forgotten to ask, but aside from Lonny's accident, how have yours been?"

He rolled his eyes and told her that those stories would take a while. When she shrugged her delicate white shoulders, he sank into the large leather wingback chair that he had helped her pick out ten years ago. His recent business had taken him to the Far East and he had brought back with him a varied cargo, including silks and spices. He told her about the people he'd met along the way and the myriad trouble they had encountered. In the last six years, his Chinese had improved vastly, but there were so many dialects that one could still step in it sometimes.

"Has your little heiress gotten herself into any more trouble?" he asked.

"Not that I've heard, but I'm not always sure I will hear of it. The gossip columns usually hear before I do, but they keep it vague," she admitted. "I know she's unhappy here in London. It's stifling compared to what she's used to, but she's very careful when she goes out. I fear someone may be following her, and is just looking for dirt to use against her, and when they didn't find enough they decided to threaten her with exposing her brother."

He raked his hands through his hair. "I'll admit that I've racked my brain, and I probably knew Kit better than anyone. I can think of nothing that would incite a blackmailer. Has he given her no clue, no price for the safe keeping of this information?"

"At this point, no price but her reputation. He started out suggesting she attend all sorts of disreputable establishments, with the lure that he will meet her there and tell her the price and presumably what secret he thinks he has."

"I take it you cautioned her against such assignations?"

"Of course I did but that must have incited him because it was after that when he began to have her followed. It may not be so bad were it not for their aunt. She's one of those devout Methodists who believe any sort of pleasure will send you straight to the devil. And for a woman to succumb to those wild desires, well, she's convinced it's madness. Literally."

"I remember her. One look from her could wither the stoutest cock. I never did care for her. I recall Kit mentioning that she had disapproved loudly when his father eloped to Gretna Green with Veronica."

"So the story goes. As long as Veronica did not marry, her fortune was in Charles' guardianship. Kit never believed Charles liked losing that control, despite having his own, albeit modest, fortune."

"If it can be called a fortune, it isn't modest," Rath said dryly. "I have a very discreet runner I can use. He's doing some work for me now, but I will put him to this task too."

A knock at the door interrupted them, and Mr. Hobbs, Cleo's butler, presented a note for the earl.

He glanced over it quickly. It was the information he was waiting for.

"I must go," he apologized and returned his empty glass to the sideboard.

"It's not Lonny?" Cleo asked, concerned.

"No, sweetheart." He kissed her cheek. "Lonny is fine. This is just business," he assured her.

She narrowed her eyes at him and caught his hand. "Whoever she is, she must be something else. You won't forget I need your help."

"Never. I will meet you and the girl here tomorrow at say three o'clock, and we will think up a solution together."

* * * *

They had found the girl.

"There she be, my lord," the runner said, pointing to her as she exited the bookstore across the street. Rath watched as she arranged her few purchases in her arms. She was walking his way. He dismissed the runner with barely a glance. As she neared, he slid out of the shadows of his carriage and caught her elbow.

"I thought I'd never find you." He propelled her into the carriage before a word of protest could pass her lips.

"Gray, I don't understand?" She looked up at him questioningly.

"What is there to understand?" he said, pulling her onto his lap, and kissing alongside her neck. "I missed you." He took the books from her hands and put them on the seat across from his.

"Gray, you are incorrigible." She laughed, despite herself, and he felt his own lips raising to return her smile. She was beautiful, even in her simple muslin walking dress. He knew she must have a million questions, least of all how he found her.

"I wasn't happy with the way we left things the other night."

"So, you decided to kidnap me?" she scolded.

"I wanted to see you again." He kissed along her jaw and she arched her neck, allowing him to skim his lips over her throat. "Can you really tell me that you didn't want to see me too?"

"I've thought of little else but you." She curled her hands into his hair, but it was only to pull him away as he blazed a trail with his lips across her collarbone, toward her breasts. "I can't do this now."

"You were made for doing this."

"I mean" — she took his face between her palms and forced him to look at her — "I am expected somewhere. I can't not show up. People will worry."

He groaned, not having thought that far ahead. "We'll send a message."

"I can't," she insisted. "I have to be there."

"This is a means for you to get away?" In his quest to find her, he hadn't stopped to think if she'd want to be found.

"Yes and no. I mean, I don't know if I want to get away. But I am expected elsewhere."

He tapped on the roof of the coach and had it swing back around to the bookshop. "I'm giving you a choice," he said. "Stay away, and this will be over, or come to me tonight when you can. Have a hackney bring you to this address." He handed her a card with the address to his bachelor residence upon it.

"Is this your address?"

"I have quarters there. It's not large, but I do have an excellent cook."

"Thank you," she said, adjusting her clothing.

"I hope to see you again," he said as she tucked the card into her reticule before gathering her discarded purchases with great deliberateness and care. She wouldn't meet his eyes.

She looked back over her shoulder once after his footman had helped her from the carriage. She smiled up at him, but it didn't quite reach her eyes, then she turned away, heading back toward the milliner. Rath was sure he'd lost her, and he still hadn't gotten her name.

Chapter Five

Georgie smacked her fan against her thigh impatiently. She was irritated, but not surprised when Maggie's hand enclosed hers, stilling her restless thumping. She gave a little smile to her friend, who enjoyed these choral performances.

Georgie had never found pleasure in these assemblies, listening to a tiresome selection of singers and musicians both professional and amateur, but she tried always to be patient for her friend's sake. Besides, this event was meant to show solidarity. Together they were making a stand against the ton. With Maggie and Cleo throwing their support behind her, she was well protected from the hostile glares. They just raised their brows and glowered back, daring them to give her the cut direct.

Tonight, Georgie wanted to be elsewhere. She didn't know if it was true or just romantic fancy, but she had felt a connection that night with Gray. No one, not even the fish-lipped Lord Hurley, who would have made her a decent match in every other way, made her stomach flutter the way Gray had. And they shared, she thought, some of the same restlessness.

What would he say, she wondered, *if he learns I was taught to box and fence, and I know as much as almost any sailor about running a ship? Will he find me completely unsuitable? Will he retract his request for me to visit him tonight?* She thought not.

Unnatural she'd been called. Not as a rule to her face, but she'd heard the young women talking when she was at school. She just wasn't interested in embroidery and menu planning. Running an estate, she could do. Keep the ledgers, not a problem. But mend the curtains, not likely. Sew her husband's or her children's clothing? If she was expected to then blood stains had better become a fashion because she'd prick her fingers to death trying.

She fretted all evening. She knew it was wrong to let Maggie and Cleo think it because of her worry over the blackmailer had given her a headache but it had given her the out she needed to leave early.

It wasn't until the hackney pulled up in front of the small townhouse that she began to question her decision. She frowned at herself, at her impetuousness, which was why she was forever getting into trouble.

It was raining but a footman had been standing at the ready near the door, as if expecting her, and he rushed forward so she did not have dash out into the rain. By the time she'd climbed the stairs, the door was open and Gray stood waiting for her. He wrapped his arms around her waist, pulling her inside.

"I knew you'd come," he said, lifting her into his arms and carrying her upstairs as she laughed.

* * * *

She had expected they would get right down to business, but she'd been here an hour and her virginity was still in tact. She giggled, he had however kissed every inch of her now naked body, before deciding the occasion called for champagne. She was getting impatient waiting for him.

"Good news," he said as he kicked the door closed behind him with the ball of his foot. "My housekeeper has restocked some of the kitchen." He presented the tray to her with a regal bow.

She laughed and reminded him, "You said you had the best cook."

"Gissy is the best but she wasn't expecting me to have company."

Truthfully, Georgie couldn't care less about the plate of food, though her belly had begun to growl. She was looking, instead, at Gray's bare broad shoulders and the dark smattering of curls across his chest. His ebony hair hung loose about his shoulders and his chin held a dark shadow. Those whiskers had scraped raw every inch of her bare skin. The memory of his lips making a map of her body made her shiver beneath the soft woolen blanket that she was now wrapped beneath.

It had felt glorious, but inside she was still wrestling with the decision she had made. Kit and Cleo would be so disappointed, wouldn't they? Would they even care, knowing how she felt about marriage and London? She never planned to stay there. She was an independent woman, and for all practical purposes, a spinster to boot. She had her own money. She would soon have her own estate. Why shouldn't she take what pleasure

Gray offered? It may be her only chance, and no one had to be any the wiser.

Her decision was made. She stood and walked to the small table where he was setting out the light repast. Dropping the blanket, she perched upon the table edge and took a sip of the sweet champagne he had poured.

"I thought you were hungry," he said, licking his lips as he raked his eyes over her naked form.

"I am," she said as she reached out to untie the breeches he'd donned to run downstairs.

"You're impatient, little one," he chided.

"I think I've been showing remarkable patience." She pouted, as she slid her hand against his bare cock. "I want to do more than kiss."

With that, he seized her roughly around the waist, pushing her back on the table. He spread her thighs apart with his hands, his long fingers stroking her damp flesh. She writhed, begging him to touch her.

"You want more, my little vixen?"

She growled. He knew she wanted him inside her. She wanted to feel that burst of pleasure again, but with him. She wasn't afraid of his cock, though she had been warned by her friends at *Chez de Sauveterre* that the first time may hurt.

A moment later, she realized that knowing about something and experiencing it were very different things as he thrust his cock inside her. The sharp sting of pain was instant and brought tears to her eyes, but it only lasted a moment before she began to relish the beautiful fullness of his cock inside her. She looked up at him, and she knew he knew. She could see it in the fierce furrow between his brows. "Don't stop," she begged.

"Christ!" he swore, holding himself still inside her. He didn't need to be told how stupid this was. He should stop. Withdraw now. But he couldn't when she begged him to keep going.

He pulled her into his arms, still buried inside her, and carried her to the bed. He kissed her eyes, where the tears still shimmered and began stroking her body.

"Don't stop." She looked up at him, her hands clinging to his shoulders.

"Wouldn't dream of it, but I am going to slow this down so it feels good," he promised her. He braced himself on his forearm so he could kiss her as he ran his hand down her body to the spot they connected.

His fingers danced over the little bundle of nerves above where they met until he felt her contracting around him, her hips squirming against him. Then he began to thrust, slow steady and steady, meant to drive her toward her peak. Her fingernails dug into his shoulders and her feet wrapped around his thighs.

"That's it, vixen," he encouraged her. "Cling to me. Come for me."

When her tight sheath convulsed around him, he set up the rhythm he needed to join her in that pleasure. She was so tight, it didn't take much before he felt the orgasm rushing through him. He barely had enough time to pull out of her and spill himself against her thighs.

He collapsed next to her, fighting his urge to run away. "You should have told me," he demanded.

"Why?" She nuzzled closer to him and chewed on his bare shoulder. "Would you have stopped?"

"Yes."

"Then I'm very glad I didn't tell you. I didn't want you to stop," she argued.

"I don't make it a habit to deflower virgins," he said roughly, pushing her away. And it was true. Despite his reputation, he had never spilled virgin blood.

He got a wet cloth from the dressing table and set to rinsing her blood from himself and from her thighs. She spread her legs for his cleaning, and he was instantly hard again.

"My virginity was not a virtue," she told him.

"Your future husband may not see it that way. Or another family member should they discover this." His looked at her. "Tell me, luv, should I be expecting a dawn meeting with your father or brothers?"

She stilled his hand. "Stop worrying. I don't have a father or brother who are going call you out for having your way with me. And I won't be having a husband, as I never intend to marry."

He shook his head, not believing that for a second. "Every woman intends to marry."

"Those who know me know that I don't. I'm not some fresh society miss bent on trying to trap you."

"You wish to be someone's mistress, then?"

"Are you offering?" She was laughing at the idea, but he wasn't. He didn't respond to the bait.

"I wish to be more than that. I plan to be my own woman. Surely, even you, whom I realize spends months at a time at sea, must realize that when a woman is well and truly on the shelf—which is what I am—that she will have very few opportunities to learn this pleasure," she said vehemently. "And this woman wants to learn all she can from you, before you set sail out of my life again."

"I will sail out of your life again. No matter how fucking tempting your body is, I won't marry you." He looked her up and down. "And, my darling, you are far from on the shelf."

"I don't want to marry you, Gray," she told him. "I want to fuck you." Her strong language caught him by surprise. "Now, please get yourself together and get ready to teach me all the things that I really shouldn't know."

Rath shook his head. Every clue pointed to her being a lady, a well-born society miss. Even if she did drink and gamble and, he was learning, cursed like a sailor. He looked at the creamy thighs still splayed before him. He traced the curve of her muscled legs until it rested on her mound.

He groaned. It sounded harsh and animal to him. He dipped his fingers into her, exploring. Her hips writhed against his fingers. "A few rules, then."

"There are rules in this?" She sighed, throwing herself dramatically against the pillows.

"There are always rules."

She rolled her eyes.

"We can stop this now, if you prefer." He withdrew his fingers and she frowned, her brow wrinkling, her lips pouting. He licked his fingers clean. "Good, then the rules." He walked back to the table and poured himself a shot of gin. "I think you will agree I have more experience in these matters than you do."

She nodded. "In this particular matter, I will agree that you do. But I've been to *Chez de Sauveterre*, so don't think me ignorant."

"I'm not looking for a mistress or a wife. But I like your offer, and I dare say I was a notorious rogue when you were still in swaddling cloths and I can teach you things you've never dreamed." Rath was used to experienced women throwing themselves at him. On his travels, he had learned more techniques and indulged in more decadence than he would have ever thought existed at her age. He had been taught well, and he had a lot to teach.

"I'm guessing we both have busy lives, but in this room, we are here for one thing. Pleasure. I know I've given you pleasure tonight, but there are many more ways to make your body quake and I daresay we will have a great deal of fun learning what pleases you. And I" — he returned to the bed, straddling her hips, his still semi erect cock pressing against her belly — "will teach you what pleases me. I will show you things that a ton husband would blush to ask for from his mistress, let alone his wife."

"Because wives are to be submissive and endure. Hence another reason I don't want marriage." She smiled smugly as she forcefully wrapped her hand around his length, brushing the crown with her thumb.

She had guts and he had no doubt she would prove an eager pupil. "I promise I will never hurt you or suggest that we do anything you do not wish to do. If you trust me, we will enjoy what time we have together."

"I wish we did not have to leave this room," she told him. "I may not have family here but there are those who will be aware of my comings and goings. We will need to use a certain amount of discretion."

"You agree to the rules, then?"

"They are not difficult rules." She shrugged, bringing her other hand underneath his sac, stroking his balls. "I can't hide that I was a virgin, but that does not mean I am innocent either. Think of where you met me. I daresay I've been called an original. A blue-stocking. And worse. I am not wife material, nor will I likely ever be allowed a protector. Therefore, there is nothing and no one preventing us from this pleasure. I want to be your lover. And when this is all over—whether you choose it or I—we shall shake hands, kiss one another on the cheek and walk away."

"That's a pretty speech."

"That's the truth."

He shook his head. "I will need to know what to call you."

She chewed on her lip.

"I can't just keep calling you luv," he told her. His hips thrust into her eager hands. Her touch felt good. Light, but confident.

"Ana," she said finally, her eyes wide as a drop of pre-cum slid from the tip of his cock, soaking her hand. "Does it always do that?" She looked up at him with wonder and excitement.

"Pretty much, Ana," he groaned as she raised her hand to her mouth, tasting him. He had to bite his cheek to keep from coming again with that lush but innocent gesture. "Do you want to see a man come? What my cock does when it's inside you?"

She grinned. "Yes, please."

He pushed her back so she reclined against the pillows on the bed, and brushed her hands away. His took his cock in his one hand, the other hand fondling his balls. "When you touch me," he instructed, "I like a firm hold, like this." He squeezed his hand around his cock, stroking himself roughly. "I like to hear you talk about how much you want my cock, my dick, my rod."

She nodded. "And you like your bollocks grabbed like that? Doesn't it hurt?"

"A little hurt is worth the pleasure," he told her, stroking himself faster. "You can squeeze them, suck them, nibble on them. All of that will please me." He took her hand and placed it over his sac, curling his hand around hers. "Feel me as I come. I'm close."

He took care to direct his cock as he stroked it. The feel of her delicate fingers stroking his root, were exciting. He couldn't wait to paint her breasts with his cum. To watch it splash thick and white against her creamy skin. The thought made his balls tighten and his orgasm raced like fire through his veins. He shot ropes of pearlescent cum as she watched, wide-eyed.

He was the worst sort of rogue. She'd been a virgin an hour ago, and now he had used her as his canvas. The experience had left him lightheaded, and he hung his head forward, closing his eyes and catching his breath. He was amazed at her sensuality, her openness. *Almost too good to be true,* he thought, but pushed the idea away. He wasn't going to let doubt interrupt their pleasure.

"That was" — she sounded breathless — "amazing. I mean I've seen it before, but not up close, and not been part of it."

He lifted his head to see her dip her fingers into the wet mess he'd left across her breasts. She rubbed her fingers together then brought them to her nose to sniff.

"Taste it." He was breathless as he watched her tentatively touch her fingers to her tongue. "Not now, but soon, I plan to fuck your mouth. I won't ask whether you know men and women do that."

She licked another finger, taking more of his essence on her tongue.

"You didn't stay in the gaming salon at *Chez de Sauveterre*?" He knew the answer. She may have been a virgin, but she wasn't as innocent as she looked.

"I have always been good at sneaking into places I wasn't supposed to go." She shrugged. "There is a room up there with a window, where people who like to watch can see people who like to be watched."

"Yes, I know." He shook his head. He slid onto the bed beside her, pulling her to his side. "You are a hellion."

"I've been called worse." She snuggled into him. "But for now, I'm your hellion."

It was past midnight, and they'd been nibbling on some bread and cheese when he remembered to ask her if there would be anyone waiting for her.

She sighed. "I should send a note."

Rath grabbed his trousers and ran downstairs to deliver the note to his footman who would see it to her home. He stopped in the kitchen to get more wine and something else he knew he'd need tonight.

By the time he got back upstairs, she'd stolen his dressing gown and was sitting in the chair by the window. Her feet were tucked up off the floor and he was struck by how she could look both innocent and wanton. Her lips were swollen from his kisses. Her eyes languid. Faint abrasions could be discerned on her neck where his whiskers had scratched her. He'd have to shave more often if they kept this up.

"Second thoughts?" he asked, noting her moody countenance as she looked out the window.

She looked over her shoulder at him and smiled. "None."

He was relieved. He wouldn't blame her if she had. "What did you say in your letter?"

"I'm not in the habit of explaining to my household what my plans are," she told him. "I sent the note to my maid to let her know that I was spending the night at my best friend's home. It's not unusual. I've stayed there for the night unexpectedly before. I told her I would be in late tomorrow."

"You live alone?" He seemed incredulous.

"I told you, I'm an original." She shrugged. "Besides my very discreet servants, I have an ancient companion who will not know whether I am there or not. It would take weeks, if ever, before she thought to wonder where I was. Stop worrying."

He would be the first time some little miss had tried to trap him, but though Ana had omitted telling him she was a virgin, he didn't think she was a liar or a fortune hunter.

"How about you?" she asked.

"It's been a long time since I had a guardian." He laughed and handed her a glass of wine. She punched him in the side before he could step away.

"That's not what I meant."

"I know, little one. But the answer is no, I have no one expecting me this evening. There are always invitations, but none that I must stick to. We have all night."

He pulled over a chair and sat next to her, looking outside. He put a hand on her knee, but otherwise they were quiet. He enjoyed the silence with her. It gave him a chance to observe her, like he had at the gaming table.

"Thank you for the wine," she said after a time, closing her hand over his.

"I brought something else for you, too."

She stuck out her bottom lip in a playful pout. "Your tone makes me think it's not chocolate."

"Next time I go down, I promise."

"You are sounding entirely too serious, Captain. What serious thing could you have brought with you from the kitchen?"

"Your next lesson." He pulled a fresh sponge out of his pocket. It was a good thing that all Richards had done was smirk when he'd requested one. "Have you heard the women at Lisette's talk about preventing conception?"

He felt a little chagrined. He had never had a lover to whom he'd had to explain this sort of thing. His usual choice of partner already knew the ropes and was able to handle these things without being told.

"I thought if you didn't come inside me, I wouldn't get pregnant," she said uncertainly.

"That's one way, and where I profess to a great degree of control, your future lovers may not have as much foresight." In truth, it killed him each time he had to withdraw from her tight sheath. He wanted to come inside her. "And you can take this precaution yourself unlike French letters. You don't need to rely on your lover."

"Smart. So what do we do?" She unfolded her feet from beneath her and sat forward in her chair.

"An ill-timed pregnancy can destroy all hope you may have for true independence. A sponge, like this" — he passed her the sponge — "placed deeply inside you, keeps my seed from entering your womb."

She turned the sponge over in her hands. "A kitchen sponge? So what do I do with it?"

He took the sponge back from her and dipped it in a small bowl of vinegar he'd brought with him. "Bend over the chair and spread your legs."

Her skepticism was obvious in her expression. Her brows knit together, and she pursed her lips, but it only took a moment before she stood up. She let his robe fall to the floor at her feet before she turned around, moving into the position he'd instructed.

"Give me your hand."

He put the sponge between her fingers then guided her hand between her legs to her pussy.

"It may sting a moment," he warned as he added his two fingers to hers and pushed the sponge deep. Her body tensed then relaxed. He let her fingers slide out, but he kept his inside. Stroking her, preparing her. He stroked his fingers against the front wall of her sex until she bent her head to her hands and let him wring forth another round of pleasure from lush warmth.

"What do we do now?" she asked huskily, even as her body still quaked.

"Anything we want," he promised.

Chapter Six

It was a quarter past three when Cleo glided into her library to meet with the Earl of Rathbridge. "Georgie should be along anytime now," she lied. She had just dispatched her footman to Georgiana's townhome in a hope to find her. She had not heard from her since she'd dispatched her first note yesterday requesting her attendance here today. That was worrisome.

So was the limp in Rath's step. He was leaning heavily on his cane. "Are you all right?" she asked, running his hand down his thigh. "Your leg is bothering you more now that you are home, isn't it? Should Gabe take a look at it?"

He winked at her. "I may have overdone it last night, but it was worth it."

She smacked his thigh. "You're a devil."

He grinned. "Gabe would tell me to walk it off or to warm it. And I've done both. I will do more later, too."

"I am sure you will be doing more of what made it sore to begin with too," she admonished. Not that she expected him to change his ways now. He'd been at sea for what seemed like ages. His first stop upon his return was always the brothels. Then the gaming hells, before he'd come up for air and be sociable. She knew she was invading his personal ritual by asking him to help her with Georgie's plight. "About Georgie," she began.

He shook his head. "I've given it some thought and have only a few questions."

Cleo, intrigued, nodded for him to continue.

"The girl is comely?" he asked.

"Exceedingly so," Cleo confirmed. "A lack of suitors is not her problem. Just an unwillingness to entertain any offers."

He grinned. "And she is obviously well dowered."

Cleo couldn't help but roll her eyes. As if Kit would have it any other way. "She inherited a Scottish title and the profitable estate it entails from her mother. It has an exquisite stable with breeders as well as racers. She also has a townhouse in London, and few tin mines that are part of her dowry."

"An heiress, then. That will work nicely."

Cleo fussed at the sideboard, pouring them both a small brandy. "Work nicely for what?"

"The only way to assure her reputation is to align it with another," he suggested, and Cleo agreed. That had been her thought as well.

"As I am newly returned to London and speculation will be that I am in search of a wife. Georgiana will be that wife."

"You wish to marry her?" Cleo stared at him. She knew he'd do anything for Kit, but the idea of Rath married to her Georgie was hard to fathom. Georgie was wild, but Rath was, in truth, the very devil.

"Of course not," he spat out. "And I would think that Kit would be first to call me out should I think it. But to the ton, she will be my betrothed and she will garner the protection of my name."

Cleo thought about it. It would fix their dilemma. Her aunt and uncle wouldn't dispute the match considering how close the families were. It would look to the outside world to be a perfect match. "And in a few months, at her discretion, she can call off the wedding?" Cleo questioned.

"She can use whatever excuse she needs, and she will come off looking fresh and unscathed," he said. "I only intend to be home a few months and we both know my reputation has enough tarnish on it already. A cancelled wedding won't affect it."

"As tarnished as it may be, I know the kind of man you are," she said thoughtfully.

She knew the hell he and Kit had caused together so many years ago. She remembered their prowess at the gaming tables and with women. Together they had built up nasty reputations as fortune stealers and marriage breakers. If you're reckless enough to throw a fortune away at the turn of a card, you deserved to lose, she believed.

So, too, did she believe that there were a host of good reasons for a wife to look elsewhere. Cleo knew well that young women were often married off too much older men to raise the status of the whole family and provide dowries to younger siblings. She couldn't wait to extricate herself from that marriage bed.

When her own ancient husband had died two years into their marriage, friends like Kit and Rath showed her how to make her way through society as a widow. It afforded a woman a great degree of freedom, and she was lucky her husband had had no living children. That can make a widow's life a nightmare.

"Despite any rust on your armor, you still carry a title that all the mama's want to land. You will make her the envy of the ton and protect yourself from their machinations."

She thought of the salacious gossips, whose clucking tongues would be cut short by this unbelievable turn of events. Maybe it wasn't so bad to be an original. Maybe bluestockings were the way of the future. Maybe, just maybe, this would work.

He grinned, and she saw a hint of the devil he'd been when she met him two decades before. "I am informed that Friday evening is Lady Margaret's birthday ball," he told her, "Did you know that Ash had married?"

"Be assured, I am quite familiar with the tale of their courtship." She laughed. "I mentioned that Georgiana was a little wild, not that you can blame her, being raised by Kit, but she does like to cause mischief," she explained.

He looked puzzled. Ash had not given him the story yet, she surmised.

"I'm afraid she was the impetus that got the two of them together." She smiled at him brightly, only to be faced with a scowl. Did he think that his brother would remain a bachelor? Ash was the more serious, but she thought he was also the more romantic. "I would never have allowed her interference if I had not also been convinced that he was in love with Maggie," she explained seriously.

"So what did your little matchmaker do?" he asked through gritted teeth.

"I believe she may have taught Maggie to attract a man's attention," she told him, as he rolled his eyes in exasperation. "And perhaps encouraged her to seduce him, but believe me, it was for Ash's own good."

Rath held up his hand for her to stop. "Don't go on. I may change my mind and let your little ingénue fight her own battles. At least Ash seems happy. I suppose you are both attending the ball?"

"Of course." Cleo was helping Maggie organize it until her mother-in-law could get to town.

"I shall meet the chit there, and to all the world, it will look like we're blissfully reunited." He raised an eyebrow in question. "I trust she must be quite the accomplished little actress then, as well."

Cleo shrugged without comment. No point in him knowing that she could outperform any actress now walking the boards. She recalled when Georgiana was sixteen and Kit had refused to let her sail with him. He had claimed her burgeoning figure was unsettling to his crew. She had bound her breasts, tied up her hair under a cap and stowed away as a deck hand. They had been two weeks out before he had discovered her bunking in with the rest of the crew.

"Something tells me she will do fine," he declared. He looked at his timepiece. "I must be off. As you likely know, Mother and Fiona are arriving this afternoon, and I should like to be home with them this evening."

"Fiona is turning into a lovely young woman," she told him, escorting him to the door. At least he wasn't rushing off this time. "This will be her first ball."

"It's hard to think she's the same age as I was when I met you." He reached out and brushed a stray curl behind her ear. "You haven't changed a bit."

She lowered her eyes, the memories still fresh. "You are such a liar."

"No," he assured her, "I'm not. I will see you on Friday."

"Take care of that leg," she warned him. "I will expect a dance."

* * * *

"Cleo, forgive me," Georgie begged quickly. After receiving Cleo's missive to meet today, she had quickly changed into a simple rose-colored day gown, with a soft silver cloak. Her hair she pulled into a soft bun at the nape of neck. "Your note was misplaced while I was out, and it was only found this afternoon."

"A likely excuse," she admonished lightly. "It doesn't matter. Rathbridge came across with an idea that will solve everything. It will salvage your reputation, make your aunt's eyes bug out and your uncle swallow his tongue, at the same time as allowing Rath to make discreet inquiries on your behalf regarding your admirer."

"What is he going to do, marry me?" She laughed, pulling off her short gloves and tossing them and her cloak on the nearby settee.

"Yes."

Georgie had to pick her jaw up from off the floor. "You ca-can't mean that," she stuttered. "I mean...I can't. He can't. He's like old."

Cleo tossed her hands in the air. "Old!" she exclaimed. "Oh, please," she teased. "He is the perfect age for marrying. And everyone already suspects that he is back only to find a wife and plant an heir. With he and Kit being old friends, it is the best solution."

Georgie's face turned white, and she quickly found a chair before she fell faint. "I can't. I just can't," she stammered.

"Of course, you can't, you silly goose." Cleo patted her hand. "And, of course, you won't go through with the wedding. It will just give you protection until the blackmailer is found and then you can call it off."

Georgie glared at her friend. "That was an awful tease."

"You know I would never encourage you to marry for anything but love."

"Even if I was ruined."

"You already said it yourself. He's old. Are you going to let him ruin you?"

Georgie gasped. "Certainly not." She avoided looking at Cleo lest she discern the truth. She'd already let herself be ruined on her own delicious terms, with a man of her own choosing. She'd not left his bed until late this morning, and she still could feel the ache from his attentions.

"He doesn't even know me. Why would he do this?"

"He's not doing it for you," Cleo began to explain as she sifted through her jewel box.

"Are you and he lovers?"

"Georgie, behave yourself. That is completely inappropriate." She pulled out a simple garnet and gold choker.

How often had she heard that before? But she had learned a long time ago that you gained nothing without asking, so ask she always did. She had always known that Kit and Cleo had been lovers. She had grown up with Kit, thinking of Cleo like a big sister. But unlike a big sister, Cleo had a tendency to act like a little mother. That's why there were some secrets that she would never tell her.

"He is doing this for Kit." Cleo turned so Georgie could fasten the choker for her, then she sat down. "Kit saved his life once."

"Humph," she grumbled as she racked her brain for all the tidbits she'd learned about the earl while she had been helping Maggie plan Ash's seduction. There had been something about a mistress, a child that may have been his and, of course, the fact that he would never settle down, because the only thing he truly loved was the sea.

There was also a story about a young man who had killed himself after losing his entire fortune to the Lord Wrath. He had shot himself on the earl's doorstep and Rath had left London shortly after that. She knew, better than most, the thin vein of truth hidden in any rumor. The rest was all show.

Still, his money and his name were enough to allow him to be forgiven anything, in particular by the doting mothers of this season's crop of eligible girls. Her betrothal to Lord Wrath would upset more than one hopeful mama. Perhaps this would be more fun than she expected.

"You will do as I instruct in this matter, Georgiana," Cleo said, taking on her best motherly tone. "I will expect you to put aside rumor and innuendo and remember that the Sinclairs are a good and noble family and they are like family to Kit."

"Some of them are to me, as well," Georgie argued, thinking of Maggie and Ash and his mother, Madeline, who always made her feel welcome.

"Then we are in agreement. At Maggie's birthday ball on Friday night, Rath will announce your betrothal.

And we will make sure that even your pious aunt and uncle are there to hear the good news."

Georgie smiled with mischief. This had the makings of one hell of a fun season.

* * * *

Lady Madeline Lenora Sinclair, the Dowager Countess Rathbridge, and her only daughter, Felicia, arrived at Sinclair House, amid a great flourish of activity. The carriage with her luggage and her maids had arrived before them and the footmen were still scurrying to unload the trunks.

Madeline, who still did not look her fifty-five years, smoothed the wrinkles from her sky-blue traveling gown and waited for Felicia to find her shoes and join her outside the carriage. She looked around her as she filled her lungs with London air. *Ah, how I hate London,* she thought cheerfully, then laughed at herself. She'd been laughing a lot of late and even crowded, noisy, fetid London could not dampen her spirits.

Felicia, gowned in a pale yellow muslin traveling dress, at last found her shoes so that she could join her mother outside. But Felicia had been peering through the carriage windows since they entered London. While she and her daughter made their home for most of the year at Rosehaven, she hadn't failed to notice Felicia sitting with rapt attention to every tidbit her brother and their friends provided of the city and the world outside their safe little estate.

She hung on their every word, asking for more description. What did it smell like? What did it sound like? Madeline knew Felicia lived for the day that she too would go traveling abroad and see the world.

Madeline had promised they would make a good go at the list of places and events Felicia wanted to see before they went home.

Ash and Maggie had rushed out to greet Madeline and Felicia, but Rath held back. He didn't want to force an emotional reunion on the front stairs of Sinclair House.

"Mother," he whispered as she stepped into the entrance hall. Her eyes grew wide with surprise then glittered with tears. "Rowan." A small gasp escaped her lips and she threw herself at him. He knew she feared each time that he went away that he would not return.

She clasped him in her arms for several moments, before gaining the composure she had become known for. Madeline did not blanche, she was not squeamish, and she refused to squeal at even the juiciest *on-dit* her modiste had to pass along.

"I'm so glad you're home," she said meaningfully, stepping back. "You are home, aren't you?"

She regretted the question as he lowered his gaze to the floor.

"For a while, Mother."

At least he hadn't lied. Some of her smile faded, but she nodded as a squealing Felicia ran for her brother's outstretched arms. He caught her, easily lifting her into his arms.

Madeline marveled at the differences between her eldest and youngest children. In the long months that Rowan had been gone, Felicia had lost the last bit of plumpness that marked her childhood. She was becoming a woman, who would soon need a debut in society, even if her mama still wanted to cloister her in the nursery or maybe a nunnery.

"Hey, squid, I hear you're going to Maggie's ball." Rowan lowered Felicia to the ground, but didn't let go of her hand.

"Mama had a beautiful silk gown made for me. It's the color of pale pink roses, which Mama has said I can wear in my hair."

"You'll be beautiful."

"I know that, and you know that, but no one else will." She pouted. "Mama refuses to let me dance."

Rath bent and whispered conspiratorially to her, "Maybe we shall have to see about that."

"I'm nearly seventeen, soon I shall be coming out, and then mama will have to let me dance and you will have to find me a husband."

"That's a tall order." He laughed and looked over his shoulder to his mother. Madeline was in no position to help when it came to her daughter's ideas young men and her future. She shrugged at him and turned to deal with what she could control, the removal of their trunks from the carriage. She could hear her daughter carrying on and she pitied her poor son. He would regret his homecoming before long.

"But that's why you're the head of the family," Felicia continued as she pulled him through the hallway of Sinclair House. "Ash promised that when I'm eighteen, and no older, or I will be on the shelf, you will come home for my season and ensure that a handsome gentleman from a good family takes me to wife."

"Is that what you promised, Ash?" Rowan's voice boomed across the foyer and Madeline turned to see as Ash tried to fade into the shadows of the door, looking sheepish. Maggie was by her husband's side and trying not to giggle.

"Rowan, you will listen to me," Fellicia insisted, pulling at his arm. "He must be tall, because I'm tall, but not too tall either. He will have dark hair, and blue eyes, because I like that. He will have money, because I don't want him marrying me for my money. Mama promises that I have an ample dowry, so I take it that means I'm rich." She looked back at their mother for confirmation.

"Squid," he interrupted, "couldn't this wait, until say, you unpack?"

She stopped suddenly, and looked at him, not pouting, but with glaring certainty. An intensity reflected in her eyes, which he noted was the same as their father's, and he'd been told, he shared it as well.

"I will not be put off," she announced, shocking the family into silence. "No doubt you will be rushing out of here to attend to business, and I will see you for a few moments here or there during the rest of our stay. You have but two years to find me someone decent. You and Ash need to get to work if you're going to find someone suitable. Mother says I am very choosy.

"And remember, he must be athletic. He'll like horses and to travel, because it's just not fair that everyone has traveled in this family except me. And above all, he must be faithful to me. Like Ash is to Margaret. I will be the most important woman in the world to him."

With that, she turned on her heel, lifted her skirt to show an indecent amount of ankle and ran up the stairs toward her room. The family was quiet a moment, before laughter began to reverberate throughout the foyer. Rowan chuckled, shaking his head.

"Has the whole world gone crazy?" he asked.

"No. It's just your family," Ash promised and slapped him on the back before walking away with Maggie toward the front salon.

"She is your father's child. You all are." They both knew what she meant. They were all headstrong, stubborn and passion filled.

Madeline smiled. Even Ash, despite his quiet devotion to the everyday duty of the business, was their father's son, as had been evidenced by his hasty marriage. And though she would never admit in out loud, she wouldn't have had it any other way.

Chapter Seven

He'd been kept later than he'd hoped, his mother insisting that he stay for them to talk. She was always interested in not just the business side of his voyages, but the cultural side. She wondered about his progress in learning the various dialects of China. What the women wore and did. Were their roles any different than in England. He didn't mind satisfying her curiosity, but as the hours had ticked by, he had to beg off.

His mother was too clever to buy his ruse of being tired, or needing to visit the ship. He knew as he headed back to his small townhouse that his mother suspected he was out gaming and whoring. *I would be,* he thought, *if not for a delicious morsel named Ana waiting for me at home.*

The door to his study was ajar and he could hear a fire crackling in the grate. He grinned and opened the door. Ana had been waiting for him for almost two hours, but he had sent a note around to explain his delay.

She sat in his favorite chair, her legs curled under her. She was reading a book on navy procedure, which she had no doubt borrowed from his bookcase. She had also borrowed his shirt, having discarded her gown for something more provocative.

"I trust you've missed me," he said. He had pulled his hair back for dinner, but let it loose now and slipped out of his coat and waistcoat.

"No," she said, stretching cat-like in the chair, extending her bare legs out before her. Though his shirt reached the middle of her thighs, he was offered a view of a great expanse of soft white flesh. "Did you have a good evening with your family?"

His brow lifted in question.

"Unlike what you did to me, I've not hired a runner to keep track of your whereabouts," she promised. "I simply deduced that you would hardly be likely to leave your mistress to come running here to me, and you mentioned last night that your family was staying in town."

He nodded. He leaned against his desk and stretched his legs out in front of him. He rubbed his palm over his thigh where the pain of his old injury was centered. "Unfortunately."

She looked at him askance.

"Don't give me that look," he warned. "It's not that I don't love my family. I love every one of them. But it is a little overwhelming to be inundated when I have only just returned myself." His lips quirked into a sly smile. "Especially when there is another obligation to which I am more inclined. I trust my escort ensured you got here unaccosted?"

"Richards was very efficient, and has made sure that I was well fed in your absence." She nodded to the plate of empty oyster shells.

"They're supposed to be an aphrodisiac," he told her, pulling the book from her hands and tossing it to the floor, then lifting her into his arms. "Not that I think you need the extra incentive."

She shook her head, then touched her lips to his, eager to kiss him like he'd taught her. She sucked his lower lip into her mouth, running her tongue over the trapped flesh, before opening her mouth and sliding her tongue into his. He lifted her against the nearest bookcase, and with a practiced hand released his erection from his tight breeches. Bracing his hands beneath her buttocks, he plunged into her roughly. She growled and bit down onto his shoulder through his shirt.

"That's it, my little cat," he encouraged. "Bite me. I've been dreaming of your sweet cunt all evening." She nibbled down his neck and shoulders. He squeezed her thighs, grinding into her.

"Harder," he commanded, "You won't hurt me."

She sank her teeth into his muscled flesh a little deeper with each bite. And he pumped into her with wicked adeptness. Building the rhythm to a blinding crescendo then retreating. She was purring and straining against him. The shirt she wore fell open and she pulled him to her breasts. He slid one plump nipple into his mouth.

His cock throbbed and he couldn't hold back his release any longer. He buried his face in her breasts as he came. He breathed in the heady scent of her lavender bath water and of sex as he released himself inside her.

Soon, the room would reek with the smell of it, sex, wine and lavender. She always smelled of lavender.

He slid from her body but did not release her. He carried her into his bedroom and gently laid her down on his bed, and bathed his seed from her legs, as he had last night. He had discovered last night that he liked doing this for her. Ministering to her. He had lovers, albeit it had been part of their job, take care of him after sex, but until Ana, he'd never thought to return the favor.

"I'm sorry," he apologized.

"For what?" She raised herself up on her elbows. He loved that she was oblivious to her nakedness. She held no priggish notions of propriety when they were alone together.

"I didn't mean to fuck you as soon as I saw you, but you were quite irresistible, lounging there in my shirt."

"That was the point, so don't apologize." She grasped his hand, tossing the washcloth from his hand. She placed his hand between her thighs. "I won't break, and I needed you."

He slid a finger, then two inside her.

"You think you won't," he warned her. He had only scratched the surface of what he wanted to do with her.

"I won't," she promised, grinding against his hand, searching for the friction she needed. Her face was flush with arousal. The curls at the apex of her thighs were damp with his seed. He liked that she'd been ready for him. He could feel the sponge inside her.

She braced her heels into the mattress and pressed down into his hand. "Not yet, Ana. Not until I say so."

He shifted on the bed, spreading her thighs. He pressed his tongue against her engorged clit. He ran his tongue along the side as he slid his fingers back into her quivering cunt. He nibbled her softness, dragging his teeth over her clit and sucking it into his mouth.

He loved the taste of her, the sound of her as she keened above him as he brought her closer to the orgasm she craved. She bucked into his hand and he pressed down on her hip to hold her still.

"I said not yet," he warned her again, nipping her inner thigh, leaving a bruise.

She flinched. "I'm so close," she whimpered.

He knew that. Her body tightened on his fingers as he added a third. He wanted her ready when he took her again. He didn't want to have to go easy on her. "Does it excite you to have my mouth on your cunt? To know that I have your honey on my tongue?"

She whimpered again. "Gray!"

He laughed against her pussy, as body convulsed with pleasure. She hadn't waited for his permission, not that he cared. It played well into his plan for the evening.

He kissed his way up her body, her thighs still shaking, wrapping around his hips. She ran her hands over his bare shoulders. "I've marked you," she told him as she traced her fingers over the outline her nails had left.

"I shall wear your mark with pride," he said, kissing her lips, hoping the little crescents indentations bruised. He didn't know why this woman had such a hold over him, he only knew he wanted more.

He tried not to be distracted by her casual confidence as he climbed from the bed to disrobe. Did she realize how unusual she was, not even trying to cover herself from his gaze? He couldn't remember having a more brazen lover that he hadn't paid for. She was a good match for him. "You suit me well," he complimented her as he climbed back onto the bed, straddling her hips between his thighs.

"I wonder how long this will last," she wondered aloud, looking up at him.

"I have until tomorrow afternoon," he told her, stroking his hands down her ribcage.

"You know that's not what I mean." She laughed and pushed his hands away. "We don't have much time together. Soon, the real world will intrude on both our lives."

"Are you saying you want more?"

She could hear the worry in his voice. That wasn't at all what she meant, though she suspected there were a lot of woman for whom dependence was a more reliable commodity.

"Oh, please." She laughed. "Your cock hasn't changed my life. Though I know most men would find it hard to believe that any woman would value her independence over a marriage of convenience."

He bent low over her, kissing her nose. "You constantly surprise me, but I well understand that our relationship is precarious at best."

She nodded. "People are going to begin to miss me if I keep running off here every chance I get. Should we end this?"

"Before it barely begins. Lord, no." He took her hand and wrapped it around his recovering cock. "We just have to be clever. And I know my student is very clever, aren't you?"

"Top of the class, my lord," she promised.

He smiled and let one of his fingers slide into her mouth, over her tongue. "My student," he groaned. "There is much I can show you." He gazed down at her body but held himself back. They had only just started last night, and he was ready for more interesting play.

"Are you ready for tonight's lesson?"

She'd never been more ready. "Will I like tonight's lesson?"

"I promise you." He reached over her into a small teak box on the table beside the bed. From it, he pulled a small crystal box containing to two small gold balls. "Tonight's lessons shall prove most entertaining."

"And what do you intend to do with those?" Her skin was still flushed and she felt alive with a sensuality she hadn't realized she possessed.

He did some sleight of hand, making them disappear from one had to appear in the other. "These little beauties," he said, "slip inside you."

He slid to the side, lifting her as he rolled onto his back. She found herself astride his hips, his finger dipping into the valley between her thighs. He pressed the pad of his finger against her pussy, pushing the balls deep inside her tight wet sheath. The sensation was too much and she rolled her hips, pressing her mound against his palm. One of the balls slipped out.

"How do they stay in?" she asked as he pressed it back inside her.

"Pretend it's my cock inside you and squeeze."

She did as he instructed and squeezed. The balls moved inside her and her breath caught.

"You like that, do you?"

"Yes." She sighed. She didn't know how to explain the feeling.

"You'll like this even more, I promise." He lifted her off him and dragged her off the bed. "Walk around for me."

"You think I can possibly walk now." She was squeezing her thighs together, sure she was about to drop the balls.

"Walk for me. Around the room." He gestured with one hand that he wanted her to make a circuit around the entire room. She groaned, taking a tentative step then another, until she was able to do a little better than a shuffle. She was only halfway around when the first wave of pleasure came over her. She stopped walking and braced her hand on the wall.

"Gray, I don't understand."

"Keep walking." He wouldn't relent, but he did join her, walking in front of her. He took her hand in his. "Your movement is making the balls move around inside you, over your very tender and sensitive flesh."

She made it around the room once, but he urged her on.

"Try to focus on the feeling. Can you feel them sliding over each other? Can you feel the pleasure that it is bringing you? You're hot, aren't you?"

She had stopped again, her hands holding him for support.

"Of course I'm hot, watching your cock bob up and down." She could tell he had thought nothing of his own nakedness, when he laughed.

"A little bit more, luv," he coaxed and continued walking, beckoning her to follow like one would an infant just learning to walk. She growled at him, but followed. She was almost around a second time when she cried out. The sensation was too much.

Taking her chin in his hand, he forced her to look into his eyes. "Ride out the pleasure," he whispered to her, his other hand cupping her mound. She ground against him, breathing hard as a long and lazy orgasm caressed her entire body. When she finally sagged into his arms, he carried her back to the bed.

"I trust you like that toy," he said, his deft fingers retrieving the balls from her pussy.

"I had no idea that was possible," she confided. "You didn't even have to touch me, and it felt so overwhelming."

He could tell he was amused by his grin. It was full of entirely too much ego. "These are for you. You will have as much fun with them alone as you have had with me watching."

"Alone?" She asked, as if not knowing what he could possibly mean.

"Should you find the urge, and not have a partner around, you can use them to give yourself release. You have touched yourself, haven't you?" he asked. "Brought yourself that extreme pleasure to which you abandon yourself so willingly here."

She shouldn't be surprised that he would have the temerity to ask her that. The man had no shame, and obviously neither did she because she nodded her head. "I mean, yes, I tried, but it was always just short of that surge of pleasure. It felt good, but never quite good enough. I had no idea what I was missing."

"And now?"

"Now, I never want it to stop!" She laughed. "Do all women want that?"

He laughed and pulled her close to his chest. "My beautiful Ana, I hope they do. For some women, I understand that alone is the only time they can achieve that result."

"And you? Do you bring yourself release?"

"I could give you excuses about life on the sea can be very lonely, or it being an effective way to ease the tension, but in truth love, I'm a man. It feels good. Of course I do it."

She the rough, gravelly sound of his chuckle. She had a feeling he felt things very deeply and had been through more misery than he'd ever tell her, after all, she had seen his scars, but he could still laugh at himself.

She stroked her hand down his chest, past his navel to his groin. "You are still hard?"

"It hadn't escaped his notice," he confided. "How could I not be after watching prance around the room, seeking your release like my lovely harlot."

"That was your doing," she reminded him, wrapping her fingers around his length. "Do you mind me touching you, or perhaps you'd rather touch yourself. You could let me watch?"

"I'd rather feel your naughty little mouth on me. Would you do that?"

She licked her lips, loving the sound of that. She nodded.

"Good, just trust me and listen to my instructions," he whispered.

With the small pressure of his hands on her shoulders, she slid to her knees before him. He had promised to teach her things a husband would never ask of a wife, but she hated to think this was one of them. She knew she was going to enjoy this, if only because she knew it would blow his mind.

She followed his instructions implicitly, having previously heard from the girls at Sauveterre the logistics of fellatio. She used her tongue as a feather against his rod, gradually building up force, but teasing him just the same. When he finally told her to take him in her mouth, she didn't hold back, sucking his length inside her until he touched the back of her throat. She swallowed against him and he groaned.

"That's it, keep going." With a hand tangled in her hair, he guided her up and down, in and out of her mouth.

While he controlled the movement in and out, she used her hands to stroke his balls, his thighs. She loved hearing how his breath hitched when she dragged her nails against his sac, or his moan as she rolled her tongue around the head of his cock. The bolder she was, the more frantic he became.

"Enough," he said gruffly, pulling her from her knees. His hands on her hips, he pressed his groin against her sex, as he came. His seed hot and sticky between them.

"Son of a bitch," he cursed, bringing his forehead down to hers. He was breathing heavy, and she was sure her hips would bear the mark of his fingers because he had yet to let her go. "Are you all right?"

"That was more fun than I expected," she reassured him.

He laughed, his hands letting go of her hips finally but wrapping around her, holding her to his chest. "You are a natural."

She liked the sound of that.

Chapter Eight

"I don't like it." Constance had been into her husband's study three times already that morning to complain. "It is all very short notice."

Charles looked over his spectacles at his wife. "It is not so bad as all that," he coaxed. "It was very polite of Ashleigh Sinclair to invite us to his wedding ball."

"The Sinclairs have always lived up to their name. Sinners and rogues, the bunch of them." She snorted.

He drew his mouth into a tight line, having determined that it wasn't worth the effort to enlighten his wife to the origin of the name Sinclair and it had nothing to do with sinning. "I will remind you, Constance, that the Sinclairs' knowledge of shipping and the aid they gave Christopher and Georgiana after my sister and her husband's death, has ensured that we continue to lead the lifestyle we do."

"You were the son of an earl. I don't understand why you insist in involving our family in business. Our daughters have naught but suffered from our association with merchants."

He shook his head. He was the stepson of a Scottish earl, but the eldest, his sister, had inherited, as Scottish law provided. He was not destitute, but his settlement allowed him a modest allowance.

"Our association with merchants puts gowns in your wardrobes and baubles around your necks. It funds your charity work, and your insufferable committees. Were there not a business for me to oversee when Georgiana and Christopher are abroad, we would have not but my meager allowance. Would you be happy living on that?"

He frowned at his wife in her severe gray gown, wringing the lace handkerchief in her hands.

"How dare you complain now about my charitable works. It is the least we can do for the less fortunate. It is even more required of us now that dear Michael has moved in. How could we house a minister and not be moved to greater works of charity?"

"Allowing your brother to move in was my great work of charity," he barked back, irritated.

"How can you say that about Michael?" she shrilled. "His ministry is greatly needed in London. Now more than ever. And your own niece is involved in the debauchery that so affronts us. And you do nothing, save let that woman speak to her about it. She must be punished for her sins."

"Constance," he ordered, "I will hear no more talk about this punishment. Not for her and not for our daughters."

"No, you would let them behave like little heathens," she accused, now crying into her handkerchief.

"I was never more happy than the day I sent our girls away to school, and well you know it. They are young women with lives of their own. I will not have them punished for their thoughts. Georgie is a woman grown. She will do as she must. I just ask that she temper her adventures with discretion."

"You have always sided with them and with their mother before," she cried. "I don't know why you married me, if you can't at least respect my belief in our Christian duty."

"Madam," he said sadly, picking up his hat and coat from a nearby chair. "At this point, I do not know why I married you either." He stalked from the room, fleeing to the solace and sanctuary of his club.

Constance dropped her handkerchief, her eyes now clear. "Did you hear that, Michael?" she asked. Michael entered through the open door. While he was as thin as she was round, they shared a similar height and features that would mark them as brother and sister.

"I am sorry, Constance," he said. "I did not mean to eavesdrop on your conversation, but it is certainly as bad as you say."

"He would let his family run riot."

"It's the Church of England, my dear. They allow decadence and chaos to reign across the British Empire."

"I shall not have my family's name dragged through the mud because of his thoughtlessness." She shook her head adamantly. "My daughters will learn their duty. Do you know he has sent them to a bluestocking boarding school? The same one that whore of a niece attended?"

"You are a good woman, Constance. I would not have your forbearance."

"It is with God's divine guidance that I am able to persevere, Michael." She touched his hand lightly. "Your spiritual guidance has helped me tremendously in the last few months."

"I was only happy I could travel from Brighton to be here for you. Surely, Charles will see to his Christian duty. I believe we could make great strides to improve the lot of London's unfortunates if only we had more funds with which to proceed."

"I have collected what I can from my parish and our friends. They have supported our efforts most generously, have they not?"

"But what of Charles? He allows you to give so little but your time."

"I don't know, Michael. If he were the earl, that would be different, but as it is, with the title going first to his sister and then her daughter, I truly do not believe he will part with any more funds. At least when I give my time, it spares me his presence."

"Do not worry, Constance." He patted her hands. "The lord will provide in this as in all things."

* * * *

Rath and Ash raced their thoroughbreds through Hyde Park. It was early, only just after dawn, and the park was quite deserted and would remain so for many more hours.

Rath had confided to Ash, the dilemma he now found himself in and the threat that loomed against Georgie and Kit.

Ash oversaw the business and finance side of their shipping company and had done so even when his father was alive. He was meticulous with the accounts and inventories. Ash knew of the privateering they'd taken part in, most often in accordance with their license from crown. He been their liaison with the foreign office, and knew more about what both Rath and Kit had been doing than he'd ever let on. Except now he was going to have to tell his brother.

Ash slowed his horse to a trot once they'd reached a private area where he knew they could speak freely.

"What couldn't you tell me at home?" Rath asked

Ash ran his hand through his short sandy hair, and gave a sigh of resignation.

"I've been involved since the beginning," he admitted. Knowing that he could never seek the role of adventurer that his brother had seized for himself, he had turned to the only adventure allowed him. He acted as special agent with the war ministry. His connections in business, and in aiding the administrative details in the secret war for information and knowledge.

He was also the only trusted go-between for foreign office and Kit.

"Mostly it's information that is smuggled in or out. On occasion we may have had some human cargo. Neither Kit or I have been active on that front lately. I thought us both unsuspected. I've no doubt that were that the secret revealed, Kit would be dead within a fortnight."

"Because he had access to this information."

"The information. The contacts and sources. There are any number of people who might want to see him dead, should his identify be discovered," Ash confirmed. "But if Kit is discovered, my own involvement would be as easy to uncover."

"Bloody bastards," Rath hissed under his breath.

"Georgie would know nothing about this," Ash continued. "She knows her brother was a privateer, it's part of our business, but she truly does believe he is retired from anything more dangerous than captaining a vessel."

"Do you know her well?" he asked.

"Sometimes I think too well." He laughed, then noticed his brother's startled glare. "Not that well, she's Kit's little sister." He grinned. "I already told you she connived to get Maggie and I together."

"So she's a beauty, is she?"

"She is uncommonly attractive, and I'm not using that as a front. She is entirely too educated for a female, and I have it on good authority that Kit taught her not only to fence but to box."

"The devil he did?" Rath laughed.

"You should try taking her on sometime?" He laughed too. "Not that fencing was ever my strong suit, I much prefer shooting, but the chit nearly broke my wrist."

Ash couldn't help but find the humor in Rath's mock-betrothal. He couldn't think of a girl more suited to him, or who would lead him on a merrier chase than Georgiana. And foisting his brother off on Georgie, even as a pretend fiancé, was a bit of divine justice for all of her machinations during his courtship with Maggie.

"She'll cause you hell." Ash laughed. "Maybe you should really marry her."

"That had best be a joke," Rath warned.

"Hear me out," he suggested. "She's rich and pretty and wants nothing more than to go home to Belle Fleur. You'd be saving her reputation and you'd be saving yourself from the scheming mamas who see you as best addition to the marriage mart. Plus," he continued seriously, "it would once and for all align our families and shipping interests. It would be bloody brilliant."

"Kit's like a brother, which means she's a sister. It would be incestuous."

"She is not our sister. Trust me, there is nothing similar between Georgie and Felicia," he told him. "And you hardly remember her."

"It doesn't matter," he complained. "I wouldn't do that to Kit."

Ash didn't find it hard to believe that his brother had no memory at all of her. He and Kit were grown men by the time Kit assumed custody of his sister, and Rath was already at sea for a good number of months each year. When he was home, the children running around their feet was hardly his first concern.

"I think he's holding hope she'll make a love match, but I still think it a good idea, but the choice is yours." Ash readied his horse to jump a small fallen tree. "I am willing to do my duty and provide all the necessary heirs for our line."

"You have a head start, anyway," Rath reminded him. "You seem genuinely happy with Maggie."

"Everyone always saw me as the settled one, the stern one. And I was happy to fulfill that role. I don't mind being the responsible one. But Maggie makes me want to be irresponsible." He patted his horse's neck. "It's hard to explain. She's so full of life and spirit that I just can't help but want to be that way for her."

"I have no intention of marrying Georgie."

"Too bad." Ash shrugged. "I thought it might at least keep you out of the gossip columns."

"What do you mean?"

Ash laughed. "You must not be spending much time at your club to have not heard. You've been outed for your night at Sauveterre with a masked lady. There is much speculation about who she is."

"Only speculation?"

"So far," Ash confirmed. "Do I know her?"

Rath rather hoped not, but a crazy part of him wanted to share her with his family. She was funny and wild, and passionate, but she was also quick witted and intelligent. "No. I don't intend to add to the drama at this time."

"I know you probably think we've all gone crazy since you were last home, and it's true everything has changed. But I think for the better."

"Felicia is a young woman already," Rath noted. "I'm sorry I haven't been around as much as I should have been. You know I've always thought you should have been the first born."

"You play Captain Wrath much better than I, and no one is complaining. Certainly not me. We all followed our hearts. Yours took you to sea, and mine kept me on land most of the time. I have enjoyed learning the business. And if the earldom didn't keep Father home, why should it have kept you?"

Their father had been the younger son, who entered the navy as an officer. He had sold out when his brother had died, and he'd learned that he was now his father's heir. Except there wasn't much of a fortune left at that point. So his father, being a shrewd business man and having made many connections during his naval days, sank what had been left of his fortune into shipping. He had had little to risk, and much to gain. The Earl of Rathbridge was once again a wealthy and profitable title.

"We were very lucky growing up the way we did," Rath said, and Ash readily agreed, remembering their father, who had been dead for close to six years. He had returned to the sea he loved often during his tenure as earl, but rarely without his family. Rath remembered his mother on many voyages and he and Ash learning to captain a ship from the earliest age. Not many boys had been granted the freedom they had to choose their own direction in life.

"Mother still misses him greatly," Ash told him. "It's not good for her to be alone."

"I suppose it's hard for her," Rath said. It hadn't passed his notice that she spent most of her time at Rosehaven, away from the social scene. As if she couldn't bear it without her husband. "I don't know many of our friends whose parents enjoyed a love match."

Ash reined his horse to a halt and blew out a deep breath. "I have to tell you something and there's no easy way to say this. I think she may have developed a fondness for someone."

Rath drew his stallion to a stop, then guided it a step or two back so he could stare at his brother. "You think, or she has?"

"I think she has," he squeaked.

Rath continued to stare down his brother. It was the same look he used on his crew, and it was developed to make even the most hardened man wither.

"She has," Ash said finally.

"Bloody fucking hell," Rath bellowed.

"That was the attitude I was hoping to avoid," Ash said.

"Is he a cad, a bounder, a fortune hunter?"

"He's most definitely not. He's been a good friend to her, and I truly don't believe that an inappropriate relationship has developed, but I've seen her with him, and he makes her smile, and laugh." Ash paused a moment. "Damn it, Rath, I haven't seen her laugh like that since our father died."

"You're still not telling me who it is?"

"Maggie's uncle. Our horse master at Rosehaven."

"It is completely inappropriate."

"He is a widower. He has no children," Ash continued. "He's the brother of an impoverished Scottish earl. He has made himself a tidy sum dealing in horseflesh, which is Mother's passion. While he is not exactly ton, he is not a peasant, either."

"I don't like it."

"I won't see her hurt by your disapproval," Ash warned.

Rath drew a hand back through his hair, exhausted and exasperated. "Why can't I deal with one crisis at a time?" He sighed. "It's neither of our places to judge what Mother does. If indeed he makes her happy, then she should follow that happiness."

"I hoped you'd feel that way."

"You weren't going to let me feel any other way," Rath admonished, "But next time I come home, I want one surprise a week. Not all at once like this."

"We will endeavor to provide it," Ash promised, laughing, as they set their horses at a canter back to the stables.

* * * *

Georgie cancelled an afternoon engagement with Maggie and with her dressmaker when she received

Gray's note. She couldn't deny the wicked beat of her heart when she saw it on her desk. He was quickly becoming an addiction, or at least the orgasms he gave her had. Social engagements had ensured they had only caught a few unguarded moments with each other this week, and it was driving her wild.

She allowed her housekeeper and Leda to believe she had plans for the rest of the afternoon with friends, and fetched a nearby hackney.

Gray answered the door to his townhouse himself, and she was instantly pleased that she had taken extra care with her garments. She wore a deep blue day gown, with a low-cut bodice. She had chosen a delicate chemise of Brussel's lace to wear beneath, its scalloped edge visible just above the bodice of her gown. She had splurged on the stockings yesterday, buying the most expensive, softest pair that her modiste had on hand.

He pulled off her hat and let loose her hair from its pins. "I have missed you," she told him, as her hair tumbled about her shoulders.

"What have you missed most about me?" he asked, gracing her with a lascivious grin.

"Your outrageous questions, I think." She laughed up at him. "You want me to say something lewd."

"Yes. Tell me," he prodded, pulling her tightly against his bulging erection.

"I've missed your cock." She rolled her hips against his.

"That's a good girl," he encouraged. "And should I give you my cock?"

"Yes." She wrapped her hands around his waist. "Please."

He pushed the charts and maps off his desk then, and quickly bent her over it. The bodice of her gown touched the smooth polished surface of the desk. He held her hands above her as he pulled up her voluminous skirts. "This is the first lesson of the day," he whispered to her, as his hand caressed her bottom and the cleft between her legs. "Submission."

She wriggled her backside, desperate to feel his hard length press against. When he groaned she knew he was enjoying watching her wiggle. She had worn nothing beneath her chemise but her stockings, kept in place but satin ribbons. When he smoothed a hand up her thigh, over her ribbons to her bare ass, she shivered.

"I like the stockings," he growled in her ear. "And knowing that you wore them for me. I bet you were wet and ready when you received my summons."

"Yes." She sighed heavily. "I was ready."

She was truly ready, her cream damp on her skin. She spread her thighs as he slid a hand between her legs to test her arousal. She purred as his fingers teased between her damp curls.

"I can't wait," he warned her, his hands releasing her for a moment.

"Then don't," she told him, feeling the hard tip of his arousal stroking her heated flesh. "I need you inside me."

He grabbed her hips and plunged his cock inside her.

She arched her back and cried out at his rough invasion. He withdrew and plunged in again. "Yes," she hissed with pleasure.

He set up a deep rhythm of plunge and retreat. He soon found his release deep inside her. "We don't have much time this afternoon."

"I know. I have an engagement tonight I cannot miss." She shifted her hips and felt him still hard inside her. They weren't done yet.

Chapter Nine

Lady Broughton stumbled over her words as she introduced him to her daughter, Lady Leticia, who was a pert and pleasant young girl, of perhaps seventeen years. She seemed embarrassed by her mother's obvious machinations and his heart went out to her, promising her a dance later this evening. With a shy smile, she curtsied and struggled to pull her mother away.

It was a harsh realization that he was getting old. He was old enough to be the father of any one of these debutantes. And after meeting their mothers, he wouldn't be surprised to find out he was. *How could I have fucked so many of them?* he wondered, promising himself that he would only entertain dances with petite blondes with ghostly complexions. With his dark looks, he was somewhat confident that at least he wasn't their father. Leticia had both going for her.

"Georgiana," his mother exclaimed behind him. "I am so pleased to see you again. You are a beautiful sight. That color looks ravishing on you. Come, you must see Maggie."

By the time Rath was able to extricate himself from the Broughtons he could just glimpse his mother's shape in the throng of guests. He couldn't tell who she may be with. He did however spy Cleo nearby. Her silver-blonde hair sparkled with diamond clips, and her creamy complexion was set off by the sapphire-blue gown she had chosen.

"I recognize those diamonds," he told her, commenting on the pendants she wore on her ears and the simple strand around her neck. He and Kit had presented the set to her for her twenty-fifth birthday.

"Yes, I believe an old friend may have given these to me, many, many years ago." She smiled. "They are still my favorite, you know."

"So where is my fiancée?"

Cleo looked around in the crowd. "She was here a moment ago. Your mother must have stolen her away. She is a favorite of your mother's. Did I mention that?"

He rolled his eyes. "No, but Ash has told me that Georgie is something of a fixture around our home."

Cleo nodded. "Rosehaven has an impressive stable and Georgie is an accomplished rider."

"I hear she is accomplished in a great many things," he whispered to her. "You really should have told me."

Cleo looked up at him questioningly.

"Fencing. Sailing. Boxing. Shooting."

"Yes." She nodded sheepishly. "Well, you can thank Kit for that. She spent way too much time in his company."

"Yes, no wonder she's such a catch." He had no problem understanding why the little hellion was both on the shelf, and in need of rescue. What had Kit been thinking? He looked around the room for his mother again but didn't see her.

"Between her beauty and her fortune, there are many men who are willing to overlook her more public eccentricities," Cleo reminded him.

He had no doubt she held the men in thrall. "Then I had best find her before someone makes off with my fiancée."

Georgie had slipped away from the crush, helping herself to a chocolate-covered praline and a glass of champagne. She wound her way toward the back of the ballroom and out the garden doors. She took a deep breath of clean, night air as she found herself alone the small terrace overlooking the topiary gardens. It wasn't a large property, but the landscaping was second to none. She and Maggie had shared many a picnic surrounded by the lush aroma of the herb garden.

She sighed. There were some things she'd miss once she was allowed to leave England. She would never be able to grow as lush a garden as this in the Caribbean, but there were other benefits. *Like sand between one's toes*, she laughed to herself. Kit had made a small sandbox for her, which she kept in her room where she could wiggle her toes in what she considered her native soil whenever she needed.

She hated that she was hiding out on the terrace. She had been looking forward to tonight. Maggie's ball. She needed to go in and support her friend, even though her own life was about to take a drastic change. It may be a *faux* engagement, but it would mean real, if temporary, changes to her lifestyle. Like she knew Madeline would insist she move in here both in order to plan the wedding festivities and to ensure she had a proper guardian until she walked down the aisle.

It was as if she was waiting for an axe to fall, even though she knew she should be grateful to Lord Rathbridge for his help. She wasn't sure she was quite that good an actress.

She was startled by the touch of a hand upon her bare shoulder and she turned quickly, knocking her champagne flute into the bushes below.

"Oh," she cried out, her eyes following the glass as it crashed to the stones below. She turned with exasperation to her unexpected guest. "Gray?"

She couldn't believe her eyes, and a number of thoughts crowded her brain at once. He said he didn't mix with society. Had he been following her? Again? What did he want? She settled finally on the question, "What are you doing here?"

His expression was grim, taking her elbow and leading her deeper into the shadows. "I could ask the same of you."

"I was invited, of course," she said, noting his stern countenance and his rigid manners.

"You implied that you did not mix with society."

"I did no such thing. I said I don't like to take part in these sorts of events, but on occasion one does have to venture forth and put on a good show. How many times did I have to sneak away from some event to see you?" she reminded him, as she set her hand upon the balustrade, steadying herself.

"So the ton welcomes you?"

"They're not overjoyed with me, but I do run in their circles, yes," she admitted. "And because of a few well-placed connections I've even been presented at Almacks." It was a good thing Cleo was such good friends with Lady Jersey or that may have never happened. "And you? A merchant captain, they welcome you? Are you a friend of the Sinclairs, or the earl himself? Do you captain a ship for Sinclair Knolls?"

"You could say that."

"I hadn't dared hope to see you here." She touched the sleeve of blue wool coat. He looked delicious in his buff cashmere knee breeches, stockings and polished leather shoes. His hair had been combed to shine and pulled back in a tight queue.

"You are probably the most dangerously attractive man here," she blurted out, then looked down, trying not to laugh at herself.

"Ah, Ana," he purred, and leaned down, taking her lips in a possessive kiss that made her forget everything but his touch. "I bet your cunt's still wet with my seed," he whispered against her ear, taking a nip at her earlobe, then trailing kisses down her neck.

"Hush," she admonished, but did not push him away. "Someone is going to overhear."

The clearing of a throat behind them said that someone had. Gray stiffened, and he moved to hide her in his shadow as he turned.

"Cleo." His voice was tired. "If you wouldn't mind."

Cleo? Shoot. Shoot. Shoot. Georgie banged her forehead against Gray's back. Of all the people to interrupt. She would tear a strip off her. She would demand an explanation. She would...wait. How did Gray know Cleo?

Georgie stepped to the side and looked at Cleo.

"I see you two have met." Cleo's voice was clipped and her tone censorious, as she closed the doors behind her.

"You know her?" he asked, looking back and forth between the two women. Georgie wasn't sure which of them he was asking, but she answered.

"Cleo is my aunt, for lack of better description," Georgiana explained.

"Your Aunt Cleo." He dropped his hands away from her and stepped back.

"It's all right," she tried to explain. "She has a vested interest in not making this into a scene."

"I'm sure she has, Ana — Georgie Ana. That's your name isn't it?" he replied, then he turned to Cleo. "I suppose you put her up to this?"

"I don't know what you mean." Cleo glared at him.

"Don't you?" he asked, backing away and circling around them like a predator. "She needed a fiancé, and now it looks like you've discovered a way to get her one."

Georgie didn't know what to say, but she took her cue from Cleo and kept her mouth shut. There was something lethal in Gray's tone, even though he otherwise projected a cool and detached demeanor. He didn't look at Georgie. His eyes were focused on Cleo.

"Our betrothal will be announced in fifteen minutes. She," he hissed, "should meet me inside." He strode from the balcony, the door slamming behind him.

"He is Rathbridge," Georgie cried out as realization dawned.

Cleo grasped Georgie by her bare shoulders. "What were you thinking?"

"I wasn't thinking," she uttered. "I didn't know who he was, Cleo, I swear it." Tears welled up in the corners of her eyes.

"So you kiss men you don't know on the balcony," Cleo scolded. "I don't see that as a reasonable explanation."

"I haven't seen him in more than twelve years. He was so much bigger, and larger than life then." She stammered on, "I didn't know he was Rowan Sinclair, the Earl of Rathbridge." She threw up her hands. "Captain fucking Wrath."

"Language please, Georgie. Someone could still hear you."

"How much did you hear?" Georgie asked.

"Probably not as much as I should if I am to understand what has happened between the two of you," Cleo said through gritted teeth. "Just who did you think he was?"

Georgie began to pace. It all made sense now. His presence here. His being a captain who had run away from his responsibilities. Damn it, why hadn't she put two and two together before?

She sank down on one of the small benches. "A handsome merchant captain. Someone who probably had a woman in every port, who wouldn't notice my absence when I stopped seeing him. I told Gray I wasn't planning to marry. He knew I'd be leaving soon."

"Stop babbling," Cleo ordered. "He said his name was Gray?"

"Yes. We met more than a fortnight ago." It hit her then. "At the same time Lord Rathbridge made his reappearance home. Ugh. I am so stupid." She leaned on Cleo's shoulder and took a deep, shuddering breath. *This is a mess,* she thought.

"Square your shoulders, blow your nose." She handed her a handkerchief from her reticule. "You will go in there and pretend to be in love with him, no matter what went on between you. We will sort this all out later."

"Cleo, please." Georgie grabbed her arm. "I can't do that. Not after this." She shook her head. "He hates me right now."

"I don't care what he feels for you. In ten minutes, he's becoming your betrothed. And you will smile and dance and accept everyone's well wishes, until I can figure out what to do about this situation."

"I'm sorry. You are having to rescue me from the rescue you already planned."

Cleo's face softened as she perched next to Georgie. "You don't make it easy, but I never should have expected you would." She tucked a stray curl behind Georgie's ear. "I suppose I had just hoped we hadn't raised you to be quite so much like us."

"Is that a bad thing?"

"No. It's why I'm not angrier. But he is, and I know him well enough that he isn't going to make this easy. When they call him Captain Wrath, they spell it W-R-A-T-H for a reason."

Georgie groaned. She had worked that out for herself.

"Let me worry think on this. You need to worry about being a besotted bride-to-be."

Georgie wasn't sure she could make people believe that, but for Cleo's sake, for her own sake, she would try. She took Cleo's extended hand and allowed herself to be lead back into the ballroom.

* * * *

Rath was gritting his teeth and trying not to break the champagne glass in his hand. He knew he should throw himself off the pier, or let Kit do it, because he would if he ever found out that he'd seduced his little sister. His virgin sister. *Oh, God, what have I done?*

Rath thought of his own sister, only a few years younger than Ana, no, Georgiana, and he groaned hopelessly. The image of Ana bent over his desk this afternoon entered his mind. The memory of her honeyed walls gripping him, vivid in his mind. His cock stirred at the thought.

He would tell the little chit that they would marry. Really marry. Not the convenient engagement they had arranged. Whether she had plotted this all or not, he would discover soon enough, but no matter what, he was bound by his friendship to Kit to do the right thing.

His brother stood now and strained to get the attention of the throngs of people in attendance. "Please, may I have your attention?" he asked. "On behalf of my wife and myself, I wish to thank you for coming this evening to share my wife's birthday."

A small round of applause followed his thanks. "But no one can outdo my brother's gift to us. First, he returned in time for the party, but he also brought us some wonderful news. His intention to wed my wife's dearest friend. The sister of our esteemed business partner, Christopher Knolls, Viscount Hunton. May I ask you to raise a glass to Georgiana Knolls, Viscountess Belstratten. We welcome to our family the future Countess of Rathbridge."

A few audible gasps, and a few unbelieving whispers followed, but Rath knew that whatever else the ton might think, his fiancée had just regained their fickle favor. As the orchestra struck up a waltz, all eyes watched the infamous Lord Wrath stride across the floor, and claim the first waltz of the evening with his newly acquired fiancée.

Pulling her into his arms, he swirled with her to the fluid sound of the orchestra.

She tried smiling up at him, but it looked more like a grimace, and he realized that she was an atrocious actress, despite what Cleo had promised.

"I swear, Rathbridge, I didn't plan this. I had no idea that you were anything other than a ship's captain."

"I find that hard to believe." He smiled back at her. "But regardless, we shall be married in three weeks."

"The hell we will." She struggled to pull away from him, but his hand behind her back held her firm in his arms. "I told you that I would never marry."

"You should have thought of that before you came to my bed. We will both suffer the consequences." He continued to step in time to the music. "Now, smile pretty, flutter your eyelashes and pretend that we are indeed the happy couple."

Rath was mollified when Georgiana thought better of continuing their argument. She tucked her head, staring at his chest until the music ended. She curtsied to him as the throng of onlookers put their hands together. Rath smiled down at his wife-to-be and grinned at the disappointed mamas.

As soon as was polite, Georgiana yanked her hand from his and made her escape with Maggie. His brother gave him a quizzical stare then shook his head as he followed his wife.

Rath was tempted to follow them, but decided instead to make for the nearest bottle of gin and the privacy of the library. He was cursing himself for being taken in by a chit of a girl and forced to marry. If she were not Kit's sister, he would have considered paying off her family and leaving with the morning tide. But he was obligated to protect her. *And you still want her*, he thought.

He was waylaid by Georgiana's blustering uncle and his shrew of a wife, who followed him into the library. "What can I do for you, Norris?"

It was Constance who replied "You can explain to me why you have chosen to attach yourself to my niece. As her guardians, we should have been approached. My husband won't give consent for her to marry the likes of you, and into this family of pirates and thieves."

Rath's distaste for the apple-faced aunt multiplied with each new insult she heaped on the Sinclair family, and he recalled Kit's less-than-glowing appraisal of the woman.

"I will stop you there, unless, Mrs. Norris, you would like to be thrown out of my home, with your daughters close behind. You may not like my family or my choices, but I do recall that at three and twenty, Georgiana has no legal guardian, save her brother. Lord Christopher is the only one who can object to this betrothal, and I bid you write him to protest, however, I can assure you that Kit will not support your cause."

Gathering the rotund woman by the elbow, he gently prodded her toward the door. "Now, if you will excuse me, I shall brook no further disagreement on the subject." He raised an imperious brow at Charles, daring him not to follow his wife. He had always thought Charles a decent sort, but Rath was feeling the need to hit something tonight and he wasn't picky about what. Alas Charles was not up to the challenge and followed his wife without a word. Rath let the door slam behind them.

He had polished off three quick shots of gin when he heard the door open again. He groaned and threw his goblet into the fire grate.

"Rough night?" Ash asked, pouring a fresh glass for both himself and his brother.

"What brings about that assumption?"

"You were looking daggers at your bride-to-be? I thought this was supposed to be a favor to Cleo. You're suddenly acting like a lion with a thorn in his paw, and my wife and your fiancée have disappeared with a bottle of my best brandy."

"Did anyone else notice?" Rath leaned his head against the granite mantle. His leg was beginning to ache as much as his head.

"I doubt it. You've always been good at hiding your feelings, except from, of course, me."

Ash handed him the gin. "I must be getting old," he lamented. "To be taken in by a chit of girl."

"You've just been at sea for the better part of fifteen months. I think you're entitled," he snorted. "We're not talking about woman you've been seeing from *Chez de Sauveterre*, are we? I was speculating with Maggie that it must be the newly widowed, but not mourning, Lady Pamela."

"It's not Lady Thursby, though she did offer tonight." He smiled just a little. "I shouldn't tell you."

"Of course, you should, unburden yourself," he goaded. "I'm an old married man, so I must continue to live vicariously through you, just don't tell Maggie I said so."

"It seems that I've been carrying on an affair with my fiancée," he said.

Ash's face fell, then he swore under his breath. "And you didn't know?" he asked.

"Hell, no," he denied. "She's not the girl in breeches and pigtails that I remember." Then he told Ash of how he met her playing cards and losing to him. How despite hiring a runner, he'd never gotten her true name. "I should have known. I should have been more curious and asked the runner who she was, or at least where she lived. Hell, even my footman knows where she lives, but I never asked. I was happy playing Gray and Ana. I didn't need to know more."

"Well, as much as I like Georgie, and we should feel some responsibility toward her, I can't see how you should need to marry her if she's been so free with herself."

Rath tossed another glass into the fire grate.

"Oh, shit," Ash cursed, and Rath knew he'd figured out that Rath had taken her virginity.

"Precisely, brother." He sighed.

"Still," Ash continued. "If she has no intention of telling Kit, then there's no reason to go ahead with marrying her."

"You don't believe that."

"Does she want to marry you?"

"She says she doesn't, but you know that doesn't matter."

Rath knew that though Ash wanted to protect his brother, he would never condone abandoning Georgie. Kit had been raised as part of the family, their parents having been close. Their fathers had been best friends before that. If Kit were to do the same to their sister, they'd beat the crap out of him first, perhaps make him unable to perform on the wedding night, but they'd still haul him up to the altar. Rath couldn't escape his fate.

"I can talk to Maggie and see what she can find out." He let out a long breath. "If this was some clever plot to get you to the altar, or if it was all a mistake, then she will find out."

"I appreciate that, Ash, but no," Rath told him, his composure once again regained. He straightened his waistcoast and checked his appearance in the mirror by the door. "I need your word that this goes no further than us and Cleo. I would not see my wife's reputation besmirched, even if I do decide to marry her, strangle her and drop her overboard at the soonest opportunity."

"I understand, but what are your immediate plans?"

"To escort my fiancée in to dinner, of course."

While Rath had found solace in the library, Georgie had escaped the ballrooms before anyone could see her cry. Recognizing the urgency in her friend's eyes, Maggie had rushed with her to her private suite upstairs.

"For heaven's sake, Georgie, sit down and tell me what's happened," Maggie said, trying to hand her a snifter of brandy. She couldn't afford to be drinking now. Even if it would calm her down.

"I've really done it this time," she gushed and pulled at the fine linen handkerchief. "I've really messed it up. I thought I knew what I was doing. No one would ever find out, but how could I know my Captain Gray was the infamous Captain Wrath? Lord Sin."

"What do you mean?" Maggie asked, helping herself to the brandy. "What does your captain have to do with the earl?"

"Cleo came to me with an idea on how to provide me with protection from the blackmailer. She got Rathbridge to throw his cloak of protection over me. After all, who would defy a man named Rath? But the beautiful Rath, the most delicious Earl, was the gentlemen named Gray that I told you about."

"Your Gray is our Rowan Grayson," Maggie said.

"Is that where Gray comes from? Rowan Grayson Sinclair. Why didn't I know this?" She pulled the goblet from Maggie's hand and took a healthy swallow. She didn't give her back the glass.

"Well, no harm done. It was a flirtation. Your visit to *Chez de Sauveterre* is somewhat known, but with his protection there should be no worry."

"He kind of found me after that," Georgie squeaked, and Maggie's eyes widened in comprehension. "And found me several times in the weeks since."

"You've been intimate with him?"

Georgie stopped pacing and flung herself down next to Maggie on the settee. "I've been seeing Gray, Rowan Grayson, Captain Wrath, the Earl of Rathbridge," she confessed, "every night for the past two weeks. I was even late meeting the Earl of Rathbridge that first day at Cleo's because I had been with him, but I didn't know they were the same person. I didn't know so many things that should have been clues, if only I had been looking for them."

"How could you have not known?" Maggie objected loudly, sounding for all the world a lot like Cleo had.

Why would no one believe her that she hadn't cared to find out? Georgie took a deep breath before continuing. "We were being discreet, never telling the other the whole truth about our names or identities. He never saw me home. I never visited him except in his bachelor residence, which is not even on the same street as Ash's old rooms. If there were clues, I suppose I didn't want to see them."

"So, he had no idea he was making love to his partner's sister?"

"No, but now he expects me to marry him, just because he's discovered who I was, am, oh, whatever."

"The man is a dunce. He didn't know you were his soon-to-be pretend fiancée."

"Obviously not." Georgie shook her head in dismay, wishing for the first time she carried a lady's possessions in her handbag instead of a pocket knife and a deck of cards. She could use smelling salts, because she thought she may just faint from the shock.

"But now he is willing to marry you?" Maggie had picked up a hair brush and was smacking that into her palm as she thought. This was not at all the subtle seduction the two of them had schemed when she wanted Ash.

"He's demanding it."

"And that's a problem." Maggie didn't phrase it as a question because she knew for her friend, this would be fact.

"Of course, it's a problem, you know I have never wished to be under a man's thumb."

"But you've helped me get under a man's thumb, as it were. Do you think I'm under Ash's thumb?"

"Oh, Maggie, I don't mean to insult your relationship with Ash, but it's different, isn't it? You wanted to marry him, and you both love each other. I just helped you help him figure that out."

"Surely, he can't force you to marry him."

"I don't know what he can do, if he were to tell my uncle, or worst of all, Kit." She began to cry. "Don't you see? No one was supposed to know. And Cleo suspects the extent of our tryst."

"Do you care for him at all?"

"I think I was falling a little in love with Gray. He made me laugh, and blush, and he never minded that I was well read, or knew about politics or shipping. But I care not a whit for Captain Wrath. No, certainly not the Earl of Rathbridge."

"Would you see Gray again, if none of this had happened?"

"I believe I would, but that's just passion and lust. And while I may have been losing my heart to him, I knew he never felt the same." She had regained some of her composure. "Uncle Charles was threatening to marry me off, and I was planning to escape back to the Caribbean, so it seemed prudent to follow my heart, just this once. To give myself up to the experience just once before putting myself for good on the shelf. But I won't marry any man, least of all a man who doesn't have those feeling to me."

"Then we'll think of something to get you out of this," Maggie told her, and Georgie could almost believe that there was a way out.

Chapter Ten

The Earl of Rathbridge had begun to believe dinner would drag on forever. He was seated across from his fiancée and had the unfortunate pleasure of what Lord Hurley and Lord Wright on either side of her take wistful glances at décolletage. He seethed as he thought of Ana's responsive nipples and wondered if they were still peaked and sensitive beneath her chemise. He'd teased them well this afternoon.

Georgiana frowned at him, and he smirked. The young bucks on either side of her looked heartbroken when she pulled her shawl over her shoulders, obscuring the view of her chest. He knew that had been for his benefit, and that she'd discerned his train of thought. He couldn't help but be delighted with their disappointment.

It was late when he'd made his escape to St. James Street. He had only stopped into his club once since he'd returned, having been preoccupied with his mistress. God, it upset his stomach to think of it. He'd originally planned to go visit Ana tonight, but he wished now that he never had to see her again.

No, he allowed, that wasn't quite the truth. He wished that he could see her, but not have to see Kit's little sister again. Unfortunately, he couldn't forget they were one and the same, not without a copious amount of alcohol. Brook's was as good a place as any to do that.

Like any good gentleman of the ton, he and Ash had membership at a number of gentlemen's clubs, but tonight he favored Brook's.

Ensconced in a large leather chair by the fire with a bottle, Rath made it a point to steer clear of the Subscription Room where already the Honorable Frederick Gerald Byng was playing. He'd lost to 'Poodle', as Frederick was known, a time or two and Rath had no intention of losing his fortune tonight, just his memory.

He was well on his way to a good drunk with friends from the foreign office when his presence was noted by an odious dandy, Batholomew Pratt, Baron Pratt. Rath gritted his teeth as he saw Pratt heading in his direction. He could tell by his uneven gait that he was as in his cups as Rath felt.

Pratt, his discretion lessened by brandy, announced impudently, "Trust Lord Wrath to find his fiancée in a brothel." The man chuckled as he walked by, a small dab of brandy leaking out of his loose lips.

Rath couldn't say he remembered rising from his chair. His first memory would be his fist connecting with Pratt's rotund chin. Even drunk, Rath packed quite a wallop, and Pratt, no lightweight, flew backward over a chair. The legendary Lord Wrath was upon him in an instant, shaking him by the collar, knocking his head back into the thick Aubusson carpet.

"Say it again and I'll make sure your wife is a very happy widow," he gritted out between clenched teeth.

It took three footmen to pull him off Pratt as they exchanged blows. Their ruckus brought even Poodle away from the table, though he had no doubt already wagered on the winner of their scuffle. He frowned at Frederick who shrugged in response. There was literally nothing he wouldn't bet on. Rath shrugged away the footmen, hands up in promise not to hit Pratt again. He thanked his friends for the distraction, grabbed the near-empty gin bottle and his cloak. He'd had enough of Brook's tonight.

Though he had never asked where Ana lived, he knew exactly where Kit's townhome was. He expected that was where she made her home, with her ancient chaperone and loyal servants. He sighed when he found himself standing in the alley behind her home, having not made a conscious decision to go there.

With a stealth that belied his intoxicated condition, he scaled the garden wall and slipped through the kitchen door, having remembered the secret jiggle that would make the lock give way. *Kit showed me that,* he thought, *god, how many years ago? Twenty?*

She had said she kept only a small household so he didn't worry as he slipped upstairs and peeked into bedrooms. When he opened the door to her room, she was seated in front of her dressing table, combing her hair before the mirror. It was in the mirror that she saw him, leaning against the doorjamb watching her. She dropped the brush.

"Rathbridge, you have to believe that I never meant for this to happen." She turned in her chair to face him.

He stalked across the room. "Rathbridge, is it? Whatever happened to— Oh, please, Gray, fuck me, Gray?"

She flinched at his words. He cupped his hand beneath her chin when she tried to look down into her lap, to avoid his gaze. He wondered if she was trying to be demure, or if she was trying not to blister his ears. Her language could be as blue as his own.

He squeezed her chin and forced her to look up at him. "I wish I could believe you, but you see, you wouldn't be the first."

He saw surprise and defiance in her eyes. She wasn't going to admit that she'd been trying to trap him. Maybe she hadn't been. Perhaps she'd been sincere, but if so, she'd also been worse than stupid. So had he. He took a deep breath, but it didn't clear his thoughts.

"You need to leave," Georgiana said, smacking at his forearm and forcing him to let go of her chin. His hold had been tight, and she feared there would be bruises she couldn't hide. There was coldness in him she didn't recognize. And he was drunk.

She dashed across the room reaching for her robe but he caught up to her, pulling the robe from her hands.

"Is that how I taught you to talk to your lover?"

"You don't really want to do this, Rathbridge." She shook her head, crossing her arms in front of her breasts, the thin chemise doing little to hide their form or her stiff nipples. A day ago, it wouldn't have embarrassed her for him to see her like this. Tonight, it did. "You're drunk."

"Not drunk enough."

"You don't want to do this," she repeated, but he wasn't listening to her.

"I think this is exactly what I want to do." He grabbed hold of her wrists and pulled her to him, his head angling down to kiss her. She wanted that kiss. Gray's kiss. But she couldn't allow herself to kiss Lord Rathbridge, not when even a kiss would force her to the altar.

She kicked out at his shins, like her brother had taught her to do, and threw herself to the side, trying to escape his hold, but he was much stronger than her, and she didn't have a knife on her. When she'd sailed with her brother, she always had two strapped to her person. She cursed herself for being too comfortable in her own home.

She gasped as he picked her up, feet leaving the ground as he swung her over his shoulder. She beat on his back with her fists, but he seemed immune to her assault. He sat down heavily on the chaise in front of her bed and swung her around until she lay facedown over his lap.

Her hair fell in front of her face as she wriggled. She didn't stop until his large warm palm was against her buttock.

"You wouldn't dare?" she asked. No one, not even Kit when she was a child, had dared to spank her.

His throaty chuckle sounded less threatening, more amused, and she thought of her position. Arse in the air over his lap, and she shook her head.

"I think putting you over my knee is one of the sanest and soberest things I've thought of all night." He smacked her. The thin cotton muffled the sound and intensity of his hand as it connected to her buttock. Obviously, that wasn't the result he was looking for as he began pushing up her chemise, ripping it when he couldn't get it untangled from around her legs.

She bucked against him, but it was still no use, as he smacked her again, harder this time. She bit her lip from screaming out.

"Do you have any idea what you've done?" he asked her. "Who you've tied yourself to?"

"We don't have to be tied at all," she gritted out, as he continued to spank her like a recalcitrant child. "We can dissolve this engagement right now and forget we've ever met."

His hand smoothed over the now-tender surface of her buttocks. It felt like pinpricks of fire where his hand had landed each blow, but his touch also soothed. She frowned at her body's betrayal.

"Is that what you think?" he asked as he moved his hand between her thighs. "That we can just forget that I've ever been inside you. That I've felt you come for me."

She tried to close her legs but he wouldn't move his hand. She wasn't prepared for this new assault as he slid a finger inside her. She mewled, feeling her body melt into his touch. She cursed herself for a fool, but that didn't stop her body from responding.

"You are always so wet for me." He added a second finger and she squirmed again. This didn't feel like punishment anymore, and she couldn't fight the sensations he was drawing forth. She groaned as her indignation was replaced with reluctant delight. She shouldn't still want him. It was the worst possible match in the world.

He dragged his soaking fingers out of her cunt, sliding them up her backside. He rimmed them around the tight bud of her arse. She hadn't believed him when he said how pleasurable loving that way could feel, but he'd proved her wrong. She pressed her hips back toward him as he slid a wet finger just inside her forbidden hole.

"Ana likes all the naughty little things I want to do her, doesn't she?" He laughed. "All the things a proper wife wouldn't allow. What are you going to do when you can't have this?"

She cried out in helpless pleasure as he slid a finger deeper insider her bum, and another back into her quim. She closed her eyes, trying to stave off the pleasure it created. She shouldn't continue to respond to him, but she couldn't help it. He knew her body.

"Don't fight it, Ana," he whispered as he ground his fingers in and out. "I can feel you so close. Take it. Take your pleasure," he continued to coax her as he fucked her.

"Damn you." She was shaking. In anger and delight. She hated herself for letting him do this, for wanting him this bad. Her climax claimed her quickly, and she continued to buck against him. Needing more. Always more from him.

He lifted her off his lap and pressed her back against the corner of the chaise. Her orgasm still throbbed through her. He pushed her chemise down to bare her breasts to his lascivious gaze. Her nipples were ripe and pebbled, aching for his touch.

She sighed when he bent his head to her breasts, laving them, pulling each taut nub into his mouth. He shook her hands off when she would run her fingers into his hair. He reared over her. He didn't look drunk anymore. He looked hungry.

"This afternoon was about submission. This" —he ran his hand down her side, over her belly until he cupped her sex—"this is about domination. This is where I take what I want."

She whimpered, but her hips rose and she pressed herself into his palm.

"Tell me you want me, Georgiana." His eyes feasted on her near nakedness. The torn chemise hid nothing. She loved how he craved her body.

"Yes." She shook her head. "God help me, I shouldn't, but I still do."

She closed her eyes reveling in the feel of his strong hands stroking her thighs, pressing them wide.

He knelt between her thighs, his thumbs stroking over her labium as he thought of all the things he wanted to do to her. How he could use her passion to punish her. Punish them both.

He loosened the ties on his breeches, freeing his cock so he could guide it to her center. She was still slick from having reached her pleasure moments before, and he used her juices to anoint his cock before he pressed, and he stroked his crown against her sensitive clit.

He didn't have to be told that he'd lost his mind, he was sure of it when he pressed his cock inside her. She grabbed on to his shoulders as he set a demanding rhythm of possession. His fingers dug into her thighs as he slammed into her again and again. He heard her begging him to take her hard, to make her come, and he growled, knowing the she loved what he did to her. That's why he'd fallen in love with Ana. She was his equal in all things carnal.

He shook his head. *You don't love her. You love her body, and all the myriad things she allows you to do to it,* he reminded himself. He wasn't going to make the mistake of losing his heart when what he loved was her tight, hungry pussy.

He buried his hand in her hair, as he ground his cock against her. Her honeyed walls quivering against his shaft. She sank her teeth into his chest, muffling her shout of pleasure as she came. He shouted out an incoherent curse, as his balls drew up tight and his cum shoot into her. He rode her until his cock ached, and he could bear to pull himself away from her.

They couldn't do this again. He sat back on his heels, ignoring the wanton portrait she made. Her eyes languid, her breasts heaving. Her cunt wet and still quaking.

He tied his breeches and stood. He tossed her the robe she'd been desperate to reach earlier.

"This won't happen again, my lady," he promised. "I'm sorry to have disturbed you."

He grabbed his bottle of gin and left. He could hear the muffled sound of her crying through the door. He knew he couldn't stay with her, but he also dreaded going home to a bed that still smelled of her sweet shampoo.

* * * *

Cleo arrived before lunch the next day, dragging Georgie from her fitful slumber and out shopping for what she called "a wardrobe fit for the next Countess Rathbridge."

"I'm not going to be the next Countess Rathbridge," she told her emphatically, but Cleo said regardless of that, the public had to believe she was to be if she were to be protected from the blackmailer. "Especially after every gossip column this week is likely to be remarking how the two of you found safe haven together at a brothel."

Georgiana's stomach sank. Safe Haven. They'd found out about *Chez de Sauveterre*.

"Come on," Cleo rallied her. "There is no time now for regret. We plow forward. Head up, and make you the most sought-after countess-to-be to be found in London this season."

Georgiana allowed herself to be dragged about the fashionable London shopping district, and splurged on three new dresses, one ball gown and two tasteful but extravagant walking dresses. Cleo demanded they be ready by weeks' end, making Georgie shake her head. As if they could shop their way out of this mess.

Georgiana's world closed in on her when Cleo insisted they look at patterns for her wedding gown. While Georgie didn't doubt the value of keeping up the pretense, she was terrified that she may be forced to wear the gown.

She let Cleo choose the style, only offering her opinion on the color. "Not the rose silk. I look deplorable in pink. I think the silver would suit."

Cleo chirped, "Silver it shall be. And let it be my wedding present to you."

The Dowager Duchess Grenville was at Madame Ortique's, sorting through the fashion plates for a new cloak. "I am told congratulations are in order, my dear," she cackled. "Landed Rathbridge, I hear."

"Lord Rathbridge and I are to be married, Your Grace."

"And quickly too."

"His latest trip abroad kept him away longer than expected, and now that the betrothal is announced, he is, of course, anxious to wed." Cleo smiled graciously, daring Georgie to disagree.

"Yes, well," the Duchess demurred. "One can see that he would be lured by your beauty. A pity that your family does not approve. I was informed this morning that your aunt and uncle were seeking to have the marriage stopped."

That's no shock. Georgie harrumphed indignantly, keeping her thoughts to herself. She had heard of the disagreement last night between Constance, Charles and her betrothed.

"Georgiana's brother, Lord Hunton, and Lord Rathbridge are like brothers. I can assure you that Christopher is overjoyed that the two families will finally be joined. He has been planning this connection for many years."

"I am sure that's true," she said, "though this season has been so dreadfully boring, one could use a little scandal, I think."

"There is always some delicious *on-dit* about for the ton's amusement," Georgie said, hoping it wasn't her own.

"I am sure there is. Cleo." The old woman commanded Cleo's attention with a rap of her cane. "You have taught this one well. I think she just might tame our Lord Wrath."

"Yes, Your Grace." Cleo accepted the compliment and watched as the woman was led into another room to look at fabrics.

"Cleo," Georgie said, watching Cleo sort through the plates of gowns. "Rath insisted that we go ahead with a true wedding. He plans to marry me. He told me last night."

"Of course, he does," Cleo said, unsurprised. "I don't know what game you played, but you're well and truly stuck this time."

"I wasn't playing a game. I had every intention of going home to Belle Fleur and dying there a spinster. I just wanted a taste of pleasure with someone who didn't care who I was before that happened." Georgie pouted and tears stung her eyes. She shouldn't be crying. Not here.

Cleo sighed, closing the door to the salon but continuing in hushed tones, "I thought we would discuss this later, but now is fine with me."

Georgie couldn't help it as the whole story came tumbling out, from meeting Gray at Lisette's to his drunken visit to her home last night.

"I suspected as much," Cleo said. She didn't sound as horrified as Georgie had expected her to be. "The two of you have no choice. Well" — she shook her head — "you have no choice."

"I don't see why this changes anything." She sniffed. "If he had been anyone else, he wouldn't be any the wiser."

"But he is, and likely Ash and Maggie know. And I know. We can't all be privy to your folly and let it continue." Cleo ran her hands over her face in obvious frustration. "I didn't want this for you any more than you. But I have to insist that you allow him to wed you."

"But he thinks I trapped him."

"Yes, he would think that. There's been more than one scheming mama who tried to ensnare him, catch him in a compromising position with her daughter, when nothing had happened. But in your case, it happened and we can't pretend it didn't."

Cleo's paused a moment, collecting herself before she continued. "Speaking of things that just happen, can I trust he has explained that there are precautions a woman can take to prevent a child?"

Georgie's face flushed, heat spreading across her chest and cheeks. She was mortified, but she nodded. *We even used those precautions most of the time*, she thought. Not last night, of course, because she hadn't been expecting him, but she wouldn't tell Cleo that.

"God love him, but I never thought I'd be happy to hear he'd explained contraception to you." Cleo laughed. "You know your brother will kill me for this?"

"But what am I supposed to do?" Georgie pressed. She just wanted to hold off her aunt and uncle until she could leave London, not until she was truly married.

"There is nothing more to do." Cleo passed her a linen handkerchief. "The course is set. Now, we must be off, or we shall be late for tea at your aunt and uncle's."

"If I didn't think you hated me before, I do now," she groaned. "I didn't know we were having tea with them."

"After last night's announcement, it would be surprising if we were not, but you did receive a formal request. I intercepted it this morning before waking you. Don't worry, we shall face the lions together. All of them, my dear."

Chapter Eleven

Rath laughed at himself as he stumbled up the stairs at the townhouse after a hellish, but satisfying night in Tothill Fields. After leaving Georgiana's, he couldn't face going home, and the grog shops held the promise of cheap drink and easy women, of which he'd enjoyed both. *Perhaps a little too much,* he thought as he tried to navigate the front steps. It was at the top of the stairs a few moments later, that his valet had found him and helped him inside.

"Never fuck with a woman," he counselled Richards.

"Well, sir," Richards said with a laugh, "we do prefer them to sheep, so I think we may be stuck with them."

"They are better than sheep," Rath agreed, leaning into Richards' side.

"Well, I am glad to hear that," a stern voice echoed from across the hall. Rath looked up to see his mother standing in the doorway to the main salon. Her hands were crossed in front of her chest, a frown on her lips. He straightened up quickly, grateful that Richards gave him a shoulder to lean on, even if he hadn't warned him of his visitor.

"Mother." He smiled, but it felt more like a leer.

"Don't you mother me. It's well into the afternoon, and you are just stumbling home. Richards, bring him some black coffee now, and some bread, as we try to soak some of that liquor out of him." She turned back to Rath. "I am surprised at you."

"Mother." He followed her on unsteady legs into the parlor. "I am thirty-eight years old. If I choose to drink the night and morning away, I can do that. I am also the infamous Lord Wrath. In some ways, I'm sure it's expected."

"You have just announced your betrothal to a lovely woman from a good family. How do you think it looks to the world, if on the night of your betrothal, you hie yourself off to a bawdy house, to engage in elicit acts with a harlot and drink yourself into a stupor? The ton is not blind."

His head had begun to ache. He hadn't thought that people would be keeping such a close eye on his movements, but this was London, after all. "It was two harlots actually," he said, before realizing he should never correct his mother. Especially not about the number of prostitutes one had bedded the night before. "Never mind."

"A ruse or no ruse, I will not have you embarrassing this family, or hers. Yes, you are Lord Wrath, and I know you have earned the name a hundred times over, but tonight, you will escort Lady Georgiana to the theater, and you will dance attendance on her, as a loving fiancé."

"Mother, you don't understand what's going on here."

"I understand enough, even if I hadn't had every scandal column brought to my attention today." She sighed, trying to catch her breath.

"I would gladly welcome Georgie into the family, but now I know this is strictly for her protection from her aunt and uncle. God, but I hate them." She shuddered. "I am pleased to see you have not lost your selfless nature, and that you still value your friendship with Kit so as to help his sister. Since it looks like you will never settle down, at least I have Ash providing me grandchildren. But you must understand me, I will not allow you to throw a cloud of shame over the family while we are all in residence."

Richards paused at the door, but entered at the countess's nod. "Now drink some coffee, and for god's sake have a bath. You stink of cheap liquor." She waved her hand beneath her nose for emphasis. "And get some sleep. We will expect you at the theater tonight. I've already sent word to Cleo and Georgiana that you will pick them up in your carriage and meet us there. After that, there is a small dinner party at Lord and Lady Galwaighs'."

Rath watched his mother storm out, then leaned his aching head into the palm of his hand. "Mothers," he mumbled to Richards.

"Better yours than mine, sir." Richards laughed. "Come on now, let me get you upstairs and Gissy and I will get you cleaned up and put to bed. I'll bring the coffee up after your bath."

"I like the sound of that." He wrapped an arm around Richards' shoulder for support.

"Your mother was right," his valet said as he leaned away. "You stink."

* * * *

Tea with Constance was going as well as could be expected. Cleo had explained, bless her liar's heart, that Kit and the Earl of Rathbridge had contracted this alliance years prior, and it was not sure until the earl returned whether he would honor the agreement.

"I don't believe this," Constance blathered, her face red. "As your guardian, your uncle should have been informed."

"I don't wish to argue semantics with you, Aunt, but neither you nor Uncle Charles were ever made my legal guardians or my trustees. Uncle Charles is a business manager, and while I understand, as family, you may be distressed that you were not entrusted with this happy news, I think we can both agree that Kit would only do what was in my best interest."

Georgie knew she was laying it on a little thick when Cleo rolled her eyes. Did no one believe she could be both sweet and polite when she wanted to be? She was a little put out by that but hid it by batting her eyelashes.

"But, my dear," her aunt said, her hand stroking Georgiana's sleeve. "He is known as Lord Sin. He's a man of vice and debauchery. Not only has he and his family lowered themselves to the level of a merchant, but he has visited many exotic lands, and rumor has it that he has taken part in some very improper things."

"Listen to your aunt, Georgie," Cleo admonished. "If anyone knows improper, it is her."

"Thank you, my dear." Constance beamed at her, not noting her obvious sarcasm or choosing to ignore it. "Georgiana, I am sure Cleo and Kit must not know this side of him, or they would never allow you to marry him. But I must for your own good tell you what you are in for."

"Aunt Constance, I am not in the mood for idle gossip." She shook her head. Wasn't it idle gossip that had gotten her into this mess?

"Let her continue," Cleo encouraged, "this could be enlightening."

Cleo ignored the irritated glare Georgie shot at her and prodded Constance to continue with what she must hope would be amusing fodder from the gossip mills.

"Thank you for your kind support, Cleo." She nodded. "Having spent so much time in the country, I'm sure you are not familiar with the earl's dangerous reputation."

"I'm sure I am not," Cleo agreed, but her smile said she knew everything anyone could know about Rathbridge.

Constance poured herself more tea, then thought to ask if either woman would like more. They shook their heads.

Georgie tried not to let her frustration show. "Please go on," she prodded, hopeful that they could be on their way soon.

"There is so much to tell." Constance clutched her teacup and looked up toward the ceiling as if trying to remember, when Georgie knew darn well the woman had a list of Rath's so-called sins that she'd no doubt spent all morning making.

"I've heard that he has fought numerous duels, and has even killed a man on the dueling field," she began.

"Two, actually," Cleo supplied with a sly smile.

"Thank you. And the first time he went to sea, he left another young heiress, with child, and refused to marry her, or acknowledge their child as his own."

"It turned out that Lord Danleigh was the child's father, in that case," Cleo again corrected, and Georgie was beginning to see a pattern in this conversation.

"Oh. Thank you. I hadn't heard that conclusion." Constance smiled grimly. "And the first time he came back from Asia, he brought a concubine with him who was no more than a child herself, then sold her to another man to be his mistress."

"I do know this story." Georgie clutched her hands over her chest for dramatic effect. "Madeline, the dowager countess of Rathbridge, loves to tell this tale."

"It was so romantic," Georgie continued. "Pirates attacked the vessel that Mai Jing and her family were traveling on. Rath's crew overtook the pirates, saving Mai Jing, although her parents and the ambassador perished. He carried out their wishes though and brought her to England where Madeline saw to her education. She went on to marry Lord Alfred Leslie and they've since had two children. They live together near his family's estate in Scotland, do they not, Cleo?"

Constance ground her teeth and her growing frustration was evident in the tautness of her brow. She harrumphed. "Well, I do know that after his accident, he became quite dependent on opium." She looked at Cleo to disagree.

Georgie did not know the full story on that, but it had come up in the family before, more as a testament his strength than any weakness. Cleo let the comment pass, so Georgie knew she could get the whole story from her later if she even cared to press.

Constance was bolstered by Cleo's silence and continued, "The next matter is quite delicate, but it's said that he has rather exotic tastes."

"All right, Constance." Cleo put her cup down hard enough that it rattled. "I think we both know that we can never know what goes on in any one's bedroom, and it would be improper of us to discuss what we think we know of his carnal tastes in front of an as yet unmarried woman. Georgie will do her duty in that regard. That is all she needs to know."

It was obvious by Constance's frown that she had some salacious *on-dit* she wanted to share and was angry to have been put off. "Then there is the war," she said, setting down her own cup. "It was never proven, but he may have been on the wrong side. His mother is French, you know."

Georgie interrupted this time, "I hope that is not a comment you will ever repeat in front of his family or the earl. Or do you want Uncle called on the field of honor?"

"No one is saying he was a traitor, just that he may have had some suspicious dealings." Constance backtracked. "I daresay if there had been proof, he would no longer be the earl."

"Is that all you've heard, then?" Georgie stood, her skirts brushing the tea cart and causing the little dishes to rattle. Cleo followed with a little more care.

Constance looked at them in disbelief. "Isn't that enough to warn you off him? He is a dangerous man."

"I have been told that we will suit well." Georgie slipped her hands into her gloves and proceeded to the door. "And I believe that to be true."

"My dear," her aunt called to her, "do you know where your fiancé was last night?"

"I don't need to, Aunt."

"It's all over town. He left your betrothal ball to visit a bawdy house. And it is common knowledge that this past week he had been in the process of installing another woman as a mistress, and had even inquired after clothing and trinkets for her."

Georgie's stomach plummeted, and her lower lip began to quiver. She touched the bruise on her chin lightly. He must have gone out after he left her. She took a steadying breath when Cleo's hand touched her shoulder.

"I don't see as how you can put so much stock into malicious rumor." She turned to her aunt. "Besides," she said, pointedly, "some of the best husbands keep mistresses." Everyone knew Charles had been keeping a mistress since the time he was married.

Constance understood the barb and glared at Cleo and her niece. "You are just like your mother."

Georgiana straightened her spine and smiled. "I understand if you do not support this marriage, and while I would have hoped you could be happy for me, I understand, and in truth would appreciate it if you did not attend the ceremonies."

With back stiff, she left before any more ill-intentioned accusations could be laid.

"Thank you for a lovely visit, as always, Constance." Cleo followed Georgiana out of the salon, then paused. "Wait outside and catch your breath. I need to see Charles."

Georgiana wanted nothing more than to be out of the house, and raced down the steps toward their carriage. She longed to give in to the turmoil inside her, but she noted that she was not alone on the street. She straightened her shoulders and began to pet the nose of their horse.

She breathed deeply, the way Kit had taught her to during a battle. *To think clearly, you needed to breathe. Forget to breathe and you die.* Georgie hadn't needed Constance to remind her of the infamous history of Lord Sin. She'd grown up on tales of his and Kit's exploits.

She knew he hadn't killed anyone in a duel, but he had been called out. One, she remembered, he had wounded in the shoulder, but not mortally. The other he convinced to meet him in the boxing ring instead. There was no mistaking, however, Rathbridge could be dangerous.

She sighed, resting her head against old Brutus' neck, and wondered if they could ever get back what they had. Had he really been inquiring about trinkets for her? She wondered what those would have been. A jeweled comb for her hair? Silk stockings? It may sound silly, but just the thought of them proved to her that at one point he had cared for her. For Ana. And she'd ruined it all.

* * * *

Cleo didn't bother to knock before she stalked into Charles' office. It hadn't changed much over the years. Still a man's sanctuary with dark wood, leather and brocade.

"Lady Welles." Charles stood up from behind his desk. "An unexpected pleasure."

"I think there is something we need to discuss," she began, not bothering to sit. "How to keep your wife on a leash."

"I don't like your tone, Cleo," he warned her.

"I don't care what you like, old friend." He had never frightened her. She remembered him from his bachelor days, after she was first married. "You weren't always like this, Charles, and I know there is only one person responsible."

She didn't blame him. Constance had been different, too, twenty years ago. She had been a beautiful young woman with a moderate dowry, whose stern father was looking to sell her for a title.

She and Charles had been a glorious couple as Connie engaged in a brief rebellion from her upbringing and enjoyed the sights and pleasures London had to offer. A lifetime of stern upbringing and the ongoing barrage of criticism from her parents, and Connie had slipped into old habits only a few months past their wedding.

"Will you pass my apologies to the Sinclairs and Lord Rathbridge?" Charles requested. "Constance was out of line last night, but the announcement took her by surprise."

"I know you don't dislike your niece, Charles."

"She reminds me so much of Veronica."

"That's what everyone says." Cleo smiled, and touched his arm for support. Veronica had been an uncommon beauty, like her daughter, and she'd won the hearts of the ton with her charm. Cleo remembered wishing to be like her when she grew up. "Send Constance to the country, or do whatever you have to do to keep her from ruining what should be the happiest time in a young girl's life."

Charles shook his head. "I can't send her away," he explained. "Our girls are making their debut and are getting new wardrobes and the like."

"You know your girls will have a rough time of it with Constance around," she reminded him. Constance was ill-prepared to launch young women into society, let alone to make them advantageous matches.

"I never wanted it to turn out this way. I have protected my daughters as much as I could from their mother's beliefs," he said.

Cleo knew this to be true, and that while Constance was not an affectionate mother, Charles had attempted to emulate his own father, taking the girls on picnics and to Gunthers for ices. He was a gentler influence on them than their mother had been.

"Think on it, Charles," Cleo asked. "And then when the season begins, send the girls to me. I will sponsor them in society, make sure they are given a chance to make up their own minds and find appropriate husbands."

Cleo knew the offer would gall Constance, and she would not sanction such a decision, but Charles wasn't stupid. He knew Cleo's influence, and of her friendship with Lady Jersey. If his daughters wanted a voucher to Almacks, Cleo could make it happen. He nodded. "Your offer is kind."

"I would like to help your other children as well," Cleo offered, meaning his children by his mistress. "They are what, fourteen and sixteen?"

"You always know too much, Cleo." He laughed.

Cleo liked to see that at least his other family made him laugh. She knew his mistress was a former governess, well read and well spoken, and had given him first a son, then a daughter. They kept a household in a respectable, if not fashionable part of London.

"I will let you know when I can use your assistance."

"They will need sponsorship in a few years, as well. The boy, you will want him to further his studies. Law or medicine, perhaps? I can be a very benevolent aunt," she reminded.

"You will stop at nothing to get your own way." He kissed her hand then. "I will do all I can to keep Constance from doing any further damage."

"And I will pass on your apology on to Rathbridge," Cleo promised.

"Tell Georgie that I am very happy for her."

"I will do that, too." She held his hand a moment longer, then saw herself out. She was just taking her umbrella from the footman when she heard what sounded like a *pop* and watched Georgiana fall to the ground.

Chapter Twelve

The Earl of Rathbridge would never forget where he was when he learned his fiancée had been shot.

He was lounging in a tub of steaming water, smoking one of his treasured cigars brought back from the East, and dreading the evening they had ahead at the theater. Richards, his valet, didn't bother to knock before entering. His face was ashen.

"One of Lady Welles' footmen was just here. It's Ana. She's been shot. Your presence is requested at her townhouse."

Rath felt as if he was drowning. It was like being underwater. He couldn't see straight or think right, and he felt like he was gasping for air. Still, with Richards' help, he was dressed and out the door.

Cleo was on the stairs when he burst through the front doors. She looked at him, her brow furrowed as she took in his countenance, and he remembered that his damp hair was still loose around his shoulders, and he had dressed in haste. Richards hadn't tried to stop him as he pulled on boots and trousers, a loose lawn shirt and a coarse wool jacket, then declared himself ready to go.

"She's in her room. Gabe is with her." Cleo shook her head. There were tears in her eyes. "He asked me to leave."

He wanted to comfort Cleo as she began to cry in earnest, but he had to see Georgie. He paused on the stairs to lay his hand on Cleo's shoulder. "We will take care of her, I promise."

At least he knew the way to Georgie's room. Gabe was standing by her bedside, but he didn't spare him and his blood-covered hands a thought, before his gaze fixed on her. She wasn't moving. Her tawny complexion looked pale and drawn.

"Is she...?" His voice trembled.

Gabe shook his head, wiping his hands on a towel. "No. I've given her some laudanum to help with the pain, but she's been more or less unconscious since I arrived."

Gabe motioned to Leda, Georgie's maid, to pull aside the gauze she was holding to Georgie's left shoulder. "I'll need to remove the bullet. It's deep, but I don't think it splintered or shattered anything."

"You don't think?"

"You know I won't know until I go in and dig it out." Gabe was not exuding his usual calm. "If it's not splintered now, it still could. And then there is a risk of infection."

"I know, I'm sorry." Rath rested his hand on Gabe's shoulder. "But you will get her through this," he reassured his friend.

"We'll need a footman or two to hold her while I dig it out."

"I'll stay. I'll help," Rath told him. He'd assisted Gabe numerous times in surgery at sea.

"Rath, you shouldn't stay."

"If you are going to tell me it's improper, have no fear. I've seen her naked."

"I was thinking if we lose her, you would blame yourself."

"I will blame myself, regardless, so I'm staying." His voice was gruff. He was already beating himself up over her injuries. "You may need me. I do know something about gunshot wounds. Besides she might wake up."

Gabe nodded. Whether because he recognized Rath's experience with wounds or because he understood the depth of emotions that would not let Rath leave, was unclear. When two somber footmen appeared to assist, he instructed each of them how to hold her. It was hoped that she would remain unconscious through the procedure.

Gabe worked with a speed and efficiency that won him Rath's admiration all over again. Rath was holding her left shoulder stiffly, and he willed himself to look not at her face but at the wound. He and the doctor exchanged a meaningful glance when halfway through the procedure, a small cry escaped from Georgie.

A steady stream of tears fell over her cheeks, but her eyes were clouded. Rath couldn't be sure that she saw him, or was even aware of what was going on. But from her struggling, he knew she felt Gabe digging for the ball. He and the footmen held her firm.

"It's almost done," Gabe told him.

"Keeping going, but be fast," he told him, as he watched her eyes close and she slipped back into unconsciousness.

"I've got the ball. It's intact, and I don't see any splintered bone. I'll just clean the wound and stitch it up."

Rath said nothing, but waited for it to be over. When the wound was ready to be bandaged, he dismissed the footmen, instructing them to pass on word that Georgie was recovering well.

"Rath, you look dead on your feet, why don't you go down with Cleo?"

"I won't leave her."

"There's nothing more you can do."

"How do you know? What if she needs me?" he snapped at Gabe. "What if she gives up? What if she dies?" The whole wall shook when he punched the door frame.

"Rath." The doctor grabbed him by the shoulders. Both men were of equal height and faced each other eye to eye. "I won't let her die on you."

Rath tried to calm his breathing. "I know. I know you're doing your best."

"I am going to get her through this," Gabe told him, and Rath wanted to believe him. "There will be fever. You know there often is. And my experience in battle shows better results if we change the dressings frequently. I'll keep her on laudanum for the time being."

Rath rolled his eyes, but he nodded. He knew she needed the drug and that Gabe would be more careful than any apothecary, ensuring she took only what was required.

"How did this happen?"

Gabe turned back to his patient, preparing the dressing for her shoulder. "All I know is that they were leaving Charles and Constance's house. Cleo heard a shot she thinks came from across the street, then Georgie fell. Who would do this?"

"I don't know, but I intend to find out." His scowl warned Gabe that a physician would not be needed for the person who had shot Georgie.

As Gabe prepared a salve for the wound, Rathbridge searched her armoire for a suitable shift. Between the two of them, they removed the blood-stained sheets beneath her. Rath himself bathed her shoulder gently, removing the blood that had dried on her skin, then slipped her into a sleeveless shift which tied at the shoulders and would make changing the dressing easier.

He brushed her hair, trying not to remember the last time he'd done this for her. When she'd been naked and lying in his bed.

"Rath." Gabe touched his shoulder, "I'm not sure I can hold Cleo out of here much longer."

He nodded and made sure his Ana looked more like herself before nodding to Gabe to let Cleo, and the small retinue of friends and family who had gathered, into the room.

Ash and Maggie had arrived with his mother. He thanked Maggie for bringing him a fresh change of clothes. He'd not noticed his shirt had been spotted with blood, but he wasn't surprised. He popped into the room across the hall to change before rejoining his family and Cleo, in a small upstairs bedroom that had been converted to a library.

"Well, I guess this means the theater is out," he said sharply to his mother.

"That's enough, Rowan Grayson," she told him. "I like the girl and won't be abused because I demand you do what's best for her."

No one could disagree with that, not even Rath, at this juncture. He wrapped an arm around his mother and kissed her temple. "I know, Mama. I'm sorry."

He then pulled Ash aside. "I want every runner we have in our employ investigating this," he told him. "If you can get a record of her family accounts, we should go over them and see what we can find there."

"Good thinking. I will see her solicitor and find out all I can about her parents' will as how it affects her."

"Don't we have a copy of that?" Rath was sure there would have been a dissertation on the division of assets as it pertained to the shipping company their fathers had shared.

"Only the sections that pertain to the business," Ash replied. "That doesn't mean I can't get the rest."

Rath nodded, and pulled Maggie and Cleo aside next. "I know you want to concentrate on your friend, but more than sitting next to her and reading, I need you to think. Think of everyone who has ever caused her trouble. A would-be suitor? A jealous friend? A disgruntled employee? Write it down and give it to Ash for the runners to check out."

"Rath," Cleo interrupted, "this was found while you were with the Gabe." She handed him an envelope addressed to him.

He tore it open.

Break the engagement, or my aim will get better.

He resisted the urge to crush the letter and handed instead to Ash. "Give this to the runner, as well."

"Maybe the engagement wasn't the best idea," Cleo suggested wearily.

"What's done is done, Cleo, and you can't blame yourself. We'll see this through," he assured her and leaned in to whisper, "My mother wants grandchildren, you see. For that, I need my bride to live."

"Gabe and I will be spending the night here, to take care of her if she wakes," Cleo told him.

The Countess shook her head. "No. You need all your strength for her tomorrow. I will stay and watch over her tonight."

"Madeline—" Cleo began, but was cut off.

"I won't hear another word. Let Ash and Maggie take you home. You rest and be back in the morning." Madeline looked at the small group. "I do have experience with this sort of thing. I know what to do."

Rath smiled at his mother, grateful for her backbone. He got his stubbornness from her. He gave Cleo's hand a squeeze before Maggie urged her away with them. Hopefully she would rest. He was beginning to understand the depth of her commitment to Ana. *Georgiana*, he scolded himself. It was best if he stopped thinking of her of Ana.

When they had left, Rath hugged his mother. "Thank you," he whispered.

She wrapped her arms around his back. "It's what a mother does. Besides, it would be frowned upon if I were to leave you alone with her before you're married."

The servants prepared a light dinner for which they were all grateful. After a few bites of bread, Rath went to look for Gabe. He was standing near the window in Georgie's room, looking out at the night sky.

"Has she woken yet?"

"Not yet." Gabe turned to him. "She murmured once and began to move about in her sleep. I gave her another sip of laudanum, and she settled down."

"Mother's seeing to some dinner downstairs. Why don't you join her in the dining room," he suggested.

Gabe started to argue that he didn't need to eat yet, but Rath cut him off. An argument was the last thing he had patience. "You will insult her if you decline."

Gabe sighed. "I could use a bite to eat."

He double-checked the dressing and her vitals one more time, then left Rath alone with Georgie.

Rath pulled up a small chair next to her bed and held on to her hand. He didn't know how long he sat there, holding her hand, stroking her arm, hoping she'd awake. The maid brought in some bread, pork and cheese, along with a bottle of brandy. He chose the brandy first. And began the endless wait again.

He supposed he must have drifted off to sleep, because when he woke, he found her looking at him.

"Hi there, Georgie."

"Gray." Her voice sounded dry and weak, and he hastened to pour her some water mixed with laudanum and helped her sip it.

"Does it hurt much?" he asked her. She shook her head. He climbed onto the bed with her and held her against him. "Go back to sleep, love. You'll be better soon."

"Thank you," she murmured and closed her eyes again.

His mother frowned when she came to sit with them. He shook his head. He wasn't going to let anyone tell him how he could or couldn't comfort her. His mother didn't push, just sat down, opened a novel and began to read aloud.

When he awoke a few hours later, his mother had been replaced by Gabe, who was slumped in the chair, asleep. He wondered what had woken him, then Georgie shivered. Her chemise, he noted, was soaked through with sweat.

"Gabe, wake up," he called out, kicking his friend awake. "She's fevered."

Gabe opened his eyes and cursed, dragging his hands back through his hair. He sent the footmen for ice and cloths, and together the two men began to bathe her with cold towels.

In her fever she screamed, begging them not to touch her. The men looked at each other, knowing she delirious but curious as to whom she was speaking. "Big John. Make them stop. Please make them stop," she cried.

Rath soothed her, as Gabe continued to bathe her. "It's all right, love. Big John will make them go away. They can't touch you anymore." She seemed to calm at the sound of his voice.

"Please don't let them lock me in here."

"No, sweetheart. You won't be locked in." Rath looked at Gabe with concern.

"It's so dark in here, and I can't move," she whispered. Her voice was almost childlike and laced with fear.

"No, it's beautiful and sunny and you're on *The Eagle*, sailing into the wind." He hoped in her fevered state the name of Kit's boat would reassure her.

"I'm not a bad girl."

"Oh, Lord, honey, no, you are not a bad girl." He stroked her damp hair, pushing it away from her face. "You're my girl, and I won't let anyone hurt you."

In her sleep, she clung to him, but her sobbing stopped and her breathing calmed.

"Rath, we're going to have to call for a tub of iced water," Gabe told him. "Her fever's too high."

"Son of a bitch," he cursed, but nodded.

With the tub filled, they gently began to bathe her in the icy water, until her skin cooled.

"When will we know if she's going to make it?" Rath hesitated to ask.

Gabe shook his head. "The sooner the fever breaks, the better I will feel."

The fever broke thirty hours later. Both men whooped with relief. Cleo came bursting in, after hearing them. "The worst is past, then?" she asked hopefully.

"Yes, my love." Gabe twirled her around. "The worst is past."

"Thank God." She sighed, clinging to Gabe's shoulders. "I have never been so scared."

"I have only once been so scared and that was when you…" He paused, conscious of Rath's presence. "Well, you know when, my dear."

She nodded and kissed him.

"I will take over her care from here," she told them. "You've done your work. Let me do mine."

Rath and Gabe were too tired to protest, and let her pushed them toward the door. "You come back when you've had some sleep and some food. She's not out of the woods yet, but we'll get her there."

* * * *

Georgie sat on the edge of her bed. It had taken all her strength to move this far, but she was determined that she would make it to the chair by the window. She looked at her legs. She looked at the chair, then she looked at her legs again, trying to will them to take her there.

"Good morning, sunshine," Rath said from the doorway behind her. "We've got to stop meeting like this."

He realized her intention and scooped her into his arms and deposited her in the chair by the window. He took a blanket from the bed and tucked it around her.

"The servants are beginning to talk," she warned him.

"That's what happens when you let a man spend the night in your room."

"Let a man?" she grumbled. "I was unconscious with fever."

"Just the same, they probably expect that Lord Sin, Lord Wrath — whichever epithet best fits — would have taken advantage of you, anyway."

She gave a small snort to that. No doubt they would. Since her fever had broken, he had kept a respectable distance from her. Though flowers had arrived from him each morning.

"How is your shoulder today?"

"Not bad, according to Gabe. He visited about an hour ago and changed the dressing. He says it looks good," she told him. "I, on the other hand, think it an ugly mess, all purple and black. Though he did good stitch work.

"I once had to stitch a man who had cut his arm on the plantation. The local doctor had arrived but was too drunk even to see the wound, so Kit asked me to do it, as he had to hold the man's arm. I remember all we had was some strong spirits and a strip of leather for the man to bite down on. After the doctor passed out, we found some laudanum in his bag and gave him that. Belle Fleur now has its own doctor."

Rath quirked his eyebrow at her and she grimaced. "I'm sorry. I talk when I'm nervous."

"Kit's given you quite the education, hasn't he?" He laughed.

She grinned. She had warned him that she was unusual, hadn't she?

"Do you think the blackmailer and the shooter are the same person?"

"We've had the runners looking into every aspect of this, and into every aspect of yours and Kit's life. It's likely that if they are not the same person, the shooter was hired by the blackmailer. But we have to look at all angles. And unfortunately, nothing has yet to turn up. Ash and our estate manager are going to go through the account books as soon as your uncle can provide them."

She shrugged but winced from the pain in her shoulder. "I keep trying to relive the scene and think if perhaps I saw someone — a face, a coat or anything — but there's nothing. I was waiting for Cleo by our carriage, and then I remember hearing a large bang and thinking, my God, that didn't sound good, and then feeling a sudden burning in my shoulder. I turned to see Cleo standing at the top of the stairs and then I passed out."

He knew all that, and nodded at her, his rough thumb stroking her cheek.

"Thank you for looking after this for me."

"That's what I was commissioned to do," he told her. "Though I think you should thank Gabe. I thought him too jaded to blush, but that tirade of cuss words that you used when you were fevered turned him as red as cook's raspberry syrup."

She groaned, "What else did I say?"

"You were quite chatty," he told her as he pulled close a second chair.

"No, don't tell me. So long as I didn't say anything silly like 'I love you'."

He laughed. "No, nothing silly."

He looked at her in silence for a moment, and she knew he had something more to say.

"What did I say?"

"Most of it was gibberish, but" — he paused — "all of it was gibberish. Just forget about it."

"I talked about it, didn't I?" She stared down at her hands, now folded in her lap. She hadn't thought about it in more than fifteen years, since Kit had rescued her.

"You don't have to talk about it again," he told her.

"I think maybe I do." She looked at him.

"You sounded scared and I don't ever want you to be afraid." He stroked her cheek with the back of his hand, wishing he could take her in his arms.

She couldn't help but grin. "You are very much like Kit. I'm surprised he didn't confide this to you. It's his secret too." She thought for a moment. "And Cleo's. She is aware too."

"I think you need to share this. Maybe you should share it with Gray," he encouraged. "You trusted Gray with your secrets."

"It could take a while," she warned him. She hadn't even begun and tears already burned her eyes.

"Hang on," he said.

She watched him dash from the room, only to return two minutes later with a bottle of brandy and a couple of glasses. He moved a small table between them and set his treasure upon it. He then pulled his chair up to face hers, so she wouldn't have to turn her head and hurt her shoulder. He was considerate like that.

"Now," he said, sitting and pouring them both a glass, "we have all day."

She wiped her eyes with the back of her hand. "I've never spoken of it to anyone. Kit and I don't even speak of it," she began. "Do you recall my parents' deaths?"

"I do," he acknowledged. He and Kit had been at sea. They hadn't heard of the deaths until sometime later.

"I was in the carriage when they died." It had been a long time before she could remember more than just bits and pieces of that day. She had hit her head when the carriage careened off the road and blacked out. When she woke, she was wet and cold, the carriage having been laying on its side in one of the swampy ditches that bordered the road to their plantation.

"Father was already dead. My mother was dying. She couldn't move, but she smiled at me, and told me it would be okay. Help was coming." She wiped at the tears that ran down her cheeks. "She told me that they loved me. And then she began to sing to me, my lullaby, and then it just faded out."

She didn't have words for the fear she had experienced as night had fallen and no one came to their aid. It wasn't until after dawn that she heard horses and voices. She'd been left to cling to her mother's corpse all night.

"You were just six years old, right?" He put the glass of brandy in her good hand and encouraged her to take a sip.

She took a deep breath, but nodded. "The funeral took place at Belle Fleur, and then I was on a ship to

England with my aunt and uncle. They spent most of the time, I remember, arguing about what to do with me. Kit was all I wanted and he was at sea. But I couldn't tell them what I wanted, that I wanted my brother, because I couldn't talk. I was too scared to talk or maybe I just forgot how, but I couldn't get out any words. Nothing above a whimper or a grunt."

"You were traumatized."

"'Damaged' was Aunt Constance's word for it." Rath frowned and his eyes darkened with anger. She didn't blame him. She was still angry at Constance too. "She sent me away. To an asylum just outside of Hertfordshire. It was for children mostly. I don't know how long I stayed there, wanting so badly to talk."

She shuddered just thinking about the place. She hadn't been there a day when they'd cut off all her hair and taken away the trunk of pretty clothes and toys that her aunt and uncle had packed for her. She was given a rough cotton dress and an apron. They were made to wear hard leather shoes. *It was all very serviceable,* she thought.

"When you were fevered, you begged them not to touch you." He squeezed her hand, and she thought he understood, perhaps better than most, how hard this was to discuss.

"We shared rooms, often six of us in one, and there were men who came in to clean up after us, to feed us, to bathe us. Sometimes they wanted to do more than that. You fight them, but there are always punishments, spankings, whippings. And the dark room."

She noticed that she'd slipped into present tense, so real were the memories sometimes that it was hard to put them into the past.

"What's the dark room?"

She resolved to put it back in the past. "It was the size of a wardrobe. They tied your hands and your feet so you can't" — she paused — "so you couldn't beat on the walls. And they would cover your mouth so you couldn't scream. Then they close the door." A shiver of revulsion washed over her. "And you were naked and scared. And you could hear things moving in the dark, and you couldn't look for what was making the sound, because it was dark. But sometimes you would feel it crawling over you, but your hands are tied so you couldn't push it off."

She shook her head. She knew her eyes were open, but she could still feel the blackness. She was only vaguely aware of Rath lifting her onto his lap. "Sssh, it's okay. The dark room is gone."

She sighed into the side of his neck, taking comfort from his presence, his scent, his touch. She knew she had to continue. "A few hours in the dark room and you didn't care if the men touched you. After a while, it hurt too much to fight them and you let them do what they want. I always fought, and when I was too tired to fight, Big John would fight them to keep them away from me. Even though they beat him so much worse than they beat the girls."

"But John fought them for you." She couldn't see Rath's face, but his voice was stressed with emotion.

She nodded. "And then Kit came. He rescued me. After that, he was reluctant to let me go. I was always with him or with Cleo after that."

"And still you didn't talk?"

She closed her eyes, remembering the six months at Cleo's home, The Cedars, where she still couldn't find her voice. Kit hadn't left during that whole time, but he had to go to London for some reason, and she'd been so frightened he wouldn't come back. She'd run to him, yelling, *'I love you, Kit.'* She remembered his arms shaking as he swept her up and hugged her to him. *'Tell me again, baby girl.'* And she had told him over and over. And Cleo too.

"It took a few months for the trauma to fade. And probably much to everyone's chagrin, since that day I've never stopped talking."

"How old were you then?" he asked.

"I had just turned seven. It had been just a little more than a year since I talked."

"Kit never told me, but it makes so much more sense now. Why he began taking shorter runs. As much as he loved the sea, he was loath to leave you. And your aunt and uncle," he blew out a deep breath, "you must hate them."

"I don't hate them. Kit investigated, and is sure that Charles had no idea the type of facility it was. But I don't like them much, and the way Constance has tried repeatedly to hold sway over my life. Kit is my legal guardian, and in his stead, it's always been Cleo. I give very little credence to what my aunt and uncle have to say."

"My beautiful girl." He stroked his hand across her cheek and kissed her temple.

The tenderness in his voice worried her. It sounded like Gray, not Rath.

"You must realize," she said, "that after everything that happened, I'm not a future countess. I've been in an asylum. Men, not you, have seen me and touched me."

"We don't need to talk about that now," he said.

She frowned. "We do. I can't marry you. I won't marry anyone."

He lifted her back onto her own chair, tucking the blanket around her and snagging her book from bed. He poured her another small glass of brandy.

"On the contrary, Georgie." He loomed over her, the bottle in his hand. "What I see is that you and I aren't like everyone else. We are haunted by things we've done, or things that have been done to us," he said. "But we aren't defined by them. That makes us better suited than anyone suspects."

"You can't mean that."

He winked at her. "I do, George. This changes everything and nothing. We are getting married."

She stared after him as he left. He was whistling. She didn't like that. She didn't understand that. She thought this — her past — if nothing else, would convince him she wasn't marriage material. But he sounded more sure and pleased now than ever. She sighed back into the chair, grabbing the small glass of brandy and bringing it to her lips. She'd never understand men.

* * * *

His man, Ragney, couldn't follow orders. He had almost killed the girl. That was not the plan, and it wouldn't be as helpful as keeping her alive and indisposed. The stack of bills wasn't getting any smaller, and there were very few ways to guarantee their payment. The easiest was to gain control of her money.

She was more valuable alive. Upon her death, he would gain a small sum but also a heap of suspicion. Kit would feel compelled to return home and he was smart and relentless.

He would discover it all, but so too could her fiancé. If he'd succeeded in getting her wed to his man, there would have been no worry. That would have worked. Now he needed the girl alive, but out of the way. That was a hundred times harder.

She thought she was smart and she'd been raised too damn independent by far. Not like a woman should be. Simpering, witless females.

No, Georgiana was stronger than that. He had heard rumors that she read books, not just the gothic novels, but philosophy and economics. And history. An unsuitable, unnatural bluestocking. *Maybe that's the key,* he thought. No one would welcome a bluestocking chit into a wealthy and aristocratic family, would they?

He needed to figure this out. He sighed, worrying his hand over his chin. He would bring her to heel, one way or the other. It was just a matter of time, and cleverness.

Chapter Thirteen

"Ash, I am fine," she complained, and he felt for her. He and Maggie had taken to fussing over her. If she wanted something, Maggie was there to fetch it. When she wanted to move from the bed to the chair, Ash was there with an arm around her, ready to pick her up should she stumble. When she asked to sit in the drawing room downstairs this morning, he swept her into his arms and carried her down, despite her protests.

"Rath and Kit both would have my hide if I let anything happen to you," he reminded her. "And as your soon-to-be brother-in-law, I have a responsibility."

"He may not want to see me dead, Ash, but I don't think Rath would mind if I was unable to marry him anytime too soon."

"I'll be the first to admit, you're a hoyden, but I don't think you trapped him into this." He didn't believe there was any point in pretending he didn't know they'd bedded prematurely. "We both know that you've let him off the hook, and Kit would never have to know about your relationship."

Even Rath, though he wouldn't admit it, had come to believe that she had meant to bed him not wed him. She had told him countless times he could break the engagement, but it was his own honor that prevented that course of action. "If he didn't want to marry you, he wouldn't be."

"I think if I was anyone but Kit's sister, he wouldn't be marrying me, but..."

He set her down in the rocking chair by the fire in the front receiving room. "No buts, Georgie, you didn't ask him for anything." He pulled the blanket from the nearby footstool and spread it gently on her lap.

"He hasn't been to visit me in a week," she reminded him, and Ash shrugged. Rath may not have attended the house, but he had made sure her room was full of flowers, and had sent her some new books to read.

"He sent you gifts," he suggested. "He's thinking about you."

She narrowed her eyes at him and he cringed.

"But not one personal note," she reminded him.

He didn't think it was going to get him anywhere to say that his brother needed time. That Rath wouldn't know what to do with the emotions of falling in love. It was a concept foreign and terrifying to him. No, he was going to keep his mouth shut.

"Maggie will be in with your tea shortly," he promised as he threw another log on the fire and bid her a good afternoon, bussing a kiss onto her cheek.

He stopped his wife in the hall, putting the tea service on the table next to them. "I need a kiss," he told her, and she laughed up at him.

"You always be needing a kiss, boy."

"You are correct," he said, taking her lower lip between his own and sliding his tongue inside her mouth. He would never tire of kissing his wife, or feeling their babe growing inside her. He ran his hand down her side, noting the slight thickening of her waist. He couldn't wait to be a da.

She pulled back. "The tea will get cold."

He groaned. "One more thing for Georgie to complain about, then."

"She's just going a little stir-crazy." Maggie shook her head. "She's not one to be cooped up."

"She's angry at Rath too," he confirmed. "I'm not sure where he is, but he better understand that his presence has been sorely missed."

"He's trying to track down leads on who shot Georgie, is he not?"

"Aye. I think so," he said, though Ash thought they were to do that together. "But that won't do much calm the tigress in there. Fair warning to you."

Maggie shook her head with a laugh. She knew how to deal with her friend. "Thanks for the warning, husband."

She was not surprised to see Georgie pacing the room when she brought the tea service in. She had kept the sling on her arm, holding it immobile, as per Gabe's instruction, but she was chafing at the bit.

"Should you be walking around like that?" Maggie asked, putting down the tea service. She heard Cleo arriving at the front door and a moment later she joined them, a plate of strawberry tarts in her hands.

"Yes, I should be." She continued to pace library, even as they poured tea and doled out the tarts. "I'm not just walking, I'm running."

The women looked at her questioningly.

"*The Vixen* is scheduled to break port in five days, and I have every intention of being on it," she told them.

"I don't think you've thought this through," Cleo began, looking at Maggie for backup.

Maggie knew well that Georgie wasn't thinking this through. Even if she did get the ship to sail, with her as passenger, Rath would just take *The Eagle* and chase after her. The worst thing she could do would be trying to outrun Captain Wrath. He would live up to the name no doubt.

"Hear me out, Cleo," she implored. "I have done nothing but think of this. This was the plan all along. I would break the engagement, and break it, I shall. I will be out to sea and on my way home. The scandal won't touch me there. And neither will the blackmailer, lest he follow me home."

"I'm not talking about the scandal. I'm talking about Rath," Cleo said, and Maggie thought it was as if she'd read her mind. "He won't let you get away that easily."

"This is what he wanted in the first place. He didn't want a wife. He wanted a mistress trained to see to his every lascivious request. And you can still use his contacts once I'm gone to see who was trying to blackmail me."

"But I thought you cared about him," Maggie said.

Georgie reached out to Maggie with her good arm, and touched her cheek.

"Mags, it's more than that. Part of me loves him, and has since his eyes caught mine, and he smiled that first time. But you know how I feel about marriage. He would marry me, offer me the protection of his name, and position, but he would not offer me his heart," she said sadly.

Maggie pulled Georgie's hand into hers. "You can't be sure about that. I've seen the way he looks at you. His eyes hold a softness for you."

"A softness," she scoffed. "That's not what I want to build a marriage on. Were I to decide to wed, which I won't, I want love."

Maggie sighed. Ash had promised her that Rath was as close to love as he'd ever seen him, but that wasn't the same as saying he was in love.

"And Lord Sin doesn't love, does he, Cleo?"

Maggie looked at Cleo who had been staring into her teacup. "His perception of love has been jaded by experience. I don't know if he will ever love you, and if that's what you need, then it's best you run now, but run hard and fast, because if he catches you, he will never let you go."

"You make him sound like a monster," Maggie snapped, glaring at Cleo.

"I'm sorry, Maggie, but I've known him longer and probably better than nearly anyone. And I have never seen him as angry as he was when he found out who his Ana really was or as when he thought she might die." She paused. "I would say he cares a great deal for Georgie, but I don't know if that's enough."

"Then it's settled." Georgie grinned.

"It's not," Maggie argued. "You could fight for him. Why shouldn't he fall in love with you? Why shouldn't his softness for you turn into something heated? You made me fight for Ash. Why won't you fight for Rath?"

"Because I don't want to wed," Georgie reminded her.

"Pish," Maggie scoffed, stalking toward her best friend. "You don't know what you want. And if you carry his bairn?" Maggie knew she wasn't playing fair, but she knew that Georgie had missed her monthly courses.

Cleo grabbed on to Georgie's good hand. "Are you with child?"

There was a dangerous glint in Georgie's eyes as she narrowed them on her friend. "No. I'm not. Gabe said it's common after the body has a trauma like being shot not have one's womanly flow."

"You can't leave if you are carrying his child," Cleo said quietly, and Maggie watched a look pass between them. "But if you are sure you are not, then I will help you."

Maggie threw her hands into the air then sank back down onto a chair. She didn't care if they knew she was in a huff. "I don't like it."

"But," Georgie prodded.

"But I won't stop you from sailing away on *The Vixen*."

Georgie hooted with glee, and proceeded to shake her hair loose until she looked like a hoyden. "Then *The Vixen* will leave with me on it. "

* * * *

He had told himself it was the pain that made him drink. The pain was caused by the spasm in his leg, which grew more intense with the fog. He studied the ledgers he had received from Charles. On the surface, things looked in order. The ledgers were neatly kept, and organized, but he knew in his gut, which he admitted was talking to him through the gin, that something was wrong.

"Any luck?" Ash leaned against the doorjamb to the captain's cabin on *The Raven*.

"I can't even succeed in getting myself drunk." He shook his head, and handed a new bottle of gin to Ash, who uncorked it and poured a glass for himself. "I am sure that Charles and Constance are involved in this."

"You sure that's not just because Constance is opposed to your marriage?" Ash countered.

"I'm opposed to my marriage, and I don't suspect myself."

"Well, that's good." He sat down with his gin across from Rath and picked up one of the ledgers. "If you and Georgie are both opposed, why not just call it off?"

"We will be married," Rath insisted. He didn't want to have to explain why he was so determined for the wedding to take place. *Because you care about her,* a voice he did not like to call his conscience said.

"Do you really think Kit would want you to force his sister into marriage?"

"Do you think he would be happy to know I took her virginity and left without a backward glance?" he growled. "Besides I owe it to him and Cleo to see her safe, and the wedding will accomplish that in more ways than one."

Ash grinned.

"What?" Rath demanded. He hated seeing his brother looking so smug, like he knew something funny.

"You don't care about propriety. You don't care about what people, especially the ton, think of you."

"So what are you suggesting? That I am in love with her?" He hated that word. He wasn't meant to be a husband. He had thought about it when he was younger, before his injury. Before he became damaged goods himself. He rubbed at his thigh.

"You said it, brother." Ash shrugged. "And of course, your wedding will make our mother deliriously happy, so I guess that is a good enough reason as well."

"Yes. She will be happy," Rath agreed. His mother had told him as much yesterday afternoon when she'd visited his townhouse. It was why he'd chosen to work on his ship. His mother was too comfortable visiting what was supposed to be his bachelor residence.

"Shall I take the ledgers and go over them again?"

"I wish you would," he admitted.

"No problem. Maggie and Georgie don't need me hanging around anymore."

"How is she doing?" He was still finding it hard to think of her as Georgie, not Ana.

"If you had stopped at all to visit this week, you'd know that she is being clucked after by a bunch of mother hens, including our mother. Even Felicia is excitedly chattering on about the wedding."

"How does she feel about that?"

"You could visit and ask her?" his brother suggested.

"I am asking you."

"She still says she has no intention of wedding, but she's indulgent with Fe. She only fights the idea to Maggie and Cleo and me."

No, she wouldn't do anything to insult Madeline, or to scold Felicia. She was kind that way. He always knew that. "And her shoulder?"

"A little stiff, but she's doing exactly as Gabe directed her." He smiled again, and hesitated a moment. "Our good doctor was very impressed with her. He was marveling at her remarkable recuperative powers."

"What's that supposed to mean?"

"It means she's strong and fit. I would think those positive attributes." Ash scowled at him.

"Has Gabe been there often?"

"Well, I think you threatened him with physical violence if he didn't ensure her complete and painless recovery." Ash's eyes twinkled with humor.

"Yes. Well, the doctor can have his fill of her attributes, once she provides the Rathbridge heir."

"Oh, for Christ's sake." Ash rolled his eyes. "I cannot believe you said that."

Ash snatched the ledgers from the desk. "You bedded the chit, now you're going to marry her, and against her will, I might add. The least you could do is give her a few months of believing you care just a little before shipping her off to a backwater estate to act the broodmare."

"I am tired of yours and everyone else's interference in this farce of a relationship between Georgie and myself. I fucked her, and for that we will pay the price, like it or not."

"You arrogant self-righteous prig." He slammed the ledgers back down on the desk. "You liked it well enough at the time. Now you seek to punish her for it."

"We are both punished for it. She was an admirable mistress, with much enthusiasm for the task. I seduced my best friend's little sister. Not that she did not want to be seduced, but it's just not done."

"So, that's what this is about. Maggie didn't think of this when she sent me to speak to you."

"What?"

"Maggie thought that you were still fuming because you thought she intentionally tried to trap you. Maggie insisted that I convince you that Georgie had no idea who you were. Damn chit, always was impulsive. When I think of the schemes she and Maggie cooked up to engage my interest…"

"You've yet to tell me all of that story." Rath tried to get Ash to change the subject and his temper.

"Do you really want to hear it?" Ash leaned on the edge of the desk, noticeably calmer. "Or should I tell you now while you're still mad?"

"I'd rather the story."

"Well, you know when Maggie came with her uncle from Scotland that Mother took an instant liking to her, and ensured that besides just knowing the horses, she also went to school. That's where Georgie and Maggie met—Lady Hilbert's Academy for Young Women. Both were equally rambunctious in nature.

"Mother, of course, loved that the two had become fast friends, and that they spent time together at Rosehaven, once school was finished. I had only seen Maggie once or twice before she went away, but even then, she was a beauty."

Ash's affection for his new wife was evident in the wistfulness of his tale.

"And when she got back from school?" Rath prompted.

"She was still a hoyden. I was visiting for Felicia's birthday and had just come from riding around the estate. She was wearing an impeccable riding habit, and had one foot lifted onto the first rung of the fencing. I had seen her in a lot more revealing clothes, but she made my heart pound. She challenged my riding skills, saying I hadn't improved in the year she'd been away.

"She brought out Pepper, and we raced across the meadow, through Drummond's creek and into the forest beyond. She took the lead into the forest, but I had overtaken her again by the time we hit St. Matthew's Church."

"This is getting maudlin. Let me guess, you knew at that moment, it was love." Rath finished his glass of gin, but resisted pouring another. He discovered the pain in his leg had dulled.

"It was certainly lust. But it took more scheming on Maggie's and Georgie's parts before I knew I realized it was love. The point is, their scheming was obvious. It was sweet and completely without malice. She would make sure to be around when I was at the stables. She accidentally bumped into me in the library late one evening. I 'accidentally' heard Mother talking to her uncle about arranging an alliance for her with Viscount Hudson's younger son. I don't know if they were in on the scheme, but I knew I didn't want her to marry anyone else."

"So, what did you do?"

"The next time she 'found' me alone, I compromised her, and made sure Mother, Georgie, and Maggie's uncle would see it. It didn't hurt that we were swimming nearly naked in Drummond's creek when they found us."

"Why not just ask her to marry you?"

"Too easy. As it was, Mother made us wait until she could plan a proper wedding. But it was worth it."

"From what I can see of your Maggie, she is a kitten compared to the tiger that Georgie is." He ran his hands back through his hair.

"She might be a tiger, but I can promise that she is nothing like Sarah," Ash reminded Rath of his one-time fiancée. It had been luck that he had discovered, before they were wed, that she was carrying another man's child. "And she's nothing like your mistresses." Ash quietly put down his glass. "Think about it."

Rath began pacing. He could get used to having Georgie around. He liked Georgie. But liking a wife was another thing all together, he was sure. Ash didn't know that he wasn't comparing Georgie to Sarah or any other mistress he'd had over the years, of which there were few. He didn't have time for them.

He was comparing his fiancée to Ana. He wanted to marry Ana, and he hoped that by getting Georgie to the altar, a little of Ana would get there, too. He had gone to great lengths to make sure the wedding happened.

Chapter Fourteen

He and Emily weren't Georgie's only guests, Kit surmised. From the entrance hall, Kit could hear someone demanding to know where she had gone. She, he assumed, was Georgiana, and he wondered what mess she had stepped into this time. It was always something.

He was relieved when his wife assured him the babe she carried was a boy. He'd already raised a girl. He wasn't sure he could face that again. And yet, seeing his sister, and having her there for his first child's birth was one of the reasons he was had acquiesced Emily's insistence that they needed to be in England for the birth of his heir. He couldn't resist her as she waddled around the plantation packing, declaring that it was only fitting the next earl be born in London.

Kit, for his part, had prepared his personal ship, *The Golden Eagle*, for sail.

Emily looked now at her husband questioningly. He shrugged and was crossing the hall to the library, when the double doors swung open. "The stupid chit, I'm going after her." Rath, with Cleo on his heels, turned and ran into Kit.

Both men stopped and stared at each other. Emily and Cleo stood waiting for one of them to say something. Both men were shocked but for very different reasons. Kit broke the standoff, pulling Rath into his arms.

"Good god, man, it is good to see you." Kit clapped Rath on the back. "I didn't know *The Raven* was in port."

"I had not expected to see you so soon either," Rath said. "In fact, you're the last person I thought I'd run into today."

"Emily," Kit called out, "this is Rowan Grayson Sinclair, Earl of Rathbridge, my oldest friend." Kit made the introductions, but he wasn't blind to his friend's anxiety. Cleo had been keeping a hand on Rath's shoulder as if she was afraid he would bolt.

"Now, where is Georgie, and why must you go after her?"

"Kit," Cleo interrupted. "Emily looks dead on her poor feet. I'll ring for tea and we can explain this all in the parlor."

Explanations hadn't taken all that long. Kit rubbed his swollen knuckles. It had been too long since he'd hit someone. He hoped a bruised jaw would serve as a reminder to Rath to keep his hands off Georgie.

Kit would give Cleo credit. He was sure she'd left out the more salacious bits. The blackmail was fairly straightforward and his heart had nearly stopped when she told him about the shooting. But it was Rath's involvement in all this which he found the most confusing.

Rath paced as Cleo had demurred, indicating she'd caught them in a compromising position, and while it was not common knowledge, it was best for Georgie if she married.

"Best for whom?" he asked, staring at Rath."My reputation will survive."

"So will ours. With a little time and her generous fortune, she can buy back respectability." Kit dared Rath to argue with him.

"Are you going to stop me from going after her?"

Rath was so adamant, that Kit knew there was more to the story than either were going to tell him tonight. He had a feeling his sister had really stepped into it this time. Rath had always been protective of his friends but this was going far beyond what any friend would expect.

"No. I want her back her too." Kit said finally, sitting down at his desk to write a few lines to *The Vixen's* captain. "But the decision to marry or not will remain hers alone."

He swore he could hear Rath's teeth grind, but he nodded, clutching the letter to his chest as he left. Kit couldn't help but laugh. This was not the homecoming he thought he'd received, but he should have expected it. Where Georgie was, mayhem followed.

"Are you planning on telling me the truth. What did she get herself into this time?"

Cleo poured him a drink, passing it to him, before picking up her pelisse. "That's her story, and I am going to respect that. She's not a little girl anymore, Kit."

"You aren't going to tell me she knows what she's doing?"

She laughed. "Oh hell no. She's so out her league with Rath, but trust me when I tell you that he loves her. He just doesn't know it yet."

"And Georgie." He rolled his eyes. "Is she in love with him?"

Cleo smiled and cocked her head to the side, but she said nothing. She didn't have to. His sister had chosen to align herself with one of the most difficult but most loyal men he knew. He hoped she learned sooner rather than later what she'd gotten herself into.

* * * *

They were five days out from port, when *The Raven* bore down upon *The Vixen*.

Georgie wanted to order the cannons ready, but she wasn't stupid. They weren't going to fight each other. When *The Raven* pulled alongside, she allowed the ship to be boarded by *The Raven's* band of pirates. She rolled her eyes. *Okay,* she thought, *only the captain is a pirate but a notorious one.*

And he looked every inch the pirate now. He wore black leather breeches and his gleaming knee boots. His white lawn shirt was tucked into his pants, but it billowed with the wind. The wind was whipping his loose, dark hair around his face. And he was well-armed, as if he suspected she may put up a fight.

She wouldn't do that to her crew. She had hoped he wouldn't care enough to follow, but she should have known better.

As he stalked across the deck toward her, he didn't seem surprised to see her at *The Vixen's* helm, but his hard gaze was anything but pleased.

Well, she thought, her hand resting on the sword at her hip, *I'm not thrilled by his presence, either.* She wouldn't engage their crews in the fight, but she had every intention of resisting him herself.

She stepped out from behind the ship's wheel, and a shiver of anticipation raced through her when his eyes raked her from head to toe. Did he think she was all about pretty gowns, silk stocking and lace undergarments? She'd given those up as soon as she had boarded in favor of dark breeches and stout boots, a fashionable shirt and vest. She'd tied her hair back with a scarf so the wind wouldn't play havoc with it like it was his.

Why am I thinking about plunging my fingers into that thick mass of hair and brushing it straight? She scolded herself. *I shouldn't be remembering the mat of hair across his chest, and the narrowing trail down to his groin. Or how, farther south on his body, he groomed himself for his partner's pleasure.*

That's right, she told herself, *think about the word 'partners.* He wasn't in the marriage mart. He was unsuitable as anything but a lover, and he'd had plenty of those. She squared her shoulders and imagined closing her desires into a treasure chest and dumping it at sea.

She frowned at him as he brushed past her, his shoulder jostling hers with enough force to knock her off her balance. She gritted her teeth and forced herself not to charge after him, as he presented himself to *The Vixen's* true captain.

After a moment of pleasantries that had Georgie rolling her eyes, Rath handed a letter to Captain Parks before turning to her and holding out an envelope, between his two fingers, in her general direction. She snatched the envelope from him and turned away to read it.

The letter was short but the litany of expletives that fell from her lips was not. Kit was in London and was ordering her to return. She turned back to Captain Wrath and she saw that her own ship's captain was much subdued.

She shook her head. "I may have to go to London, but I don't have to go with you."

He cocked his head to the side, a look of amusement in his eyes, and he laughed at her. "I think you will find we disagree on that."

She looked to Captain Parks, who shook his head. He had been ordered, she realized, not to interfere.

She shook her head. "I won't let you win, Rathbridge. If you are going to take me, it will be by force." She pulled the sword from the scabbard at her side.

He frowned at her, but she could tell her stand amused him. "Your shoulder, love, it will do you not but harm to fight me now. Come aboard, and we will fight later."

In bed. He didn't say it, but she heard the words on his lips, anyway.

"I am not your love," she reminded him, "and we will fight now, Captain."

A small gesture of his hand had both crews stepping back to give them room, and she noted that most of the men turned as if to offer them privacy. That only made her temper flare. How dare he take charge like that, and to think he was going to succeed.

She lashed out with her sword before his was unsheathed. He jumped out of the way with a grunt that made her smile. But their blades connected on the next pass. The reverberation of steel against steel, made her shoulder ache, but she schooled her features so he wouldn't know it. She knew Rath was holding back because of her injury, and perhaps for the sake of her reputation.

However, what she lacked in strength, Georgie made up for in technique. She anticipated his attack. She managed to draw first blood, by accident, slicing a neat, thin stripe across his arm.

He sighed with irritation as he wiped at the blood with his hand. She felt a small fraction of regret and shrugged.

He grinned and responded with three quick thrusts. Georgie would have deflected all three with ease except she lost her footing on the last one. Her left foot slid out from under her and she fell onto her injured shoulder, crying out in pain and dropping her sword.

Rath didn't hesitate to rush to her side. Heedless of the pristine condition of his clothing, he knelt in the sea spray that had caused her to slip, soaking the knees of his breeches.

"You can't do this," she hissed as he bent over her. She blinked her eyes in an attempt to keep the tears at bay. The fall had hurt, both her shoulder and her pride.

"I'm afraid you're wrong, love, I already have." He was careful as he picked her up and threw her over his shoulder.

"I won't go back with you." She swore and hit at his back with her good arm. But her tantrum caused him to tighten his grip around her thighs and he spanked her hard through her light breeches.

She had never in all her life felt so defeated. And angry, because she had only herself to blame. She couldn't help but dwell on that when both crews were letting out whoops of approval that Captain Wrath had stolen back his bride-to-be. She had learned from Captain Parks when she'd arranged passage that all the crews had heard of the union there was to be between the two families who owned New Horizons Shipping.

Rath didn't put her back on her feet until they were behind the locked door of the captain's cabin on *The Raven*.

"You whoreson. When Kit finds out what you've done." She pushed both hands into his chest. It was like hitting a wall. He didn't move, but he didn't retaliate either. He simply stood his ground.

"Think you that your brother would be happy with your actions? With your reckless and wanton behavior?" he asked.

"You didn't think I was such a wanton when it pleased you." She stomped to his desk, and snatched up the open bottle of gin in her good hand. She took a long swallow, the liquid burning her throat. She tried not to sneer as she pushed the bottle out of her way on the desk. Her left arm felt useless. She rubbed at her wounded shoulder as she hoisted herself up to sit on the edge of the desk. The wound ached from the force of the fall.

Rath sighed, and walked over to her. He took the bottle from beside her and took a long swallow himself, before he pushed off her jacket, then began pulling open her shirt.

She wanted to stop him, but she knew the battle was over, if not the war. She wasn't going to pretend her shoulder was fine, not when she saw the small stain of blood on the front.

He pulled off the bandages to see the stitches beneath. He pressed his fingers over the bruised skin and examined the wound. "Silly chit," he chided. "I'll send Doc to check on you."

The wound was still bruised, but had otherwise been healing well. Looking at it now, she saw she'd pulled the stitches and it wept lightly.

"I can take care of it myself," she grumbled, tucking the shirt back over her shoulder.

Why am I still fighting him? she asked herself. There was no way out of her current situation. She was going back to London whether she liked it or not.

He didn't answer her, surprising her instead by hugging her close. One hand cupped the back of her head, the other her shoulder and he pressed her against him. He sighed against the top of his head, pressing a kiss there.

She couldn't help but relax too, in his firm embrace. She didn't know what this was between them, but she knew she had missed him. Had missed him since the night of the ball. She rested her head against his chest and breathed in the clean, masculine scent of him. It would be too easy to forget why he was there.

He stepped back from her, his hands falling away, his spine rigid, before he stood back. She looked up at him.

"Get changed now. You'll find a robe in my trunk," he said as he headed for the door. "I will have your belongings brought across."

She heard him lock the door from the outside, and she screamed in frustration.

She paced the cabin. It was not enough that she had been caught, but to be reminded of her downfall by being deposited upon his bed. A bed they would have shared only a few weeks ago. "Where did it all go so wrong?" she wondered.

But she knew the answer to that. It had gone wrong when they became more than nameless lovers — when they had learned names and titles and alliances. It had gone wrong when he had assumed it necessary to marry her. She was no longer so sure that even Kit would have let her get away without following these rules. God how she hated rules.

* * * *

"Thank you, Captain Parks, for your understanding in this matter. I know you've known Georgiana for a number of years and are aware of her temper for things."

"Georgie is like a daughter to me and most of Kit's crews." He fingered the paper that Captain Rathbridge had first presented to him when he swung aboard. "If you did not have Kit's blessing, you wouldn't have had mine. Even if we do technically work for you."

"I am glad it did not come to that. I would hate to raise arms against an old friend." Captain Parks had served his father for years.

Rath's gaze returned to his men and saw that the last of Georgie's trunks was being hefted o'er the side of *The Raven*. "Thanks again, Parks."

"Take care of yourself, Rathbridge. That girl has got a mighty temper and I think it is all directed now at you."

He didn't doubt it.

He had sent three men down with her trunks, as well as Doc Hardy who had some skill with cuts and scrapes. While they reported the mess of the cabin, he was pleased to hear that she had no injuries requiring attention.

"Are you sure her shoulder is fine?"

"Gabe did a fine job. There's no infection. It's just going to ache like a bugger for a while longer," Doc Hardy told him, as he began prodding at the slice Georgie had given his arm. "'Twas a good cut she gave you."

"She's a devil." Rath looked down to where a thing a thin red line had bubbled up. "It's a scratch."

Compared to the various wounds and scars he'd received over the years, the cut was nothing. It had already stopped weeping.

"Figures Captain Wrath would find himself a she-devil." Doc grinned. "But the men were right proud at how you handled her. I can't believe Captain Kit would teach a girl to fight like that."

"She is handy with a sword, but still no match for a man's brute strength," he told his first mate, but he felt a thrill of pride that his woman wasn't scared of a fight. "Have a meal prepared and brought down to her."

"You don't mean to see her yet."

"Let her stew in her own juices for a while."

Hardy, who had been married more than twenty years, shook his head and laughed. "Captain, let me tell you, nothing good has ever come of stale stew."

Chapter Fifteen

Hardy returned to pick up the mealtime dishes. Georgie had relished eating the thick vegetable stew and roast chicken, and was sipping the very good burgundy that Hardy had the forethought to bring.

"It was very nice of you," she told him, "to see to my comfort."

"Any of the men would do the same for the captain's bride."

"I'm not his bride yet," she insisted.

He looked at her thoughtfully. "May I say, my lady, that both crews were very proud of you."

She seemed startled by this and looked up at him. "What do you mean?"

"There are not many men, and certainly fewer ladies, who would stand up to Captain Wrath. You showed rare spirit and the men are happy to have you become part of the 'crew', as it were. Or at least you will be, once you marry the Captain."

"Your Captain went easy on me." Her arm was already aching, and her backside was surely bruised from an indignant swat he had given her with the flat of his sword.

"And you could have done damage yourself, with that swipe you took at him. That showed spirit tempered by compassion. Captain Kit taught you well, though I am surprised he would have taught you at all."

"You know my brother?" she asked, sitting taller in her chair and gesturing for Hardy to pull up one for himself. She poured him a glass of wine.

"Oh, ay, and you as well. I remember you as a wee mite." He laughed. "You were with the captains Kit and Rath, and Rath's da at the shipyards. Kit had to keep pulling you back down from the rigging. You kept crawling up, but once there you would yell for help down."

Georgie put her glass on the table and lay a hand on his arm. "I'm sorry, Hardy, I don't remember you at all."

"Never be sorry, lass. You were no more than seven, maybe eight. The last Lord Rathbridge, rest his soul, had advised us all to keep a civil tongue in our head with you around lest we be getting familiar with a prayer stone."

"They should have known that I would learn the words, anyway," she said.

"Is the gossip true, then, lass? Do you really captain your own ship?" He had heard the rumor from some of the sailors who moved between Kit's ships and the Rathbridge fleet.

"My brother has been ever patient, and it is true. *The Vixen* is technically mine, but I've only made small voyages as captain, back and forth between the islands, but I've seconded Kit on a number of voyages. I'm afraid our crews are more used to seeing me as a boy than your esteemed captain."

"That I can imagine. His very own Anne Bonny." Hardy winked at her, as he likened her to the pirate queen.

"Not Anne. My voyages were completely legal, I assure you." She couldn't help but grin at the comparison. "Is Rathbridge a hard captain?"

"To be sure, he is not an easy captain, but our trade routes require discipline from a crew. There are too many things that could go wrong should a man step out of line, you ken."

She nodded. Growing up in shipping, she knew that the East India routes were perilous for the inexperienced.

"You know the Rathbridge emblem used to be a raven. They were considered a harbinger of death, and certainly the Captain Wrath comes from a family of old and mighty warriors."

"He was wearing a silver raven when we met, and I've seen his tattoo," she told him, pulling the pendant out from beneath her shirt.

"He gave you that."

She her Hardy's surprise in his question. "I won it from him actually. Playing cards."

Hardy laughed. "Aye, that makes more sense."

"How did he get the name Captain Wrath? Is it just because his name is Rathbridge?"

"No. His father was Captain Rathbridge, and we had called the son, Captain Sinclair, or Lord Sin if he was off wenching." He glanced up at her, suddenly shifting in his chair. "This is probably a tale best left for the captain to tell."

"No, please." She put a hand on his arm to still him. "Tell it to me as you know it. It's bound to be more embellished than the version he would recite, and I would so like to hear how he became the feared Captain Wrath."

He poured them both more wine, then settled back in his chair. "It was when we first began the Eastern runs. He was in his late twenties then. Still new from war, and recovering from his leg wound, he was. But he was a strong man, and the men trusted him. We followed him easily to the East, despite the possible dangers. Pirates were everywhere, and an unknown ship was easy prey."

"Was *The Raven* the ship you took?"

"No." He shook his head. "We took *The Siren*. One of our faster brigs. We were well armed, but so were the pirates. It was only that they wanted our ship as prize that we were not blown out of the water.

"In truth, it had been too easy a voyage, with few storms. We had seen a few pirate ships at a distance, but they had kept their distance. The men had thought it was because we were so well armed. But the captain knew. It was because our hulls were empty. They were waiting for us on our return. The battle lasted for days. The captain even allowing himself to be captured."

Hardy was an animated storyteller and he had her full attention. She pulled her legs up, sitting cross-legged in the chair, her chin resting on her hands as she listened.

"The pirate captain had a grudge and meant to make our captain bleed. He'd received near as I could tell more than a third of the lashes with the cat before he gave the order for our counterattack. We were all crazy mad by this point, but not the captain. A sort of calm had come over him and he yelled out our orders." Hardy paused to grin. "Word of our victory spread like wildfire, as did our survival. *The Raven* was a force to be reckoned with, as was Captain Wrath, which is what the pirates who survived called him."

"Hurrah!" Georgie cheered as she raised her glass to Hardy's, toasting *The Raven* and its captain.

"I think our guest has had enough history lessons, Hardy." Rath stood in the frame of the doorway. He schooled himself to keep his expression still. His temper had flared when he heard his friend talking about his past, but it was a shared history. One that belonged to Hardy and the rest of his crew as much as it did him. He had bit back his anger, remembering that without Hardy's friendship he would have died a time or two.

"Aye, Captain. I should take o'er the watch." He put down his wine. "Good evening, my lady." As he passed the captain, he whispered, "Just keeping the stew stirred."

Rath grimaced.

"And I thought Kit had had a dangerous history," she said, then drained the last of the burgundy.

"Kit's had his share of danger, I am sure." He went over to the small chest in the corner and pulled out its key. "I didn't want your tantrum to destroy anything of value," he told her, and pulled out a bottle of gin and two fresh glasses. "If you wanted to know about Captain Wrath, you could have just asked." He was pouring the gin.

"It's very difficult to get anyone to talk about your history. Cleo told me that a man is best left a mystery, or a woman might become bored. But then she says the same for women."

"That would be Cleo." He smirked. She enjoyed being an enigma.

"When I was recovering at home, your mother regaled me with stories of your childhood. Your first word, your first horse, your first days at school. Who your friends were, who your family is. I know all of your cousins, their names and titles both from England and from France."

"Then you know it all."

"I don't think I do, though." She moved toward him, and he realized that she was wearing one of his shirts. She stood in front of him. He imagined he could see the outline of her breasts beneath the gauzy cotton. "I think there is a great deal about you that I still don't know. The wicked side you've alluded to since we met." She ran her fingers through his hair. "What are your demons, Captain Wrath?"

"A secret for a secret?" he suggested, alluding to the game they'd played at *Chez de Sauveterre*. The night that started this adventure.

"You know my darkest secrets."

He shook his head. "Fine, I'll tell you some sea tales." He offered her his chair and sprawled upon the bed himself. "Some of it starts before the East India run, some comes later. Kit and I were great rakes for our time. We gambled much, drank much and had many women. But that's probably what you already know."

"No one talks about how you injured your leg. Or what happened afterwards."

He searched for the right words to fill in the blanks for her. "Kit and I were sailing on one of my father's ships during the war when we were attacked." Rath closed his eyes, and he could see the fighting again. "We were boarded and it became hand-to-hand combat." He remembered his opponent. The Spanish captain had been well armed, but when it came to the fight, they'd been fair-matched.

"It was a good fight, but cannon fire knocked us both off-balance. He recovered his feet more quickly and took the advantage, slicing into my leg."

Without thinking, his hand rubbed his thigh. He felt what it was like, the cold steel slicing into his muscle, nearly to the bone, then falling hard onto his knee.

"I couldn't stand. I went down and the Spaniard was standing over me, grinning, his sword to my throat. Then, with a yell, Kit was on him and the bastard captain was dead."

"So that's what you mean when Kit saved your life."

"Actually, it's not." He couldn't help but laugh. "Having each other's back was pretty usual for us back then. I'd saved his backside as often as he'd save mine. When I say he saved my life, I mean because of what came next."

Georgie abandoned his chair and joined him on the bed. She sat cross-legged next to him. Her hand on his thigh. "Tell me."

"The surgeon wanted to take my leg. Kit wouldn't let him. He and Gabe tended my injury themselves until our ship limped back into port. The leg was in a bad way. You've seen the scar, nearly hip to knee and through muscle. They gave me laudanum for the pain. But it wasn't strong enough."

Rath gritted his teeth as he remembered Georgie's wound, and Gabe's reluctance still to leave the bottle with him. He took a deep breath, letting it out with a sigh. He hated that after all these years he'd not earned his friend's trust back.

"I can't imagine what that must have been like."

He shrugged off her hand. "The worst was the months of not knowing whether I would ever be able to walk, let alone sail or captain a ship again. Three times infection set in, and throughout the fever, all I could think of was the saw that was ready to take my leg. There were days" — he paused — "no, weeks, where I cursed Kit for saving my life if it meant I was to be no more than a crippled shadow of who I was."

"That doesn't sound like you. Not the man I know." She touched the rough stubble on his chin.

"It wasn't me. But for months, I couldn't even walk to the chamber pot myself. I had to teach my leg to walk again. Teach the muscle how to move. Even once I began getting around, and insisted on returning to my own townhouse, the pain did not go away, or the fear, except with opium. Then suddenly all the things I hadn't wanted to lose, I had lost to the pipe."

"But you did walk again. Sail, captain your ship."

"Thanks to Kit and Gabe." He smiled. "Kit was the brute force, keeping me from using, and Gabe helped me manage the pain without it. They saved me. They saved Ash or my mother from seeing me at my worst. They are my brothers."

"You've been injured since. Thanks to Hardy, I know how you got those stripes on your back. How do you manage?"

He raised his glass and winked at her. "Gin gets me through."

"You are very strong." She leaned her head into his shoulder.

"Sometimes, I'm not strong at all." He shifted on the bed, lifting her over his lap so she straddled his thighs. "It's been years, but I sometimes, I can feel it like it was only yesterday."

In her new position, she was able to stroke his neck, her fingers kneading the muscles of his neck and shoulders. He shuddered against her.

"Now, we know each other's secrets."

"We shouldn't do this," she said and her voice sounded unsure.

"We should do nothing but this." He wrapped his hands around her face, his thumbs tracing the high arch of her cheekbones. "In bed, if nowhere else, we don't argue."

She laughed and held on to his shoulders as his hands stroked a path down her neck to the thin shirt. "I don't want to forget this."

"You won't." He skimmed his hands over her breasts, his thumbs stroking her nipples, which pebbled before him. "You are mine."

It was a statement of possession, and he'd meant it. He would never let her go, whether she wanted him or not. The violence of his feelings startled him. He hadn't felt like this before, but nearly losing her, had done him in.

"Please, make love to me."

Blood roared in his ears. "I don't know that I can be that gentle."

"I can handle Captain Wrath," she promised, her mouth fusing with his in a fierce kiss that betrayed the wildness she felt.

He didn't stop to wonder at his constant aching hunger for her. He surrendered to it. *She feels like paradise, and warms me better than a hundred suns.* He groaned at that thought. Laughing at himself that he would ever wax poetic over a woman, but Georgie was no ordinary woman.

He lifted her off of his lap. "Have I told you how much I hate you in boy's clothes?"

"I thought I looked rather nice in these breeches?" She grinned as they both left the bed. She walked a few steps away from him, lifting her shirt so he could see the breeches stretched over her backside. They were indecent, and in truth he loved them on her.

He cupped his hand over his erection and cocked his head at her. "You know what the sight of you in those breeches do for me. The things it makes me think about."

"Like what?"

"If you want to be a boy, I could take you like a boy." He saw he had startled her with that. "You hadn't thought of that, had you? That if you were a young man, I could peel down those breeches just enough to get my cock into that tight little ass of yours. That seeing you in those breeches makes me want to fuck you there."

He saw her bravado fail, but a flush crept across her chest. His salacious words had piqued her interest. *That is one of the things I love about her,* he thought as he peeled off his shirt. Her sexuality matched his own.

"Have you done that?" she asked. She mirrored his movements, moving with care because of her injury, but pulling off her shirt. She then began to work on the cloth bindings around her breasts.

He took the cotton strip from her hand and began unwrapping her.

"Not to another man, or boy, since I was a boy myself." He bent low, whispering in her ear, "But I could take your ass. I have thought about little else since I abducted you from *The Vixen*."

She smiled up at him, and he realized the gift of her trust that she had given him weeks ago. It hadn't diminished.

"Bend over the desk."

Her smiled faltered, but she walked confidently over to the desk, swinging her hips as she went. She laid her bare breasts against the hard wood, her head resting on her hands, looking at him.

He cupped his cock, giving it a hard tug through his trousers to alleviate the ache. It didn't help.

"You are a very naughty girl, wearing breeches and teasing me like that." He walked to his trunk, and dug around to the bottom where he had secreted a few gifts for his fiancée. He looked at what he'd brought, the jade phallus, the silk scarves, and the scented oil. That was what he needed now. He closed the box, but left it on top of the chest.

He strolled back to the desk, feeling Georgie's eyes following him. "You are giving me that look, luv."

"What look is that?"

"Like you can't wait to get fucked."

"You haven't fucked me in weeks. I've missed your cock. The taste of it on my tongue, the velvet feel of it between my lips. The way it stretches my pussy."

He stopped and ran a hand over his face. When she talked like that, he wanted to nothing more than to turn her over and fuck her long and hard and deep. But he had plans tonight that included introducing her to more of the body's natural delights. "God, grant me patience," he whispered under his breath. To her, he said, "Keep talking like that and you'll get another spanking."

"Promise?"

He dove for her then, his body bending over hers, pinning her to the desk. He thrust his hips against her, intent on ensuring she felt how hard she made him. How much he wanted her.

"Say it. Say it here, when it's just the two of us," he growled in her ear, as he slid his hand down her hip. "Say you are mine."

Georgie threw caution to the wind. Here, if nowhere else, she would always be his. "I'm yours," she said, as his hand made contact with her buttock. The sound of the slap echoed in the quiet chamber. She wondered if they could hear it outside. She tried not to whimper when a second blow landed and he stood up behind her.

He kept one hand between her shoulders, reminding her that she wasn't to move as he gave in to his desire to punish her for running away. It wasn't a punishment to her. She knew she shouldn't have run, but this, between them, would always be about pleasure.

She loved every wicked, decadent thing that Rath did to her, taught her. She knew tonight would be no different. She was on the verge of orgasm, when he decided she'd been punished enough.

He nibbled a path of kisses down her spine as he pushed her breeches down her thighs. Her legs felt trapped. She wanted to spread them, to encourage Rath to dip his fingers into her cunt. To play with her, but he was unsympathetic. He knew what he wanted tonight.

With her ass bared, he continued with the trail of kisses, down her tailbone, into the sensitive hollow at the top of her crease. He soothed her enflamed buttocks, though the breeches had done much to soften the blows.

He continued to massage her bottom, dipping his thumbs between her cheeks and tracing the path between. He stroked her delicate opening and she pressed back against him. She moaned in desire. She knew, like every other wicked delight he'd introduced her to, he'd make sure she loved it.

He squeezed one of his large hands between her thighs. The breeches didn't give her a great deal of space to spread her legs for him, but that made it feel all the more forbidden.

His palm ground against her opening as he cupped her mound. His finger toyed with her clitoris. "It turned you on to fight me, didn't it?" he murmured. "You knew you couldn't win, but you couldn't help yourself."

She bucked against his hand. She wasn't sure she like that he had come to know her so well in such a short time. "I've missed this," she confided, and she felt rewarded for her honesty when he slid a finger inside her. He rubbed the pad of his finger in circles along the sensitive flesh inside her and her belly clenched. It was too good. How could she thought to have lived without this? Without him?

"Me, too," he whispered against her neck. His teeth grazed over her shoulder. He continued to press kisses and bites over the back of her neck and shoulders as her body wound up toward a fevered pitch. And when he bit down on her neck, marking her, she couldn't hold back. The orgasm rushed through her body.

She mewled with disappointment when he slipped his hand from between her thighs, but he didn't leave her. He picked up the bottle of oil from the desk. The warm oil dripped onto her back. He used it to make his fingers slick as he teased them toward her back entrance, his thumb caressing the sensitive flesh, testing its limits.

She loved when he did this. She loved the feel of him teasing her, but this was more than a tease. He had promised to fuck her there. She was the good kind of scared, she decided. She liked the anticipation, the heightened awareness.

She felt the dribble of more oil against her crease and the pressure as he pressed a second finger — was that his other thumb? — inside her, stretching her. Preparing her for his cock. It was too much. Too full and too good, but she bit her lip and let him continue preparing her. She needed this as much as he did. She wanted to be owned by him this way. Even if they parted after the voyage home, she would always have this to remember.

Gray was silent behind her, except for his breath, which was more ragged than before, and she could imagine the intensity of his gaze as he watched himself penetrate her.

"Gray?" she rasped.

"Is it too much?" he asked, and she could hear the concern in his voice. A tear slid down her cheek, but it had nothing to do with what he was doing to her body, just her heart.

She shook her head.

"Good," he panted. "You should see how ready your body is to accept me. How much it needs what I can give it."

"Yes."

"I need to stop a minute to prepare my cock, then I'm going to be inside you," he told her. She didn't think she needed the warning until he wasn't touching her. She felt bereft, lost, where a moment ago, she'd been anchored to him.

"I'm still here, Ana," he reminded her, and he placed one hand back on her hip.

It wasn't his thumb that grazed her entrance now, it was the solid length of his erection. She bit her lip as she listened to his instructions, as she pushed back against his cock, feeling her body bloom against its invasion. She was shaking. She couldn't stop. It was so unlike anything she'd ever expected. She felt full of him.

He rocked forward gently. Her body yielding a little more with each thrust, and he continued to praise her. Telling her how much he needed her. How beautiful her submission was to him.

This didn't feel like submission—more like possession as his body curled around hers, rode over hers. He snaked a hand beneath her to stroke her clit as his hips continued their gentle thrust. She took more of him with each stroke, enjoying the strong, sure slide of his length in and out. The sensitive nerve endings fired at once, lighting her up from the inside. Fireworks centered in her womanly core.

"Give it to me," he commanded.

She growled. How could he think she wasn't already giving him everything that she was? That she had? He must have sensed her moment of panic because his arms anchored her to him. One hand slid through her hair, gripping it to the point of pain, but it calmed her.

"I know," he promised her. "I know how out of control it makes you feel. I want that. I will hold you while you break apart. I am not going anywhere."

Hot tears burned her cheeks as the vortex broke. She shuddered in his arms, as he continued to thrust in long steady strokes inside her. *This,* she thought, *is what it is to be broken, to be tamed.*

She was still riding the high of her release when he shouted out his own. His seed flooded her as his hips ground against her bottom. His hands shook as they held her, and she thought, perhaps, they had broken together.

Chapter Sixteen

I'm growing used to seeing her in her boy's clothes, he thought, as he watched her enter their cabin from across the deck. She had been helping one of the crew repair sails. She'd said she had no skill with a needle when it came to the finer things, but sails she could repair. There was little she couldn't do on a ship, he'd discovered, as he'd watched her scale the rigging this morning to the crow's nest.

They hadn't spoken of their situation over the last few days, though he had come to the realization that she hadn't meant to trap him, or herself, for that matter. She wasn't built that way. If she thought it, she said it. She did everything on purpose. Including swearing with his crew, or singing inappropriate shanties. They treated her more like one of them than a lady, and that was how she liked it.

Despite their week of respite on the ship, they would be ashore before nightfall. The inevitability of it had thrown a pall over their last night and morning together, and Rath worried when her stomach seemed upset this morning. She said it was nerves.

"Do you think it easy having to face Kit after all that happened?" she snapped at him.

He knew it was not. He had to face him too. "He already knows," he assured her. "And he's not inclined to hold either of us to account."

"Just because he won't make me marry you doesn't mean it's over." She sighed before she turned away.

Lord, I hope not. He hadn't changed his mind about what needed to happen. And after a week at sea, carrying on an affair in full view of the crew, he hoped she and Kit would see it his way.

He knew it was a bastard move, but he would press the issue once they were on land. There was also the chance that she was carrying his child. The chance was remote, but it was still there. In the almost two months they had been together, but especially this week, he had not been diligent in that regard.

Because you want her to have to marry you, his conscience nagged. Yes. He did. And perhaps the cause of her queasy stomach was the leverage he needed. To that end, he'd gone to the galley for tea and biscuits, and followed her back to the cabin.

Georgie was on the floor. He dropped the tray at the sight of blood on her breeches and was at her side in an instant.

He searched her body for some type of injury, even as she tried to stop him.

"What's happening?" he asked.

She looked up at him, tears on her cheeks, and he knew. She was losing their child. He sighed and gathered her into his arms.

"I didn't know," she promised him, clutching his shoulder.

"Maybe it's not what we think?" he asked hopefully, pulling back from her. "Let's get you cleaned up and in bed." He helped her to her feet, watching as she stripped out of her soiled garments. Too much blood.

"I've seen this happen on the plantation." She sighed, going to the basin and washing her legs clean.

"I've said it before, you've seen too much."

She tried to laugh. "I told you I was unusual." Her tears began to flow again, and she buried her face in her hands.

Rath's heart was breaking for her. He pushed her hands away, his thumbs dashing her tears away. "What do you need?"

He followed her instructions, helping her change and lie down, as she continued to grimace through the spasms in her belly.

When the ship made dock, he helped her into a gown, and didn't argue when she insisted on walking off the ship herself. She didn't want the crew to know that anything was wrong.

"Where are we going?" she asked once she was seated on Rath's lap inside the hired carriage, a blanket tucked over her lap.

"My townhome. Gissy will know how to help you. And I want Gabe to check you out before we deal with anyone else." At least no one was expecting them. He hadn't sent word of their arrival, though he knew he wouldn't be able to keep her with him for long before it got out.

Gissy helped Georgie upstairs, and Richards sent off a footman to summon Gabe.

"Shall I get you or the miss something to eat, sir?" Richards asked as Rath slumped back onto the settee in the parlor. It was a stout piece made for a bachelor's residence. He had fallen asleep on it more than once.

"She's a lady, you know," he said solemnly. "And despite the fact that she's warmed my bed for weeks, she won't marry me. I think the world has gone mad."

Despite their more intimate friendship at *Chez de Sauveterre*, Richards knew his place in the household and didn't offer comment. Rath grudgingly appreciated his continued discretion. Richards counted on the distinction of his station here versus his role at Lisette's. He needed a bit more from his valet tonight.

"She lost our child." Rath ran his hands back through his hair in frustration. "Part of me hoped that if she was carrying our child, she'd see sense. She'd see that she had to marry me."

Richards went to the sideboard and poured a glass of gin and brought it to Rath.

"Do you think a glass is going to do it?" he asked, grabbing it and knocking it back in one swallow. He swung his legs off the sofa. "Her brother is going to be showing up in a few hours and I'm going to have to explain to him what this means."

"Yes, sir." Richards stepped back formally and Rath frowned at him.

"Jesus Christ, Richie, I'm pouring my heart out here and you are standing there like a statue."

Richards cleared his throat. "I never thought to see you in love with anyone, sir. That means everything is changing."

"Not everything."

Richards harrumphed, dropping into his usual accent, "Really, Cap'n? So, you'll be inviting me into your room to suck you off before bed, then?" He walked over to the bottle of gin and poured himself a glass, not waiting for Rath's reaction.

"If I want to keep my place in your household, then we have to remember our positions, Cap'n. I am your valet and your butler here. You and your lady, when you marry her — and you will marry her — will move into the family home or find a new home. Maybe you take me and Gis with you. Maybe not."

"Sit the fuck down, and pass me the goddamn bottle," Rath commanded. He hadn't thought about what the change in his status would mean for them. They had been with him through the good and the bad. "I will take care of you and Gisele. Whether that's here or somewhere else, I can't imagine another valet serving me."

He caught Richards' grin.

"There is no way to say that that doesn't sound dirty, is there?"

"No, sir." Richards laughed into his cup.

"Our situation was already changing since you and Gis wed," he reminded him. "But our friendship hasn't."

"Ana's really a lady?" Richards questioned. "She talks like a tart."

"She swears like a sailor," Rath agreed. "But she is a lady. Lady Georgiana officially. Please try to remember that. A lady who doesn't like London or the ton."

"She sounds perfect for you."

"Aye, she is." Rath looked at the clock above the mantel. "We should expect to be descended upon by any number of family and friends soon. Can you make sure we have tea and bread at least for them?"

"Yes, my lord." Richards put down his glass. "I am sorry about the babe. Gissy's been through it and can help your lady."

"Thank you, Richie." He sighed and leaned his head back against the sofa, waiting for Gabe and the first wave to arrive.

* * * *

Georgie hoped there would be a guest room she could stay in, but Gissy wouldn't hear of her being anywhere but in the captain's room. "It's the best room in the house."

"I know," she responded, remembering it was only a few short weeks ago that they'd lounged around in bed for the night and half the day. She loved that the room still smelled of him. She wanted to wrap herself in his bedding, her head sinking into his pillow. She may never have the chance again.

"So which was it? You forgot the sponge, or he was too impatient for it? Men are sometimes."

"A little of both," she confided. She'd used the sponge often, but there were those times where he'd taken her by surprise, leaving her no time to prepare.

"Careless men, it's so easy for them." Gis clucked, as she helped Georgie change her clothes, again. Georgie was beginning to tire of getting dressed and undressed.

"There will be enough people tonight blaming Rath," she told Gis. "We don't have to heap more guilt on to him."

Gis stopped fussing at her and stared at her. "You're in love with him."

"No," Georgie dismissed, frowning. "That's not it at all. But my brother will bring holy hell down once he finds out about this."

Gis didn't look like she believed her, her eyes narrowed together, causing a crease between her heavy, dark brows.

"'Cause you're a lady and have no business being at some lord's bachelor quarters?" Gis laughed. "And don't try to tell me you're no lady. I know who you are. You're too good a friend of Lisette's for her girls not to talk."

"Yes, I'm a lady." She rolled her eyes. "Fat lot of good that's ever done me." Wearing a fresh chemise and morning gown, she climbed back onto the bed.

"Even ladies make mistakes." Gis shrugged. "As long as you got a cunt, you're the one to pay the price. I lost my first babe when I was four and ten."

Georgie tried not to look stunned. So young to experience such loss. "Do you and Richards have children?"

"Aye, we have a son and a new daughter. And we can talk about that another time," Gis said forcefully, not allowing Georgie to pull the blankets over her legs yet. "We have just enough time to have a look at you."

"I thought Rath had summoned Gabe?"

"He did, and if you were shot again, or had fallen and hit your head, he'd be the best person to see to you. Do you want him feeling up your snatch?"

The thought that Gabe would do anything of the sort hadn't occurred to her, and her stomach lurched.

"That's what I thought."

* * * *

Cleo rushed up the stairs ahead of Gabe and Rath. Rath frowned after her as she lifted her skirts, taking the steps two at a time. "Are you sure she miscarried?" Gabe asked, taking off his coat and handing it to Richards.

"It looked like it. She seemed sure."

Gabe nodded. "It would have been quite early and it's not unexpected, given the fever she'd suffered when she was shot."

"That's what I was thinking."

By the time Rath and Gabe made it to the room, Georgie was flanked by Cleo and Gisele. Their expressions were serious, making Rath uncomfortable. "What?"

"Gabe," Cleo said, softly. "You aren't needed here."

"I'm going to examine my patient, Cleo."

She shook her head. "No. That's been taken care of. She's fine."

"Cleo," Rath began, "I would feel much better if Gabe—"

Georgie interrupted, "And I'd feel much better if he didn't. I've been examined by someone experienced, and I'm fine."

Cleo stood and pushed Rath and Gabe back into the hall.

"You know this is my job."

"And I know she doesn't need to be traumatized anymore," Cleo argued.

"But how can you be sure that what happened was anything more than her monthly flow?"

"Only a man would ask that. Her monthly flow wouldn't start and stop like that. She described it to me, and to Gisele, who you may not know has been midwife to more than half the women at Lisette's.

There was a babe. Now, there isn't. Her body has expelled the last of it, and with the exception of being tired, and sad, she's fine."

Rath hugged Cleo to him. "Thank you."

"She did all the work," Cleo insisted. "Gabe, can you please assure Rath that there is no reason they won't go on to make beautiful children together?"

"You just did." Gabe laughed. "And no, there is likely no reason to expect otherwise. Get some rest, Georgie," he called through the open door.

Richards was welcoming their latest guests as Cleo, Rath and Gabe came down the stairs.

"Why is she here, and not at home?" Kit demanded.

"Perhaps this is best discussed in the morning," Gabe suggested, but both Kit and Rath shook their heads.

"This really must be done now," Rath said, leading them back into the library. He hated that he was about to lose his best and oldest friend. He loved Kit like his brother, and he would have liked to spare him the full disclosure of the situation, but that was not possible.

"Where is Georgie now?" he asked before anyone could begin to explain. "And not that I am not overjoyed to see you again, Gabe, what the hell took you two so long and why has a doctor been called again? Is her shoulder not healing?"

"Cleo filled you in. then. That's probably good, and no her shoulder is fine," Rath assured him. "You should have seen her climbing through the rigging. What were you thinking letting her have the run of the ship?"

"I was thinking that she loved it, and I would give her anything she wants." He sighed. "So the reason for the doctor?"

"Let me preface by saying," Rath began as he handed a brandy to Kit. His best friend had never taken to the taste of gin, "that I have asked Georgie, even told Georgie now on several occasions that we would be wed. Unfortunately" — he shook his head — "to date, she refuses to do anything but use our betrothal as a way to trap her blackmailer."

"I told you before you left that I wouldn't force her to marry you," Kit confirmed. "Nothing has changed."

"You would rather risk public censure."

"I won't argue this with you," he told his friend. "I don't care if you were caught in a compromising position. She's my sister, and I won't force her to wed you, or anyone, to save the family from malicious gossip."

"To hell with gossip." Rath stared him down. "I'm not talking about kissing in the alcove. I'm talking about her sharing a bed with me for more than a fortnight, and for every night last week."

Rath knew it would be coming. The punch was clean and swift, a right upper cut, which knocked his jaw together and threw him off balance. The next hit was to his stomach and it sent him crashing into the sideboard.

A once-prized Ming vase landed in pieces on the floor. Kit held him to the floor. "What did you do to my sister?" Another blow landed against his jaw, his head hitting against the floor.

Gabe pulled Kit off Rath.

"Is that why she ran?" Kit demanded.

Rath sat on the floor, rubbing his bruised jaw. "I didn't know she was your sister the first time I slept with her, nor most of the nights I slept with her."

"You're not doing yourself any favors, Rath," Kit warned, shrugging off Gabe.

"I met her at Lisette's. I didn't think to find your sister in a house of pleasure," Rath argued.

"So, you thought she was just another whore?"

"She lied to me about her name. I believed her mistress material, and I treated her as such."

Gabe and Richards held Kit back again, and Rath was glad he hadn't brought Emily with him. He stood, rubbing his side. He was pretty sure that Kit had broken one of his ribs.

"When I discovered who she was I insisted that she marry me. She was running to you because she was sure you wouldn't force her to wed me." He took a swig from the brandy bottle before handing it to Kit.

Kit sat down, and the others followed. Watching him in case he decided to let his do his talking for him.

"What was she doing at Lisette's?"

"That's the part I told you about," Cleo offered. "Your aunt and uncle got under her skin. They've already arranged a marriage for her to a hideous old toad. Some friend of Constance's from church. She ran to *Chez de Sauveterre* to play a few hands of cards."

"And that led to your aunt and uncle having more leverage to force her to wed. She was recognized there."

"But aligning our two houses brings her respectability." Kit nodded in understanding. "It was a good idea."

"It was, until she ran," Rath confirmed.

"She is in the country with your mother, planning your nuptials," Cleo told him with a wink.

"Sneak."

"I was trying to do my best by her, and your mother agreed." She shrugged. "Your money and title will protect her, but at this point it only works if you wed."

"I won't force her marry you or anyone," Kit repeated between gritted teeth.

"Kit," Cleo admonished, slapping his shoulder. "I am the last one who would try to force anyone into a marriage they didn't want. But by deed, if not by word, she's proved time and again to find Rath to her liking."

Gabe choked on his brandy, and Rath hid his grin behind his glass.

"Why are you here again, Gabe? Did you ever say?" Kit tone expressed his exasperation.

"That's still my story to tell," Rath said, stopping Gabe from answering.

"No, actually, it's mine." Georgie stopped at the edge of the room. She was wearing the morning dress that she'd donned upstairs, but had put one of his warmer robes over it. She looked less than respectable, as she walked in.

She grabbed hold of Kit's right hand, examining his bruised and skinned knuckles. "You'll live," she pronounced, then looked over at Rath. He caught the resigned look in her eyes. She didn't look happy. He stood up, waiting for her.

Cleo sighed. "Sweetheart, this is not your fault. I should have taken better care of you."

"When have I ever let you?" She laughed. "Truth is that I saw the opportunity to do something I wanted to do. And perhaps I was naïve, but I hoped no one would find out."

"You just wanted to play cards." Rath smiled at her.

"Not once you sat down across from me." She shook her head. "I wanted you."

He held his arms open to her, and she ran into them. "It's okay." He kissed the top of her head, not oblivious to Kit's furious stare but not caring.

She ran her hand over his chin. "I see you told him."

"Not quite everything," he confirmed.

She nodded and turned to the small assemblage. "Mrs. Richards is bringing in some refreshments." Even as she said it, Gisele arrived at the doorway with a tray.

"Kit, come with me."

"We can discuss this later," he assured her.

"No. We will discuss this now." She didn't look back as she walked out of the room, hoping that her brother would follow her.

Chapter Seventeen

There was a harsh finality to the sound of the parlor door closing. She couldn't hide from her indiscretions as Kit unleashed a tirade she'd not only been expecting but deserved. She knew that even though hitting Rath had probably helped, he wasn't going to get over it until he had it out with her.

He paced and yelled and ran his fingers through his sun-lightened hair. She smiled, because it was Rath's habit, too, this pacing and worrying his overly long hair. Only his hair was black as midnight while her brother and she shared the same auburn curls.

Finally, with his anger spent, he sat next to her, taking her hands in his and asked, "Why?"

"Why what?"

He sighed, looking down at their hands. Hers seemed very small and pale in his large tanned ones. "Why Rowan Sinclair? Why at all? Why everything? Why is Gabe here?"

"Which question would you like me to answer first," she laughed.

"This isn't a joke. Would you stop being such a bloody pain in the ass?"

She pressed her lips together, and nodded. "Gabe is here because I miscarried a child this morning."

Kit's eyes widened, as the full scope of what she'd done bloomed in his mind. She felt sorry for him as he struggled for words. That was why she told him. He couldn't pretend that hadn't happened. That her actions hadn't had consequences. "I'm fine by the way," she said.

"He's old enough to be your..."

"Brother." She nodded. "I know. And I know he is like a brother to you."

"Not anymore."

"You don't mean that." She shook her head. "Let's remember for a moment that I am nearly twenty-four. Most women my age are married with children, and your own sweet Emily is three years younger than I am and about to give birth to your child."

"Big difference there," he growled. "I'm married to her."

"Please," she sighed, pulling her hands from his. "I know you didn't wait for the wedding night."

"I should have been more careful with you around."

"You were the best brother I could ask for," she assured him. "So my education is a little unusual. You'd be surprised what I knew was going on. You took me to Lisette's yourself. You let Lisette and Big George babysit me while you took your pleasure with her girls. And please do not think I don't know why they call Big George 'big'. His cock is huge. The girls may have enjoyed your visits, but they loved Big George."

He cupped his hands over his mouth and stood. She had embarrassed her brother. Mortified may be the better word. He had protected her, but she had never wanted to be sheltered.

"Kit, please don't berate yourself for the way I was raised," she begged him. "You taught me to fight, not just with swords or a gun, but hand-to-hand. I'm surprised Rath hasn't chastised you for that. I drew first blood against him when he kidnapped me off *The Vixen*," she said proudly. "You raised an original."

"I raised a hoyden. Now, I know why Aunt Constance was so incensed that I was your guardian."

"She's incensed when I don't wear a lace cap indoors," she complained, narrowing her eyes.

"Do you remember what a crush I had on Rath when I was nine or ten years old? I thought he was the most handsome of your friends," she cajoled. "Maybe deep down, I recognized him, but both of us have had years of practicing discretion. He didn't give me his name, and I didn't give him mine."

"At least you learned something from me."

"That and how to cheat at cards." She laughed and he rolled his eyes. She was winning him over to her side.

"He is intent on making our engagement farce a reality."

"After what he did, I'd expect no less from him."

She nodded. "The charade was a good idea. The reality is not."

"I beg to disagree."

"He didn't ask me to marry him because of what I am to him. He asked because of what you are to him.

What our families are to each other. And that's why I won't marry him, Kit, because I do love him. Every inch of his arrogant hide. But I won't be married for the sake of your honor."

"What about your honor?" he asked, gazing into her deep amber eyes.

"Still intact, even if my virginity is not."

"Aagh," he yelled. His face was aghast as he clamped his hands over his ears. "You can't keep saying those things."

She laughed at him, then he began, deep belly guffaws that were hard to stop. They were hand-in-hand on the sofa, backs against the hard cushions. Kit had put his feet up on the tea table in front of them.

"So what do we do now?" he asked, looking over at her.

"I don't know if he can ever love me, and I won't marry for less," she told him.

"What if he does love you, Georgie?" He squeezed her hand. "I've seen the way he looks at you."

She shrugged. "We need to find out who is coming after us. After you. Since there is no rush to wed now that we know I'm not carrying the Rathbridge heir, we continue our ruse."

"What am I supposed to do? He's my best friend, but you're my sister." He looked at her robe. "And I expect I can't convince you to come home with me tonight."

She shook her head. She was staying with Rath tonight. She knew she needed him, and she had a feeling he needed her too. Even if it was for just one more night.

"No. He needs me tonight. He lost something too," she explained. "But I'll be back tomorrow and hopefully, if we all put our heads together, we can figure this mystery out."

"Don't think this discussion is over," Kit promised. "I can't even promise I won't hit Rath again just because I feel like it."

"I know." She nodded, standing. She was getting tired and she wanted some time with Rath before they had to say goodbye.

"I'm will delay my final decision on whether to press you to wed." He kissed her forehead, as they said goodbye in the foyer. "Don't think I won't force you to if I decide it's the right thing to do."

She nodded. She'd had won the battle, if not the war.

She wandered back to the library. She was surprised to see Rath alone, nursing a glass of brandy in front of the fire.

"Are they gone?" she asked, wondering if Cleo was still lurking around.

She walked over to him and sat down on his lap when he nodded.

"We should go up to bed," she suggested.

"Kit is gone and he left you with me for the night?"

"I have a one-night reprieve. I need to be home in the morning," she told him, wrapping her hands around his neck.

"Marry me?" he asked, looking down at her. She could read the sincerity in his eyes.

"Kit hasn't decided whether he will press the issue."

"That's why I am asking, not demanding."

"I am not ready to answer that question," she told him.

"You want to say yes," he gloated, his smile broad and his eyes full of mischief.

"I want to go to bed and feel your arms around me tonight."

His hand fell to her belly. "I'm so sorry."

"Is it crazy to mourn something I didn't know existed a day ago?"

He shook his head. His hair still loose and wild about his shoulders. He looked tired.

"I feel like I'm in mourning, but I don't know if I'm mourning our child or losing you." He frowned. "If the babe had survived, would you have married me?"

"Yes." She nodded.

He breathed out a deep sigh, letting his head fall back against the chair, but his arms held her more tightly. "What are we doing?"

"I don't know." She shook her head. She should have gone home with Kit, but she couldn't. "I just need to be with you."

He nodded and lifted her off his lap, propelling her in front of him, as he followed her up the stairs. It wasn't forever, but they could enjoy each other for one last night.

* * * *

The night went by too fast for Rath's liking. He hated that he was taking to her home, where he couldn't wrap his arms around her and convince her that their marriage was the best option. It was the one thing that would stop his heart from breaking.

"I don't like that you are all in the city," Ash said.

Georgie had insisted they pay a visit first to Maggie, so she could reassure her friend she was fine. And because his brother had uncovered some information regarding the blackmailer, the four of them were now into his carriage as they headed toward Knolls Court, Kit's London house.

Rath had brought some excellent quality Spanish cigars as a peace offering for Kit, and as Maggie and Georgie ran off to find Emily, he hoped for a détente between him and Kit.

Kit looked at the cigars, taking one out and holding it beneath his nose as he inhaled the rich smell of tobacco. "These are good."

"I know." He grinned. "It's why I stole them."

"I did not hear that," Ash reminded them as he took one from the humidor.

"But it won't stop you from enjoying one." Kit laughed.

"Are you kidding? My brother has been holding out on me. I didn't know he had these."

"That's because they were meant for bribes," Rath confirmed, looking at Kit thoughtfully. "I want to marry her."

"She wants to marry for love."

"I do love her," Rath told him. He hadn't said the words before, but he'd known since the night he'd seen her lying ashen against the sheets as Gabe dug a bullet out of her shoulder. He wanted her in his life. He told his brothers this.

Kit nodded. "You have one month to convince to walk to the altar with you. Otherwise, she may hate me, but I will force the outcome."

"Don't force her." Rath shook his head. "Just give me time. Ash is concerned we are all too exposed here in the city and thinks we should move to Rosehaven. I'll have the bans read at the local parish as part of our ruse. We'll be ready to wed as soon as she agrees."

"I don't like the idea that Georgie could still be in danger, or that I'm putting Emily in danger. She has only a few weeks until our child is to be born. It would be best if we were away from the city."

"Mother will be happy for our company," Ash promised.

Rath nodded. He like any plan that meant that he could be closer to Georgie, day and night.

Kit narrowed his eyes at Rath as if discerning his intentions. "Where are we with the investigation?"

That was Ash's cue to take over. He passed out the dossier he'd put together with some help from his contacts in intelligence.

"We favor your uncle for this," Ash announced. "He's been stealing money from the business interests he handles for you and Georgie. The stables, the tin mines, some of the imports."

Kit thumbed through the file. "Still roughly a fifth of the profits?" he asked.

"Most of the time," Ash confirmed suspiciously. "Occasionally more, but this usually coincides with an event in his household. Like the girls being sent to school, or attendance at an extravagant ball."

"It's not him," Kit told them shaking his head adamantly. "Uncle Charles has been supplementing his income this way for as long as I can remember. Mother and Father let him get away with it. Once they were gone, I let him know that I would not notice should those funds continue to go astray."

"But why not just raise his quarterly stipend?" Gabe asked.

Kit shrugged. "He prefers it this way." He passed the dossier back to Ash. "Who else are we looking at?"

"He was the most promising suspect," Ash confirmed glumly. "Since Constance's brother moved in, she's been desperately trying to raise funds from her friends and family for his ministry."

"Constance's brother?" Kit questioned, his brow arching in concern.

"Yes." Ash searched the dossier. "We don't have much on him. He had a ministry in Briton briefly. He's, supposedly, a fairly dictatorial Methodist, but there was some rumor of him taking advantage of a woman or perhaps some women in his ministry. Using their devotion to God as getting some devotion to himself. They were married, and therefore, no one is willing to talk about it, but it looks like they may have quietly run him out of town."

"Michael is now a minister." Kit laughed. "I'm sorry but that strikes me funny. Not that Constance's parents weren't devout, and Constance has always been absolutely dutiful, but Michael was about as pious as a wagtail. Family disowned him years ago."

"Constance has welcomed him into the bosom of her family."

"There was always some talk about how close to her bosom he was." Kit rolled his eyes. "And he's her stepbrother. We need to look at him."

"Any particular reason?" Rath requested.

"He's a cheat and a liar and we have an old grudge. I don't suspect he'd hesitate to kill to get what he wants."

"That's a pretty good reason," Ash agreed.

Rath looked at Kit thoughtfully. He wanted to know what that old grudge was because he thought it may have to do with Georgiana.

"I'll have a runner put on him immediately," Ash promised. "What could he be hoping to gain?"

"Money. He was always after money," Kit conceded. "I think it's likely that he's trying to bleed some money out of Constance and Charles. He may hope to obtain access to greater funds through Georgie."

"I'll go take care of this," Ash promised, finishing off his cup of coffee, then heading out.

When they were alone, Rath poured another cup for himself and Kit. "I'm surprised you're still on good terms with your uncle, considering what they did to Georgiana."

"What do you mean?" Kit sipped his coffee and pretended to look at some papers on his desk.

"When they had guardianship of her, after your parents died."

Kit looked up, and Rath saw a mix of emotions in his best friend's eyes. Regret. Remorse. Fear. "She told you?"

"During the fever." He took a mouthful of the coffee and grimaced. "Do you have any brandy for that?"

Kit opened the bottom drawer of his desk and poured a healthy measure from the bottle into each of their cups. He left the bottle on the desk.

"She said that the two of you never discuss what happened," Rath continued.

"No. It's not discussed." The warning in his tone was clear, but Rath was not put off.

"That's not good enough," Rath told him. "I wasn't just your partner. I was your best friend."

Kit frowned but sat back in his chair. "And you were fighting your own demons. I was more than capable of handling that one on my own."

"One more thing I was too weak to be able to help with?"

"You couldn't even walk at the time. That was not your fault," Kit reminded him.

Rath sighed. "I take it the place no longer exists." He hoped so, or he would tear it down stone by stone.

"No," Kit confirmed. "I bought off the owner within a month of rescuing her, and the children were either returned to their parents, sent to a proper establishment or went into the care of homes on our estates."

"And Big John?"

"If you can imagine being a child and picturing a giant, Big John would be it. We think he was about fifteen years old when we rescued him. And was already more than six feet tall with these huge, broad shoulders. He continued to fill out once we got him eating some decent food." Kit smiled affectionately. "He had no family, so he came home with us." Kit shook his head. "I don't think we could have parted those two back then. It would have been cruel. That boy had known no kindness in his life, until Georgie and our home."

Rath didn't realize his friend was crying until he dabbed at his eyes. "He's not stupid or sick, just a little slow. He has a way with animals, and that's his job now on Belle Fleur. He even has a wife."

Rath knew his friend would have done right by the boy. "He saved her."

"I know." Kit nodded. "And that is the grudge that Michael still holds against me."

Rath narrowed his eyes. "I don't understand?"

"After I rescued Georgie, I confronted Charles and dragged him with me to show him the conditions of the convalescent home they'd sent my sister to. He was appalled. He actually threw up when he saw what went on there. Michael had set up the home with funds from his church." Kit eyes narrowed with the weight of years of hate and anger. "We shut it down."

Rath jumped when the empty cup in his hand broke. He hadn't realized how hard he'd been gripping it. His lip curled into a snarl, even as he picked up the pieces and set them on the desk. "I would have killed him."

"I wanted to, Rath. I have never wanted anything as much as I wanted to wrap my hands around the man's throat and squeeze the life out of him." He stood and stalked toward the fire, taking the bottle of brandy. Kit always paced when he was upset. He tugged at his loosely tied cravat as if needing more air. "But I had no proof, Charles reminded me, that Michael knew what was going on."

Kit closed his eyes, remembering. "They were applauded for their new methods for treating childhood disorders. But what I walked into was a warehouse of discarded children. With their hair shaved off, and all wearing these coarse gray gowns, it was hard to determine male from female. Most had been beaten, some had been raped."

He swallowed a mouthful of brandy straight from the bottle. "They had tried beating her to force her to speak. I could never be sure what else they may have done."

"It would have been easy to have a doctor check her out," Rath pointed out.

"You didn't see her then," Kit explained, his voice shaking. "She weighed next to nothing. Her hair had been roughly chopped to within a half inch of her scalp, and she was filthy. They were only given baths about once a month. The conditions were worse than most orphanages or work houses, because it assumed that these children would live and die there."

Rath cringed, imagining the scenario. He'd seen slave markets that were better kept than what Kit described.

"She couldn't stand to be touched by anyone but me or Big John, so we decided she'd been through enough." Kit took a swig from the bottle, then used the back of his hand to wipe his eyes. "She was just so happy to be home and with me, it didn't matter anymore."

Rath needed a swig from that bottle, but rather than wrestle it from Kit, he reached across the desk for Kit's coffee and brandy cup, hoping there was some left. He'd already vowed to himself to make Georgie happy. It seemed more important than ever.

"She was untouched when she came to me," Rath said, breaking the silence that hung heavy between them. "I don't see that we need to speak of this again. However, I told you this morning that she loves me. Unfortunately, I believe the reason she doesn't think she's marriage material is because of what did happen there or perhaps just being there."

"I never knew she felt that way," Kit confided. "We thought it was that independent streak that seems to run in our family. I taught her to protect herself so she would never have to feel frightened again."

"And she fights well, let me tell you." Rath laughed. "I have every intention of convincing her to marry me, but that's why I need time." He paused. "Now that she's lost the baby, we have a bit of it."

"I don't want her hurt again," Kit told his friend. "You have to convince her."

"I will," he promised. "I thought it would be a lot harder to convince you that I should marry her."

"You mean because I know you so well." Kit raised a skeptical brow.

"Because of what you know."

"You kicked that particular monkey off your back." He shrugged. "I'm much more concerned that your main household staff have also been your lovers."

"Recognized them, did you?" Rath laughed, winking at his friend. "I think can reassure you that is over. Richards finally convinced Gisele to marry him while I was away. Which is good because they have two children together. She has done remarkably well learning how to take care of a household."

Kit shrugged. "I suppose that was one of the reasons we provided Lisette funds for her establishment. As a stepping stone for her girls to find better positions."

"Gis remains loyal to Lisette too. I will be faithful to Georgie," he promised. "I think Richards and Gis would do very unpleasant things to me were I not. They are quite taken with her."

"Then you have my blessing, for what it's worth. I think the two of you are well-suited, better than I want to admit, and" he sighed. "I like the idea that we will be brothers."

"That we've always been."

Chapter Eighteen

It wasn't as difficult as one may have expected to move five separate households to one country estate. Cleo had organized the arrangements, the carriages and coaches, and had given detailed instruction to each lady's maid and man's valet as to what should be packed. She had, in the end, managed the feat with her usual aplomb, though she had more than once complained that there was no reason she needed to move as well.

Georgie assured her there was every reason, not the least of which was Gabe who was going to be staying with them until Emily delivered. Cleo went where Gabe was, and everyone knew it. It was the worst kept secret in the ton, and if Cleo wasn't as wealthy as she was, it would very well be a scandal.

"One of these days, you are going to say yes to his marriage proposal, you should stay nearby so he can keep asking," Georgie said, as they sat in the countess' private rose garden for which Rosehaven had been named. They arrived the day before and to Georgie it was as if she'd never left.

Rosehaven was a small estate as standards went, similar in size to her parents' estate, Candlewood, that abutted it to the North. It's brick-and-stone façade, more stoic and forbidding than suggested by the bright interior and cheerful gardens. Madeline, Rath's mother, had overseen every detail of the gardens. She had a slew of gardeners on staff to assist, of course, but you would find her more often than not outside each morning tending to a particular section.

Georgie thought England wouldn't be so bad if she could hide out in a garden like this every day. She'd enjoyed tending the garden at Belle Fleur but she'd not given it the attention, or years of devotion, that Madeline had Rosehaven.

"What makes you think I am any more inclined to marriage than you?" Cleo asked.

"Because you want to marry for love and he loves you." Georgie rolled her eyes. "Unless you are concerned for his lack of a title."

Cleo tapped her fan into her palm. "What do I care if he's only the third son to a viscount or a son of a bitch? I will always be Viscountess Welles. And besides." She sighed. "He is every bit my equal, my better to be honest, and I have more than enough money for the two of us."

"The three of you, don't you mean?" Georgie reminded her. "The other reason you should really take him up on his offer of marriage. Your daughter."

Cleo blinked at her several times. "I really am disappointed in your sudden sense of traditionalism and propriety."

"I am neither." Georgie sighed. "But if I thought Rath loved me, I would at least consider marrying him. If I'd been carrying his child, I would have married him. You've carried around the engagement ring Gabe gave you for years, but you continue to put him off. But for some reason, oh, yes, because he loves you, he's still waiting. The question is what are you waiting for?"

"Yes." a deep voice sounded behind their bench, making both women jump and turn around. Gabe stood behind them, looking attractive in his hunter green striped vest, and his buckskins. Were it not for the mud on his boots, he looked every bit the proper gentleman. "That's a very good question."

Cleo jumped up, and Georgie smirked. She didn't think Gabe would overhear their conversation. She just wanted to point out to Cleo that her refusal was bordering on the ridiculous.

"I am waiting for you to stop asking and give up this ridiculous idea." Cleo frowned.

He stalked toward her. "That's not the answer."

She shook her head. "I am waiting until the rest of them don't need me. And I am free."

Georgie snorted. "We will always need you, try again."

"Why are you helping him?" she scolded.

"Because you love him. And I think you deserve a happy ending."

"You heard her." Gabe grinned. "We deserve a happy ending. Say yes, and we can go in there and celebrate with our friends tonight."

Cleo threw up her hands in frustration, and Georgie did feel a smidge bad for her friend.

"The first bans for their marital ruse will be read this Sunday, they could read ours, too," he continued to coax her. He stepped closer to her, his hands held aloft at his side. It looked like he was trying to sneak up on a wild horse that was ready to bolt.

"That would be lovely," Georgie agreed, clapping her hands together. "Then all the wedding planning won't be for naught."

Cleo glared at them both, and Georgie could see her trying to think of a way out of this situation. Except Georgie knew Cleo didn't want a way out. She wanted her back up against the wall with no way to squirm free. Georgie wasn't sure how she was so sure of this, but she was.

"Marry me, Cleo," Gabe demanded. "Let's make ourselves a proper family. Stop sneaking from my bed at dawn. Stay there. Wake up with me. Let me be there when Sarah comes running in for her mother. Let me be her father."

Cleo snatched up her shawl and jumped to her feet before Gabe could get to her. She turned and began to stalk up the trail toward the house. Georgie saw his shoulders deflate, but it was as close as he'd ever come to getting her to agree. She reached out and placed her hand on his sleeve in support.

Halfway up the path, Cleo looked back down the path toward them. "You can announce our betrothal, but I warn you both, it had better be a small family wedding."

She then picked up her skirts and began running to the house, squealing, with Gabe on her heels.

Georgie laughed, as Gabe caught Cleo and spun her in his arms. He was kissing her and she was giggling. And there would be a real wedding in three weeks' time. And a true cause for celebration.

A twig snapped behind her, and she didn't have to turn to know it was Rath.

"You did a good thing there," he said, coming around the bench and sitting by her side.

"It was time." She nodded. "Do you know they have a three-year-old daughter? That's how long he's been asking her."

"He's been asking her since her first husband died," he corrected. "Though at first he may not have been serious. Drunken revelry, we probably all proposed to Cleo at some time or the other, but only Gabe ever meant it. That became clear over the years."

"She told him when she got with child that she'd think about it." She shrugged. "I think she's thought long enough."

"I was warned you were a matchmaker." He grinned.

"Only in special cases, of the people I love. Like your brother and his wife," she confided.

"What about your own brother and his wife?"

Georgie harrumphed. Anyone watching those two would know they had needed no help from her. Their attraction was unmistakable and it was, she figured, one of the reasons Emily's father had left her guardianship to Kit. He could see it too.

"You know she was his ward? They did not need my interference. They just needed to be under the same roof on a hot summer night. The lightning storm did the rest." She grinned.

He smiled. "Lightning storms must be much more seductive on land than they are on the open water."

"I dare say they are," she agreed. She sat back on the bench and swung her legs, which didn't quite touch the ground.

"You think I don't love you." Rath wasn't asking it as a question, more of a statement.

"I think that it's hard to discern obligation from honor, from affection."

"Well, at least you didn't deny that I had some feeling for you."

"I know parts of you feel quite a bit for me," she joked, but from his frown, saw that he didn't share her humor. "I don't know that I can discern what you feel for me with it all mixed up like that."

"What can I do to change your mind?" he asked. "Am I to wait, like Gabe, for years?"

She shook her head. She didn't want that. "I don't think we should see each other after this is over. I know that you and Kit and Ash have come up with a manly plan to trap the blackmailer. I'll assume it's a good one since you are keeping your own counsel. When it's over, either I will leave, or you should."

"This is my home," he reminded her, an indignant brow rising above his left eye. It was an endearing affectation and one she knew he was unaware of.

"Then I will leave." She stood up and smoothed her skirts. "Just as soon as Cleo and Gabe are wed." She had places to go, like next door to their family's country estate. She could help Emily with the baby and try not to remember that for a brief time she carried one of her own.

He caught her gloved hand in his and stopped her from slipping away. "I know you love me."

Her breath hitched. She'd hoped not to be so obvious, and while she thought to dismiss the accusation, she finally decided not to. "I think I do."

"You do," he said adamantly. "And I'm going to ask you every night before you go upstairs to bed to marry me. And I will keep asking you until you believe it has nothing to do with honor or obligation."

She waited a moment to see if he'd say it. Would he say he loved her? She thought if she heard the words from his own lips, she'd be able to tell whether they were true. But he didn't go that far. No, she frowned. He wouldn't go that far.

"Good afternoon, Lord Rathbridge." She nodded, dismissing him as she pulled her hand away. She had things she should be doing in the house.

* * * *

"You must do something about your niece." Constance stamped her foot in the doorway.

Charles glanced up from his book, frowning. "What are you going on about?" He was having more trouble concentrating of late, and even his wife haranguing at him seemed dull and distant.

"Haven't you heard yet? It's all over London!"

Charles continued to regard his wife blankly. There was always some bit of gossip 'all over London', but considering she spent her time in the company of the church ladies, he doubted she'd verified the truth of any of it. He couldn't see his wife on the docks, or at Vauxhall Garden. They'd once been offered Sefton's box at the opera, but his wife thought the Almacks' patroness, Lady Sefton, to be too forward and Covent Garden too tawdry and had refused.

"Your niece has taken up residence with Lord Sin, the Earl of Rathbridge," she complained.

That got his attention, mostly because he knew it to be a patent lie. "I sincerely doubt that," he murmured.

She stalked across the room and slammed closed the book he had been reading. "You will attend me on this," she shrieked. "Lady Mortimer was very gracious in extending her sympathy to us that we should have a niece such as Lady Georgiana. She also let me know that the ton wouldn't hold it against our girls."

He shrugged. He had no idea who Lady Mortimer was but doubted she had much clout with for instance the patronesses of Almacks. "Well, that's big of her, is it not?"

"Not," she screeched. "What it means is that our girls will be lucky to receive any further invitations. The season is ruined for them, and it has hasn't even started."

"The season is not ruined."

"Did you not hear me? She is staying with Lord Sin, at his country estate."

He tried not to laugh. He'd not heard him referred to as Lord Sin for a great many years. Most were too scared of Captain Wrath to utter the epithet. He looked up at his wife in continued disbelief. *I can't believe I'm married to the harpy,* he thought with a laugh, before his stomach turned over on itself. He was going to have to see a doctor about this continued stomach upset.

"She is staying on the Sinclair estate with her brother and his wife. As well as her sponsor, Lady Welles, and the entire Sinclair family," he reassured her as best he could, knowing she wouldn't listen to him.

"So you knew, and you didn't prepare us?" she accused.

Charles had to stop from rubbing the bridge of his nose. He felt a headache coming on. "Madame, there is nothing to prepare you for. She is his fiancée. This idle gossip, to which you are no doubt contributing, will die down in a few days. We are not going to add legitimacy to it by paying it any attention whatsoever."

"But our girls," she started.

"Our girls will survive and have their season. Whether I allow you to stay in town for it is another thing altogether," he said harshly. "In fact, I received an invitation this morning from the Dowager Countess of Rathbridge. I had thought to decline due to the expense of attending, but now that I know you are one of the reasons the tongues of the ton are wagging, we will accept. Please prepare to attend, with our daughters, a house party at the Rosehaven estate this weekend."

"We are not staying at Rosehaven," she said. "That would be too much, just too much."

"That would indeed be too much for them," he agreed. "We will stay at Candlewood. Now that Christopher has returned, I think he is planning to stay there for the birth of his heir and for some time into the future. He is having the estate house reopened as we speak. We shall be comfortable enough there."

His wife's mouth moved up and down, but no further argument burgeoned forth, for which he was grateful. "Now, I suggest you let me attend to my business, and you attend to yours."

"Huh," she huffed and pulled her shawl against her shoulders as she ran from the room.

Michael, who'd been listening nearby, intercepted her before she could get very far. He saw that she'd been crying.

"Connie, what's the matter?" he asked gently, as she turned her face away from him.

He knew she hated for anyone to see her cry. She had never been a pretty crier, even as a child, her skin would get blotchy and red. While some women's eyes looked wide and vulnerable when covered in tears — he liked that look — Connie's eyes became red, sunken pinpricks.

She sniffed into her handkerchief and repeated the stories she heard circulating about her niece. "She will ruin us."

Michael pretended to listen but a plan was already forming in his mind. "Something should be done about her. She sounds unbalanced, and why should we expect anything less? Let's remember it's not the first time."

"No." She sniffed. "It's not. She should never have been let out of the institution. She's always had, well, let's call them difficulties adjusting."

He nodded, careful to infuse his words with sympathy. "If people only knew of her problem, then the shame of her behavior could never touch your girls."

"Oh, but I couldn't tell anyone. Charles would…" she began.

He stroked her shoulder. "Charles would understand that it had to be done to save his daughters' future." He smiled. "And I'll see if something can't be done about the girl. We will discuss it further at Candlewood. That is where you're staying while you attend their wicked house party, is it not?"

She looked up to her brother for guidance. "We shall never attend. I will tell Charles the girls are ill. I will make them ill if I have to, but we shall never attend."

He could tell his sister had her own scheme in mind, and he couldn't allow that. "No, you must attend," he instructed. "Don't you see? You alone can reveal her wickedness. If you don't go, how could you possibly share your direct knowledge of her scandal to the women at your church?"

She shook her head. "Charles will never let you travel with us. I haven't even told him that you are staying here. I hate that you are living in the attics like a servant."

"Don't worry about that," he reassured her. In fact, it had worked out quite well for him, giving him unfettered access to the house in the day, especially when Charles was out. "I will find my own way to Candlewood. As a man of God, it is my duty to sacrifice. It is all of our Christian duty."

She nodded. If there was one thing he could rely on his sister for, it was her devotion to duty, as he defined it for her. He'd made sure she understood that in the years before she'd met Charles and had children, he'd had a very special duty for her to assist him with. *She's always had a very pretty mouth,* he remembered.

"Of course, my duty is to go to the party. To pretend to all the world like we are a family." She shuddered.

"And to get me some information I need so I can once and for all uncover to the world how wicked and unstable that wretched girl is." His darling stepsister would play a pivotal role in what was to come.

Chapter Nineteen

Worst party ever. Sure, everyone on their suspect list was in attendance, but so far, nothing untoward had occurred. They had been able to add a few names to the list, mostly jealous business associates. He didn't think they were involved. The more he heard about Constance and her stepbrother, the more he liked him for it.

It was the why he still couldn't figure out. Why expose Kit's previous relationships and more dubious adventures during the war? He was happily married, so no one would care who he used to sleep with. And their company had letter of marques making each Spanish vessel they took complete under the authority of the king. And why shoot Georgie? What use was blackmail if she were dead?

Rath continued to roll the idea over in his head. He didn't like where it led. Neither had Kit. She'd inherited a title and a tidy fortune from her mother. If she died, it went to Charles.

Kit had fought suggestion. It didn't seem right that their uncle would, after almost twenty years, go after a minor Scottish title, he'd argued, when they were willing to let him have all the money he needed.

Kit insisted there was something off about it, and Rath knew it would take a lot more evidence than they had to convince him. He wasn't so sure of it himself anymore, but he had assigned men to watch Charles and Michael since the family arrived at Candlewood yesterday. Michael hadn't arrived with them, but he was there. Their spy said that Michael was pretending to be a tutor to the girls, but that Charles hadn't interacted with him once.

That was odd, and it made him watch the man even more during the party. This afternoon the guests were enjoying the exorbitant fee he paid to the crown to have a bowling green at Rosehaven.

"Are you still pouting?" Felicia, his sister, asked.

"I'm not pouting," he told her.

"That's not what Maman said." She grinned up at him, holding a glass of sweetened lemonade. "She said you were out of sorts because Kit was making it impossible for you to sneak into your fiancée's bedroom."

He looked down at his little sister. Not so little anymore. They were going to have to watch that. "I am out of sorts because someone hurt Georgie recently, and I don't know who it is." He lowered his voice conspiratorially. "Want to help me investigate?"

Her smile brightened. "Georgie is my hero. What can I do?"

After watching Charles this afternoon, he could tell the old man wasn't well. "Talk to the Norris girls. It looks like there father is ill. Find out how long that's been going on."

She put down her lemonade. "I can do that." She began to flounce away on her new mission, but he caught her arm.

"Be subtle," he suggested.

She got a wicked gleam in her eyes, one he knew better than to trust. "*Subtle* is my middle name."

He shook his head.

"She's going to be trouble."

He looked over his shoulder to see Georgie standing a few feet behind him. Her hair was covered in a cotton-and-straw bonnet, only a few rich auburn tendrils curling about her ears.

His eyes raked her up and down. "And to think I thought you tempting in breeches."

She smoothed her hands down over the printed floral afternoon dress. "You just like how accessible it is. Are you really pouting because Kit has set a footman at my door each night to bar your entrance?"

"I would be if said footman couldn't be bribed." He grinned. It hadn't taken him much to get the footman to look the other way. "Kit should pay his staff better."

"And it's not as if there weren't fifty other rooms in this house where you could catch me unawares."

"You were very aware, and wet for me." He winked at her, referring to the tryst not more than half an hour ago in the orangery. "Or was that simply your love of fruit?"

"You know the only plums I like to handle are yours."

"Then marry me." He'd said he would ask her each night, but he knew time was running out. He asked her all the time now. Even when he was balls deep inside her. She was still being stubborn and saying no, or like now, laughing and shaking her head at him.

"I came to find you because Ash wants to see you and my brother in the library," she informed him. "Whereas your mother has told me I must go and play *jeu du volant* with your sister-in-law."

"Well, you do have a way with shuttlecocks." He couldn't resist the joke.

"Only with yours, my lord." She grinned, bending low in a mock curtsy. *Does she know,* he wondered, *how much of her beautiful breasts I can see in that position?* Her wink when she rose said she did. If she didn't say yes, he swore he was going to kidnap her to Gretna Green.

As he turned to go into the house, Felicia came running in a not very lady-like fashion across the terrace. "He's sick," she sputtered, catching her breath.

He narrowed his eyes. "You were with them for two minutes. How the deuce did you find that out already?"

"They are remarkably chatty. They never stop talking. All I had to ask was why their father was playing bowls, and they went into a litany of his recent ailments." She began listing off his symptoms.

"They have no discretion, I see."

She shrugged. "Oh, no, they are horribly uncouth. But don't those sound odd?" she asked. "And the tonic their tutor cooked up for him doesn't seem to be helping at all."

She was right. It seemed too odd and convenient. It was all coming together. "Come with me." He grabbed hold of his sister's hand and together they charged through the house to the meeting in the library.

He was relieved when he pushed through the doors to see Gabe had been invited as well. "Felicia." He pushed his sister in front of him. "Please tell them what you told me about Charles' health."

She listed again the symptoms his daughters had confirmed. Nausea, flux, joint pain, headaches.

"And who created the tonic he is taking for his symptoms?"

"They said their botany tutor had put together a medicinal. He has it with breakfast each morning but he is worse after it."

"Thank you, Felicia." He kissed her forehead. "That was remarkably well done. Now, how about you join your sister-in-laws for battledore and shuttlecocks outside."

When she left, he and the others turned to Gabe.

"It could be arsenic poisoning."

"Prepared by Michael." Kit sighed. "That makes sense."

"He doesn't have to kill Charles, just incapacitate him," Ash said, piecing it together. "If Georgie dies, Charles is left the title and her mother's fortune. If he is too sick to control it, Michael can step in, and being Constance's sainted brother, can help her manage it."

"You mean steal it."

"Do you think murdering Georgie was the plan all along?" Rath asked Kit. He knew Michael better than they did. "Could he have had that planned even when she was a child?" The thought made his stomach roil. The man was a monster.

"Maybe. It would have been easy enough to see her come to an accidental end, but I became overprotective. She didn't go anywhere without me or Cleo. And then I took her with me to the plantation."

"The bastard's been patient," Rath snarled. "You three find Charles. Gabe, you have to look after his symptoms. It would seem he is innocent in this."

"And you?" Ash asked.

"I'm going to look for Georgie," he confirmed. If Michael figured out they were on to him, or even suspicious of Charles, it could make him desperate. "I can't let Michael get to her first."

* * * *

"When did you figure it out?" He breathed, his mouth close to her ear, his pistol pressing into her spine.

"I don't know what you mean," she said, walking with deliberate care across the grassy slope in hopes that someone would see them and follow them. If she'd figured it out after hearing only a snippet of Felicia's conversation with her cousins, then perhaps Kit and Rath would. "Where are you taking me?"

His fingers pinched into her upper arm as he propelled her ahead of him. "I can't very well shoot you again, can I?"

"You shot me?" It turned her stomach to think that he'd done the deed, though she suspected that he wouldn't hesitate to do it again to get what he wanted.

"If I'd pulled the trigger, you'd be dead," he spat, and his spittle splashed against the side of her face. She flinched. He was as disgusting as she remembered him. "I'd hoped I wouldn't have to kill you. You turned into a pretty little thing. I knew a hospital or two where I could have stashed you away again. Your brother couldn't close down all of them."

"I don't understand." She tried to turn and look at him, and to look past him to see who may be around, but she saw only his drawn face and his grin.

"Don't you, my dear?" He laughed. "Don't you remember your dear uncle Michael coming to visit you?"

She stumbled over her feet, as a wave of nausea threatened. She remembered the laugh, of him telling her to be good for Uncle Michael as he pulled up her dressing gown. Until now, she'd been confident that she'd be found, but now a new fear clutched at her heart. Michael wouldn't hesitate to hurt her, or anyone who got in his way.

She couldn't stop the bile as it rose in her throat. She sank to the ground, her stomach heaving. She could hear him at a distance still chattering, gloating about what he'd planned to do to her, what he'd done to the other girls.

She had untied her hat and wiped her mouth on the cotton crown, before he'd pulled back up by the elbow. Her legs didn't want to support her. Her head was spinning. She was still trying to understand how what had happened then was connected to what was happening now.

When she couldn't stand up, he kicked out at her in desperation. "Get up. Get up, you silly whore."

She looked up at him. She hoped he could see the hate in her eyes, but his gaze was focused past her. She was slow to find her footing, determined not to make this easy for him. She dropped the hat in the bile, lest he make her pick it up again. She hoped if they were following her they'd see it, follow it, like Hansel's and Gretel's breadcrumbs.

She could see the cedar grove that marked the edge of her family's property, but she knew that wasn't the destination he had in mind. He was heading to the pond that both properties shared. If he wanted to make it look like an accident, the easiest way was for her to drown.

It won't look accidental if he shoots you first, she reminded herself.

She wasn't going to go quietly. If he thought he could kill her, he was going to have to work for it. She kicked off a shoe, then another. They were all the breadcrumbs she had, and she hoped it would do.

She looked around for someone, anyone. A gardener perhaps. The pond wasn't far from her house. If she could get away, perhaps someone would hear her screaming. She had to try.

She pretended to stumble again, tucking herself into a small ball so Michael tripped over her. They both fell to the ground, but she was ready for it. She was holding her skirts, allowing her to regain her feet quickly. She sprinted down the groomed path toward Candlewood, screaming for help.

Because she didn't dare look back, she wasn't ready when he tackled her from behind. She fell forward, only to be turned harshly onto her back. The back of his hand cracked against her cheek, once then twice. Her head swam, but she could feel his hands on her bare legs, pushing her dress up. She began beating him with her fists, hitting whatever was in front of her. When he had to use his hands to defend his chest and head, she began to kick. Easier now with her skirts out of the way.

Bet he didn't think of that, she thought. She was able to throw him off and began to crawl away, trying to regain her feet, even as he grabbed at her skirts.

"Michael." Georgie looked up and saw Constance on the path up ahead, a look of horror on her face.

"Constance, help me," she called out, as Michael wrapped his hand tightly around the back of her dress. She wasn't getting away. She continued to look at Constance, pleading.

"Michael, I don't understand. What are you doing?" Her voice was shrill with distress.

Michael growled behind her. She could hear him chanting "no, no, no," under his breath. But Constance wasn't looking at him anymore. She was looking down the path from where they'd been, and Georgie knew they weren't alone anymore.

She dropped to the ground on her stomach, yanking the dress material from his grasp as she tried to roll away. He raised his hand as if to strike her again, and he gasped. Then a patch of red bloomed across his chest. Constance screamed louder as Michael, confused, clutched his hand to his chest.

Georgie was able to scramble away just before he fell forward. She was relieved when she found herself in Rath's arms as he lifted her off the ground.

She sank into his hold. The rest of the world fading out, even Constance's shrieks becoming a distant echo.

* * * *

Rath had his brother on his heels as he ran across the bowls yard, looking for Georgie on the far pitch where a group of young women were batting about shuttlecocks. He spied Maggie with Felicia.

"Where's Georgie?" he asked, his heart pounding in his ears as they informed him that she'd never shown up to play.

"She went with our tutor," Annabelle, the youngest of Georgie's cousins, said. "She had just stopped to say hello to us when he arrived. He bade her escort him back to Candlewood." She pointed across the lawn.

With the sun in his eyes, he couldn't see much of anything, but he began running, and he didn't stop. Soon, he heard her screams. *That's my girl. You don't give up,* he thought. *You fight and you fight and you fight.*

He wanted to rip Michael apart, and when he saw his chance, he didn't hesitate. He screeched to a half and fired his pistol.

He wasn't just a good shot. He was the best.

* * * *

Thunder? Hooves? It was hard to discern what the pounding in her head sounded more like. She frowned. If people would stop yelling, perhaps she could figure it out. The crack of wind in the sails?

You're starting to make a habit of getting injured, she scolded herself. *And it's not a good one.* She tried to sit up, but it made her head throb worse, so she stayed still, her eyes closed as she tried to make out the voices in hallway.

"You are not going to keep me away from her. She's mine." That was Rath. She'd recognize his possessive posturing anywhere.

"Don't you think she's been through enough?" Her brother. Protective as always.

"Don't you think I know that? My god, how many times do I need to see her nearly die?"

I nearly died? Again? No, that cant be right. She took stock of her aches and pains. Her feet were sore, but she remembered she'd kicked off her shoes as she'd tried to escape Michael. Her side ached where he'd kicked her, and yes, her face and head hurt where he'd hit her. But she wasn't about to die from it. She wiggled her fingers and toes to make sure everything else was functioning as it should. Yep. No problem there.

"You don't get to bar the door from me, Kit. She's my fiancée."

"In name only."

"Bugger that. You know I love her. I can't imagine my life without her. Can't imagine not waking up in the morning with her and sinking balls deep inside her."

All she heard next were a series of grunts and thuds and the occasional sound of breaking glass.

"You'd think someone would have removed the breakables from the hall by now. In fact, I think they keep restocking the hall."

She cracked an eye open and saw Gissy sitting on the bed next to her, grinning. Maggie was next to her.

"That's Ash's fault. He loves sowing discord."

"How long have they been at it?" Her voice sounded gravelly. She willed her other eye open as far as it could. *Blast it,* she thought, it must be swollen from where Michael hit her.

Gissy helped her to sit up, and she realized she was in her mother's morning room at Candlewood.

"Pretty much since they brought you back an hour ago," Maggie confirmed. "But don't blame either of them too much. Kit's in a mood because Emily has gone into labor. She's fine. She has Madeline and Cleo, as well as Gabe with her. I hear they aren't letting Gabe near her. They keep telling him it's a woman thing."

"Shouldn't Kit be there?"

"Nothing for him to do up there. He did his work nine months ago." Gissy laughed.

There was another crash in the hall. She heard something on the wall rattle then fall.

"Kit has vowed never to touch his wife again, or let any man touch you." Maggie shifted a pillow behind Georgie's head. "This whole childbirth thing seems to have him a little disconcerted."

"And then your captain says something outrageous, and instead of being out of sorts, your brother is ready for a brawl."

She had to wonder what other outrageous things Rath had chosen to say.

"You don't want to know," Maggie and Gis responded together, as if reading her mind.

"Say it again." Kit's voice reverberated in the hall, as did the sound that could only have been Rath being thrown up against the wall.

"I love her smile."

The sound of fist hitting flesh sounded near the door.

"I love her brain and her wit."

Another punch sounded, and she heard Rath let out an *oomph* before he continued.

"I love how her pussy hugs my cock."

This time, before Kit's fist could make contact again, the door groaned inward, and Rath, his shirt torn, his knuckles scraped and his chin already beginning to bruise, skidded into the room.

Kit tried grabbing on to him from behind and pulling him out.

"I love you, Georgie," he shouted, shrugging off her brother.

"What?" She looked at him, sure there was still some fog obscuring her higher brain function.

"I love you." He stepped forward, Kit finally letting him go. "I love you in breeches or in skirts. I love that you swear with my crew and taught them new and highly inappropriate chanties. I love that you fight me and fuck me and love me. Because I will do all that for you, too."

He seemed to deflate, as he sank to his knees. "And if you don't marry me, I will be a miserable bugger for the rest of my life."

She smiled. It hurt. Lord, it hurt quite a lot and she feared what her face must look like, but she couldn't stop herself.

"You are already a miserable bugger, but I love you, too."

"Is that a yes?" he asked.

She heard Maggie's hopeful intake of breath, and Gis tightened the grip on her arm. Kit was grinning, but she kind of thought he'd hoped she'd say no, so he could keep hitting Rath.

"Yes," she said. "That means yes."

She wasn't sure how Rath managed it, but he was in front of her, still on his knees. His hands slid around her waist and he laid his head down in her lap. She stroked his hair. When he looked up, his eyes were wet with unshed tears.

"I think we have matching bruises," she said, running her hand over his cheek and chin.

"I needed to let off some steam." He shrugged. "Kit obliged. Shooting Michael did nothing to alleviate my rage at him for harming you. Again." He stretched up and kissed her swollen lips gently.

Kit pulled up a chair and together he and Rath filled her in on what they'd discerned. She also told them what she could remember of his ramblings as he'd dragged her toward the pond.

"Charles should recover, but his marriage never will." Kit tried to sound sad when he said it, but failed. "Constance will be sent to the country, not to return. Charles will need help launching the girls into society."

"Mother will manage that," Ash offered, walking into the morning room. "All in all, quite the eventful house party. The ton will be talking about this for some months to come."

"So much for just a few friends," Maggie sing-songed, and they all laughed. Now that the worst was over, it was good to laugh again.

Their London butler, Satterswaite, cleared his throat by the open door. "My Lord, there is someone here to see you."

The friends tensed and assessed what new disaster could be about to befall them when Madeline walked in holding the latest edition to the household.

Georgie looked at Madeline, who was beaming.

"May I introduce you, Kit, to your very beautiful and healthy daughter." Kit took the bundle from her arms carefully, cradling his daughter in his arms.

He face beamed with joy as he looked around at them. "I have a daughter."

The friends were quickly on their feet, gathering around to look at the little one.

"What's her name?" Georgie asked quietly, brushing the little curl of hair on the top of the baby's head.

"I hope you won't mind," he began, "but yours was the only mother I ever knew, and she treated me like her own. I hoped to call her Veronica."

Rath slipped an arm around Georgie's shoulder and kissed the side of her head as she nodded. "I think that's a wonderful idea," she told Kit.

After a few moments, she let Rath steer her away from the others, walking with her onto the terrace. With everything that happened, she was surprised to see the sun had not yet set.

"You don't mind them naming the babe after your mother? I wasn't sure if you had hoped to do so."

"Kit was eight when my mother came into his life and married our father. She was a big influence on him, whereas I barely remember her." She shook her head. "Besides, we still have your mother to name a daughter after."

"So you meant it." He grinned. "You will marry me."

"Say it again."

He laughed. "I love you."

She held up one finger before her face. "One more time."

He dove at her finger, his mouth biting at the air around it when she pulled it back with a squeal. "I love how your cunt squeezes my cock when you come."

Georgie threw her head back and laughed. "That's what I wanted to hear."

She wished he could wrap her in his arms but it would be a few days before either of their bodies were up to that. *Still, there were other things they could do*, she thought as he hugged her to his side. "Do you think they will notice if we sneak away?"

Epilogue

Richards had sent a footman up with a tray of coffee and scones. He had also folded the newspaper open to an article he thought would be of particular interest to the Earl of Rathbridge. Rath poured a cup of coffee and picked up the newspaper, scanning the article quickly.

The season hasn't even begun but the bans have already been read – in most cases. We have said for weeks that the infamous 'Captain Wrath' had been seen in the company of an unconventional. We are never wrong, because just this weekend past Earl of Rathbridge wed one of our darlings, the incorrigible Lady Belstratten by special license. We are told the two won't be around for the season. Not even a new wife can keep Captain Wrath off the seas and the two shall be sailing forthwith to the Hunton family plantation in Tortola.

The wedding came on the veritable heels of that of her guardian Cleopatra Allstead, you know her as Lady Welles, to the Honorable Doctor Raphael Wright. I suppose if she can overlook his profession, so must we. He is at least handsome enough and she rich enough that they can if nothing else buy acceptability.

"Georgie," he called out to his wife who had insisted, after he'd molested her once already, that she should have no more interruptions while she finished packing her trunk for Belle Fleur.

"If you keep making unreasonable demands upon my person, I shall have to rethink this whole marriage business." She laughed as she poked her head around the corner, looking into his sitting room.

"You enjoy the demands, and make some very fine ones of your own, never doubt it." He leered back at her, his gaze alighting on her thin chemise.

"What did you want?" She laughed again.

"I wanted you to know that according to this" — he held up the paper — "you have become 'one of their darlings' and incorrigible, which obviously they find delightful."

"Well, la!" she said, flouncing into the sitting room and throwing herself upon his lap. "Respectability, at last."

"Never that, my lady," he warned, sneaking his hand beneath her chemise. "At least not while I'm around."

Want to see more from this author? Here's a taster for you to enjoy!

Bound to Happen
Zoë Mullins

Excerpt

The line at The Mudhouse was out the door. For the first time since Jaymie and her best friend had opened the little café six months ago, she was convinced it was going to be a hit. It didn't hurt that it was crazy-hot out and they were offering large iced coffees for only two dollars a cup.

The crowds were larger on the weekend when the *city* people from Toronto drove up to their cottages on the lake. Even though she had studied in Toronto and forced herself to work there for a few years, she would always be a townie and proud of it. She hated the city, hated the late hours she'd put in at the magazine, resented the commute from downtown to the suburbs where she'd lived with another graphic designer and two additional roommates.

She'd been biding her time, skipping the parties and the clubs and saving her pennies until she could move home to Port Ellis. That she'd opened a coffee shop and bakery was entirely an accident of fate. It had been her best friend's idea. Mel'd had the know-how and Jaymie'd had the capital. After finding what Mel called the perfect location, it had all fallen into place with ease.

The Mudhouse was located on Founders Street, the town's main road. The shop itself was, to put it plainly, a hole in the wall—or maybe a closet. The coffee bar and bakery case were on one side with a row of tables against the other wall. The front of the café was also wide open to the sidewalk, with doors that could be retracted for the summer. What had convinced Jaymie that the location would work was the large deck off the back. It was the width of their shop and half of the florist's next door and had direct access to the boardwalk.

"You've done a good job at reinventing yourself here," Mel said, passing her a cup of iced tea.

"You mean co-owning a café when I neither bake nor drink coffee?"

"Ssh, we aren't telling the townsfolk about that. We'll lose the true coffee aficionados if they discover you scorn them."

"I don't scorn them or the coffee," she insisted, sipping her mango-pomegranate iced tea. "I just don't worship at the altar of the bean." They served a large selection of fair trade organic coffees, but Jaymie had made sure they also had the largest tea selection in Port Ellis.

"You don't know what you're missing." Mel took a large gulp of her iced coffee.

They leaned against the back railing, watching as their well-trained staff moved people through the line quickly. Their pastries were all homemade. That was Mel's passion, and while it would be better if they had a commercial kitchen on the premises, her partner seemed content to bake at home. Jaymie hoped they might one day be able to take over the florist shop next door and turn it into the kitchen of Mel's dreams, but that was a long way down the road.

As director of finance, Jaymie was well aware of their fiscal realities. She also handled their human resources and marketing needs — all roles that did not require her to get up at the crack of dawn. She was not a morning lark.

"So Max keeps telling me." Jaymie smiled. Like his sister, Maxwell loved his coffee.

Mel sighed. "I am so excited that you and Max are dating."

"I don't know that we're dating." It sounded so juvenile — dating. She wouldn't go so far as to say they were serious, but what they had wasn't kid stuff. "We are friends with some benefits."

"Whatev." Mel waved her hand. "You were meant to be together. I've known that since high school. He looks happier than he has in a long time."

"Don't get your hopes up, okay?" Jay pleaded. "I don't want it to get weird. He's your sibling, and though I've known him my whole life, he's always been 'Mel's big brother'."

"It won't get weird." Mel shook her head. "Why would it get weird?"

"If it doesn't work out or turn into what you hope it will. We're just seeing each other."

Seeing each other. That was a good description and it was more than she'd ever expected from her online Dom, Master M. But that was before she'd discovered that her Internet lover was her hometown veterinarian — the guy who used to pull her pigtails and snap her bra strap.

Maybe she shouldn't have been that surprised. They'd met in a chat room on *Fetlife* for people from Western Ontario. They'd talked about how much they loved cottaging and Lake Huron, because it wasn't all dick pics and pussy portraits online. She liked him and she liked exploring where that could lead now that they lived in the same town.

But they had to be careful—not because they were worried someone would find out what they got up to behind closed doors, but so as not to get everyone's hopes up that they were a 'couple'. Neither of them had a good track record with relationships.

Max had married his high school sweetheart as soon as he'd finished university. It hadn't lasted. He'd told his family it had been the stress of opening his own practice. He had never been around, and when he had been, he'd been distracted. They'd grown apart.

Jaymie knew the truth. What he'd wanted out of a relationship, especially sexually, had not been something Shawna could offer. It seemed strange to her that after movies like *Fifty Shades*, there could still be people who thought thong panties and doing it in the living room was 'out there'.

"I don't care what you call it," Mel continued. "Shawna was a doll and we loved her, but they were too different from the very beginning. She was a mouse and he needs a feline."

"Excuse me?" Jaymie nearly spat out her tea. That was the first time Mel had even mentioned Shawna.

"You know what I mean," Mel elbowed her. "He needs someone who will challenge him—someone with claws. You weren't the terror of Terence Ellis High for no reason."

"You need to switch to decaf," Jaymie told her, but she didn't argue that she had always been a little forthright. *Okay...opinionated and arrogant.* It was her defense mechanism for being an introvert in an extrovert's world. She'd learned better coping mechanisms over the years.

Jaymie finished the last of her iced tea before continuing. "I need to take the deposit to the bank and get change."

Mel frowned, but she followed Jaymie into the shop. "I need to restock the bakery display. I am going to have to start making more of the chocolate energy bars. Those are a hit."

"It's a good position for us to be in." Jaymie had cute little 'Sold Out' placeholders made to put in the case when they ran out of something so that customers knew what they had missed. "We are actually making a go of this."

"I never doubted it," Mel sing-songed as she tied on her apron. "Say hi to my brother for me."

Jaymie rolled her eyes and shoved the deposit bag in her purse, but she didn't dispute her friend's assertion. There was a good chance she'd stop in at the vet clinic on her way back from the bank. *Maybe. If the line at the bank isn't long,* she bargained with herself.

* * * *

Maxwell watched Jaymie walk by the clinic windows on her way to the bank as he explained to Mrs. Dawson how to use the Advantage Flea and Tick product on Tuffington the dachshund. He checked his watch. If there wasn't a line, she'd be walking back in about fifteen minutes, just long enough for him to see Mrs. Leclair and the cat with alopecia.

Max was waiting in the doorway when she sauntered back down the sidewalk. "Will you walk into my parlor?"

"Said the spider to the fly." She grinned up at him, slid a hand into his and followed him to his office in the back. She jumped up on his desk as he closed the door, perching on the edge.

"You look beat." He brushed her hair away from her face, tucking it behind her ear. He loved that she wore her hair loose so often. It fell in gentle waves past her shoulders. Sure, she made it a little blonder than its natural color, but the highlights suited her. He pulled off her glasses and kissed her forehead.

"Gee, thanks," she sighed, sliding her hands around his waist. She did this thing he loved where she ran her fingers along his waistband. Her touch was light, which always made him smile.

"I know how much you are putting into The Mudhouse."

"Your sister is doing the tough work, all the baking and chatting with customers."

"All of which she loves. That part suits her," he pointed out. "She is never happier than when she is feeding everyone around her."

"Isn't that the truth? I've gained ten pounds since we started this business." She looked contrite when she lifted her gaze to his.

He shook his head at her gently. He had made it clear early on that he wouldn't stand for hearing her put herself down for any reason. That was one thing that could earn her a sure punishment and her remark sounded very close to a complaint. And if she had gained ten pounds, she must have needed it, because he couldn't see any change.

"I'm sorry," she apologized. "I think I spent too much time at the café today. Too many customers I had to be pleasant to. I'm peopled out."

"Even this people?" He stepped between her legs, sliding her across the desk so she pressed against him.

"No, you are exactly what I needed. But I wasn't sure you'd have time to see me."

"Late lunch. I have time," he whispered, slipping his hands beneath her hair, around her neck, then skimming them down her shoulders. She was wearing a little blue floral sundress. The neckline was modest but her arms were bare. Goosebumps broke out where he caressed his hands over her arms.

She leaned in to him, her breath hot on his chest. *Is she aware*, he wondered, *how addicted I've become to her?* They had agreed when she'd moved here that although what they'd developed online was convenient, considering their real-world connections, nothing more could happen between them.

Their agreement had lasted for the first six weeks or so while she had been so busy with Mel, getting the café set up. And, like a fool, he'd offered to help so he'd had to see her at least weekly, sometimes more often — whether he was painting the café, helping to lay the floor or sitting across from her at Sunday dinner at his parents.

It was too much and all their good intentions — all his, in particular — had gone out of the window. He couldn't let what had started between them in cyberspace just disappear. It had been as real as anything in his life.

"Are you still wearing it?"

She laughed against his chest. "Oh yeah. Since noon, just like you ordered, Sir."

He laughed with her, rubbing his chin on the top of her head before he stepped back, helping her to stand. "Turn around and bend over. Hands on the desk. I need to check this out myself."

She obeyed his command, spreading her feet wide and bending over the cool wood desk. He didn't like clutter, so there was little in her way. When she laid her head on her folded arms, he dragged her skirt up over her hips. "You are a very bad girl."

"Yes, Sir." She swayed her hips, tempting him.

He smacked her ass, not to stop her from moving but because he loved it when she teased and she knew it. It pleased him almost as much as seeing the flat blue end of the butt plug between the cheeks of her ass. And she'd not worn panties. "Has having your ass full all afternoon made your pussy wet? Ready?"

"Yes, Sir?" She swayed again and he rewarded her with the palm of his hand.

His cock was hard beneath his work khakis. It didn't worry about the clients waiting or that his office door wasn't soundproof. It wanted to be buried in Jaymie's hot pussy, made tighter by the plug in her ass. Max liked to think he didn't blindly follow his cock, but today might be the exception.

He growled and grabbed his gym bag from next to his desk, hoping he still had condoms left in the front pocket. *Yes,* he gave a silent cheer as he turned the lock on his office door and undid his pants. "It's going to be hard, fast and quiet," he warned her before slamming his sheathed cock into her pussy.

Christ, she's wet, he marveled as he slid inside her. She was tighter with the plug still in, not that her pussy wasn't always snug. She mewed and clenched her fingers. She must be sensitive after wearing it for so long. She was such a good sub for following his directions. He'd reward her for that later.

He folded himself over her back as he thrust his hips against her, jarring the base of the plug each time. He kept one hand on the desk to brace himself, but the other he slid into her hair, holding the back of her head. He bent close, whispering to her, telling her how good it felt to be inside her, how hot she was, how her cunt held him and didn't want to let him go.

He felt the orgasm as it rushed through her. Her shoulders tensed and her pussy clamped down. She hit the desk lightly with a fist as she turned her head toward him. It was taking everything she had not to cry out, he could tell. Him, too.

It felt too good, her contracting against him. He couldn't hold back and didn't want to. He growled and leaned his head against her shoulder. He bit her through the cotton of the dress, using her body to muffle the sound of his cry as he came inside her.

Too good, he thought. *She feels too good.* She was such more than he had been expecting at this point in his life. He never stopped wondering what had brought him such luck as to find her.

He braced his hands on the desk as he stood. His cock was still hard as he wrapped the condom in Kleenex and tossed it in the waste basket. He grabbed another tissue. He had one more job before he could let her stand.

He tapped the base of the plug.

"Bastard," she hissed. "You know you're going to make me come again when you pull that damn thing out."

Oh yeah, he knew and he loved it. He slid three fingers inside her pussy so he could feel her come as he pulled the ribbed invader free of her ass as slowly as possible. She was as good as her word, coming on his fingers, covering them. He pumped gently as she came, petting her hip.

"I'm never going to get enough of you," he said as he withdrew, bringing his fingertips to his tongue for just a taste of her. Later, he'd bury his tongue inside her and feast on her cream, but they both had to get back to work.

"I don't know that I can move," she said as he pulled her now-wrinkled skirt back down over her bottom.

He chuckled and wrapped a hand around her waist, helping her to stand. She was indeed unsteady on her feet, her eyes dazed, her skin flushed. He didn't think he was as visibly affected, but emotionally, he wondered if he might be more. *I love her.*

"I have to clean up" — he nodded to the little restroom off his office — "and see a client. Mr. Pugh is bringing in his bulldog Roscoe. You don't want to know what for. You sit and stay until you regain your sea legs."

"I'll be okay," she said, but he still guided her to the chair before dashing into the tiny bathroom.

When he came out, she was gone, but she'd left him a note reminding him they'd see each other that night at his parents'. *Ugh!* That meant pretending that what was between them didn't blow his mind and eclipse all relationships that had gone before.

He let out a long sigh, resigned to do something about this weird limbo their relationship was in — soon. He wanted her in his bed, in his life, more than once or twice a week. He didn't want to rush her. He knew how many changes she was already dealing with this year. She'd said often enough that she couldn't handle any more. But she was going to have to, because her Dom couldn't wait.

Home of Erotic Romance

Sign up for our newsletter and find out about all our romance book releases, eBook sales and promotions, sneak peeks and FREE romance books!

About the Author

A prolific writer, even in elementary school, she was jotting down poems and stories whenever she had the chance - usually during math class.

After many years of working in corporate communications, Zoë decided in 2015 it was time to focus her energy on the kind of writing she loved – hot romances with strong, alpha heroes and quirky, independent heroines.

Zoë's husband of nearly 20 years threw his full support behind that dream and loves to tell people his wife is a romance author. They live in Atlantic Canada with their two crazy collies. When not at her computer, you will find Zoë chasing after her muddy dogs, working in the garden or helping to renovate their money-pit of a house.

Zoë loves to hear from readers. You can find her contact information, website details and author profile page at https://www.totallybound.com